PENGUIN TWENTIETH-CENTURY CLASSICS

THE LAST SEPTEMBER

Elizabeth Bowen was born in Dublin in 1899, the only child of an Irish lawyer and landowner. She was educated at Downe House School in Kent. Her book *Bowen's Court* (1942) is the history of her family and their house in County Cork, and *Seven Winters* (1943) contains reminiscences of her Dublin childhood. In 1923 she married Alan Cameron who held an appointment with the BBC and who died in 1952. She travelled a good deal, dividing most of her time between London and Bowen's Court, which she inherited.

Elizabeth Bowen is considered by many to be one of the most distinguished novelists of the twentieth century. She saw the object of a novel as 'the non-poetic statement of a poetic truth' and said that 'no statement of it can be final'. Her first book, *Encounters*, a collection of short stories, appeared in 1923, followed by another, *Ann Lee's*, in 1926. *The Hotel* (1927) was her first novel, and was followed by *The Last September* (1929), *Joining Charles* (1929), another book of short stories, *Friends and Relations* (1931), *To the North* (1932), *The Cat Jumps* (short stories, 1934), *The House in Paris* (1935), *The Death of the Heart* (1938), *Look at All Those Roses* (short stories, 1941), *The Demon Lover* (short stories, 1945), *The Heat of the Day* (1949), *Collected Impressions* (essays, 1950), *The Shelbourne* (1951), *A World of Love* (1955), *A Time in Rome* (1960), *After-thought* (essays, 1962), *The Little Girls* (1964), *A Day in the Dark* (1965) and her last book, *Eva Trout* (1969). Many of her books are available in the Twentieth-Century Classics series, and in 1983 Penguin published *The Collected Stories of Elizabeth Bowen*.

She was awarded the CBE in 1948, and received the honorary degree of Doctor of Letters from Trinity College, Dublin, in 1949 and from Oxford University in 1956. In the same year she was appointed Lacy Martin Donnelly Fellow at Bryn Mawr College in the United States. In 1965 she was made a Companion of Literature by the Royal Society of Literature. Elizabeth Bowen died in 1973.

Elizabeth Bowen

The Last September

Penguin Books

To
Joan Grace Reed

PENGUIN BOOKS

Published by the Penguin Group
Penguin Books Ltd, 27 Wrights Lane, London W8 5TZ, England
Penguin Books USA Inc., 375 Hudson Street, New York, New York 10014, USA
Penguin Books Australia Ltd, Ringwood, Victoria, Australia
Penguin Books Canada Ltd, 10 Alcorn Avenue, Toronto, Ontario, Canada M4V 3B2
Penguin Books (NZ) Ltd, 182–190 Wairau Road, Auckland 10, New Zealand

Penguin Books Ltd, Registered Offices: Harmondsworth, Middlesex, England

First published in Great Britain by Constable & Co., Ltd 1929
Published in Penguin Books 1942
20 19 18 17 16 15 14 13 12

First published in the United States of America
by Alfred A. Knopf, Inc., 1929
Published in Penguin Books in the United States of America
by arrangement with Alfred A. Knopf, Inc., 1987

Set in Baskerville Monotype
Printed in England by Clays Ltd, St Ives plc

Contents

'Ils ont les chagrins qu'ont les
vierges et les paresseux. . . .'

Le Temps Retrouvé

The Arrival of Mr and Mrs Montmorency

1

About six o'clock the sound of a motor, collected out of the wide country and narrowed under the trees of the avenue, brought the household out in excitement on to the steps. Up among the beeches, a thin iron gate twanged; the car slid out from a net of shadow, down the slope to the house. Behind the flashing windscreen Mr and Mrs Montmorency produced – arms waving and a wild escape to the wind of her mauve motor-veil – an agitation of greeting. They were long-promised visitors. They exclaimed, Sir Richard and Lady Naylor exclaimed and signalled: no one spoke yet. It was a moment of happiness, of perfection.

In those days, girls wore crisp white skirts and transparent blouses clotted with white flowers; ribbons, threaded through with a view to appearance, appeared over their shoulders. So that Lois stood at the top of the steps looking cool and fresh; she knew how fresh she must look, like other young girls, and clasping her elbows tightly behind her back, tried hard to conceal her embarrassment. The dogs came pattering out from the hall and stood beside her; above, the vast façade of the house stared coldly over its mounting lawns. She wished she could freeze the moment and keep it always. But as the car approached, as it stopped, she stooped down and patted one of the dogs.

As the car drew up the Montmorencys unwound from their rugs. They stood shaking hands and laughing in the yellow theatrical sunshine. They had motored over from Carlow. Two toppling waves of excitement crashed and mingled; for moments everybody was inaudible. Mrs Montmorency looked up the steps. 'And this is the niece!' she exclaimed with delight. 'Aren't we dusty!' she added, as Lois said nothing. 'Aren't we too terribly dusty!' And a tired look came down at the back of her eyes at the thought of how dusty she was.

'She's left school now,' said Sir Richard proudly.

'I don't think I should have known you,' said Mr Montmorency, who had not seen Lois since she was ten and evidently preferred children.

'Oh, *I* think she's the image of Laura –'

'– But we have tea waiting. Are you really sure, now, you've had tea?'

'Danielstown's looking lovely, lovely. One sees more from the upper avenue – didn't you clear some trees?'

'The wind had three of the ashes – you came quite safe? No trouble? Nobody at the cross-roads? Nobody stopped you?'

'And are you sure now about tea?' continued Lady Naylor. 'After all that – look, it's coming up now. No, Francie, don't be ridiculous; come in now, both of you.'

They swept in; their exclamations, constricted suddenly, filling the hall. There was so much to say after twelve years: they all seemed powerless. Lois hesitated, went in after them and, as nobody noticed, came out again. The car with the luggage turned and went round to the back, deeply scoring the gravel. She yawned and looked out over the sweep to the lawn beyond, where little tufts of shadow pricked like reeds from water out of the flat gold light. Beyond the sunk fence, six Kerry cows followed each other across with wading steps and stood under a lime tree. All the way up the house the windows were open; light came diagonally from window to window through corner rooms. Two stories up, she could have heard a curtain rustle, but the mansion piled itself up in silence over the Montmorencys' voices.

She yawned with reaction. It was simply the Montmorencys who had come; whom all day one had been expecting. Yet she had been unable to read, had scattered unfinished letters over her table, done the flowers atrociously. Sweet-peas had spun and quivered between her fingers from their very importance . . . 'I apologize for the mauve sweet-peas,' she would have liked to be able to say to Mr Montmorency. 'I don't care for the mauve myself. I can't think why I ever picked them; there were plenty of others. But, as a matter of fact, I was nervous.' And – 'Nervous?' she would wish Mr Montmorency to ask her searchingly, 'why?' But she had her reserves, even in imagination; she would never tell him.

But she had seen at once that Mr Montmorency, who must be really so subtle, would not take the trouble to understand her.

Her cousin Laurence had gone upstairs with a book when he heard the motor. Now she could hear him knocking out his pipe on a window-sill. He leaned out further and asked, pointing down, in a cautious whisper: 'Are they all in?'

She signalled a warning, nodding.

'What are you doing?' he said.

'I don't know. What are you doing?'

'Nothing particular.'

'I thought I'd take the dogs down the beech walk.'

'Why?'

'Oh, I just thought . . .'

'Come up and tell me about the Montmorencys.'

She signalled another warning: the Montmorencys were in the hall. To avoid the hall she had to go right round to a side door and up the back stairs. These smelt of scrubbed wood, limewash, and the ducks already roasting for the Montmorencys' dinner. Pushing open a door at the top she let a gust of this through with her.

'Duck,' said Laurence, sniffing gratefully. It still surprised her that Laurence, who looked ethereal, should spend so much time when he was not being intellectual in talking and apparently thinking about food. She supposed that this was because he had, as he once had said, no emotional life. 'I live,' he used to say, 'from meal to meal.' When she said, 'Why?' he put up his hands and his eyebrows and made a gesture. When he did this in front of Gerald she felt uncomfortable. Soldiers did not talk about food, they ate it. They ate, in fact, rather more than Laurence, but always with a deprecating absent look.

Laurence had been reading in the ante-room, in one of the circle of not very comfortable shell-shaped chairs that no one took seriously. His room was a floor higher; it had not seemed worth while to go up. He had brought the wrong book and dared not go down for another; otherwise he would not have felt in need of her conversation. Personally, she liked the ante-room, though it wasn't the ideal place to read or talk. Four rooms opened off it; at any moment a door might be opened, or blow open, sending a draught down one's neck. People passed through it continually, so that one kept having to look up and smile. Yet Lois always seemed to be talking there, standing with a knee on a chair because it was not worth while to sit down, and her life was very much complicated by not knowing how much of what she said had been overheard, or by whom, or how far it would go.

The high windows were curtainless; tasselled fringes frayed the light at the top. The white sills, the shutters folded back in their frames were blistered, as though the house had spent a day in the tropics. Exhausted by sunshine, the backs of the crimson chairs were a thin light orange; a smell of camphor and animals drawn from skins on the floor by the glare of morning still hung like dust on the evening chill. Going through to her room at nights Lois often tripped with her toe in the jaws of the tiger; a false step at any time sent some great claw skidding over the polish. Pale regimental groups, reunions a generation ago of the family or the neighbourhood gave out from the walls a vague depression. There were two locked bookcases of which the keys had been lost, and a troop of ebony elephants brought back from India by someone she did not remember paraded along the tops of the bookcases.

'Whow – whow – whow!' said Laurence, imitating her panting. 'Why do you hurry like that?'

'I suppose it's a habit,' said Lois, confused.

'What did you want?'

'Well, I came to tell you about the Montmorencys.'

'Oh, all right; go on. Where are they?'

'Having more tea; Aunt Myra made them ... Well, they arrived, as you probably heard, and it was all rather devastating. There was a good deal of emotion. And she would do nothing but say she was dusty, and of course she *was* dusty, so there was nothing for me to say.'

'So what did you say?'

'And he said he would never have known me.'

'Honest, bluff sort of chap?'

'Oh *no*,' said Lois and flushed, for really Laurence was too insulting. She laughed and glanced at her fingernails – the only part of one's person, she had observed, of which it was possible to be conscious socially. 'Haven't you met him?'

'I think I did once. I think I thought he was rather fatuous. But I was very young at the time – I mayn't have met him at all.'

'Isn't it extraordinary,' said Lois confidentially, 'the way one's nails grow – I mean, when one comes to think: yards and yards of inexhaustible nail coming out of one. As a matter of fact,' she added, 'I once rather had illusions about Mr Montmorency – since I was ten. He came to stay with my mother and me when we were at Leamington. After dinner – I was allowed to sit up – Mother walked out of the house and left us. We were trying chickens at that time and I dare say she went out to shut them up and then simply stayed in the garden. Mr Montmorency and I talked for some time, then he got solemn and went to sleep all in a moment. I sat and watched him in absolute fascination. You know the way men go to sleep after dinner? Well, that wasn't at all the way he did ... Then my mother came, very much refreshed at having been away from us, and said I was a rather bad hostess, and woke Mr Montmorency up. I have thought since, anyone might have said she was a rather bad hostess. But everything she did seemed so natural.'

'Oh, she was lovely,' said Laurence, indifferent.

'So you see he is really not bluff, or he wouldn't have gone to sleep in that perfectly simple, exposed way. He was melancholy and exhausted and wise, which I did appreciate as a child, when most visitors were so noisy at one.'

'Extraordinary,' said Laurence, looking out of the window.

Laurence was comfortable to talk to because of his indifference to every shade of her personality. With him, she felt committed by speech itself to a display of such unfathomable silliness that she might just as well come out – and did – with assertions surprising even to herself. When he yawned, took a book up, said he was hungry or simply went away, she was not discountenanced. It was those tender, those receptive listeners to whom one felt afterwards sold and committed. It is true that when first she had met Laurence again she had wished to impress him as an intellectual girl. But an evening of signal failure when he had told her she should read less and more thoroughly and, on the whole he thought, talk less, had involved a certain re-arrangement of attitude. She had re-attained confidence, expanding under his disapproval.

'It doesn't occur to you,' he said with an air of sinister triumph, 'that the Montmorencys may have come up the front stairs while you came up the back stairs and be both in their room, listening?'

Unthinkable, but the very sound of the thing was a shock. Crimson, she ran to the door of the spare room: struggling with unreason, knocked defiantly, rattled the handle. She went in, finally, with a sense of impertinence, for the new arrivals were spiritually in possession.

The Blue Room was of course empty; with no one to listen. The trunks had been carried up and set down, unstrapped, at the foot of the wide bed. The room smelt of bleaching cretonnes and ten days' emptiness; curtains in a draught from the door made a pale movement. Lois had put a vase of geraniums on the dressing-table; now she admired their cubes in delicate balance, spraying against the light. And there was the festival air of those candles, virgin, with long white wicks. Two arm-chairs faced round intently into the empty grate with its paper fan – in them Mr and Mrs Montmorency would sit, perhaps to discuss the experiences of the day. More probably, they would talk in bed. One of the things Lois chiefly wanted to know about marriage was – how long it took one, sleeping with the same person every night, to outlive the temptation to talk well into the morning? There would be nothing illicit about nocturnal talking, as there had been at school; no one would be entitled to open a door sharply with: 'Now go to sleep now, you two; that's enough for tonight,' as had so often happened during her visits to friends. Would conversation, in the absence of these prohibitions, cease to interest? Lois had heard of couples who disturbed each other by breathing and preferred to occupy different rooms: no allowance was made for such couples at Danielstown. The Blue Room dressing-room furniture was marble-topped to allow for spills or breakages of a gentleman's bottles, and there was a virile boot-rack for every possible kind of boot. Lois, doubtfully, had put moss roses on Mr Montmorency's table.

'Didn't it occur to you,' said Laurence, 'that they couldn't possibly have gone through without my seeing them?'

Lois came out and shut the door of the spare room. 'But panic,' she said, 'is beyond one. Things like that are so awful. I shall never forget discussing a Miss Elliot – a very musical woman – with Livvy or someone, out here, and, my dear, *she* was in there the whole time and being English and honourable began to rattle her chest of drawers. I could hardly look at her straight for the rest of the visit. However, she also covered herself with confusion, because she put all her vases of flowers outside her door at night, and Brigid fell over them bringing the morning tea. Aunt Myra was terribly irritated and talked about nursing-homes.'

'I shouldn't expect there will be anything so very hygienic about Mrs Montmorency.'

'Damn,' said Lois, looking disproportionately worried and moving off towards her own room suddenly. 'I have got letters to finish.' Speaking of Brigid had reminded her that there were letters on regimental note-paper lying about all over her room and that Brigid, who took an interest, would be likely to see them when she came up with the hot water. Not that they mattered really, but at the thought of some letters people wrote her she did feel rather a fool.

Laurence had pale blue, rather prominent eyes that moved slowly, though the rest of his movements were jerky. Looking up at her now with a not unaware kind of blandness, he said: 'Do tell me, what do you write about?'

'Life in general.'

'You amaze me – now if I did write letters no one would read them if they were not intelligent. You must have the golden touch.'

'Naturally one is expected to be amusing.'

'And how many subalterns do you write to?'

This was disconcerting, also, she felt strongly, irrelevant. If these young men wrote to her, they were unimportant; besides, she only answered every third letter. These young men, concrete, blocking her mental view by their extreme closeness, moved shadowless in a kind of social glare numbing to the imagination. Whereas Mr Montmorency came out distinct from the rather rare gloom with which she invested her childhood; her feeling for him provided agreeable matter for introspection. However much he might loom and darken up to the close-up view, he would never be out of focus.

'How many?' said Laurence again, picking up his book but still looking at her inexorably. The unkindest thing he had called her friend Livvy Thompson was – a rather probable channel for the life-force; and really when he asked questions of this kind she did not know what he must think.

But it was reticence as to a lack rather than as to a super-abundance that produced her embarrassment.

'Three – no, two,' she said coldly, 'because one of them is a captain.'

Going into her room she shut the door. Laurence got up and walked round the ante-room. For the hundredth time he looked disparagingly along the backs of the books in the locked book-cases. Then he heard his aunt and Mrs Montmorency beginning to come upstairs.

2

The Naylors and the Montmorencys had always known each other; it was an affair of generations. Hugo had stayed at Danielstown as a boy for months together, and knew the place as well as his own house, he told Francie, and certainly liked it better. He had expressed this preference, which had come as a shock to her, when they were first engaged. She was pained as by an expression of irreligion. She consoled herself, and rehabilitated him secretly, by remembering he had had a step-father and could never have known the meaning of family life – she had a delicate woman's strong feeling for 'naturalness'. She intended to make up to him for the deficiencies of his childhood, but, almost immediately after their marriage, Hugo sold Rockriver. Now she would always blame herself for not having dissuaded him, but he had been so set at the time on an idea of going to Canada and she was so foolishly anxious to compensate him for what she was not by going there with him and thriving. So when the idea of Canada failed, they had no house, and she, after all, no vocation. As for Hugo, he had expected little of life.

Francie had heard all her life of the Naylors of Danielstown, her cousins and theirs had married; but Ireland is large and she had not met them till she came to Danielstown on a bridal visit. Then, of course, they had known each other always; there had been no beginning. She knew she had never in all her life been so happy as on that first visit; time, loose-textured, had had a shining undertone, happiness glittered between the moments. She had had, too, very strongly a sense of return, of having awaited. Rooms, doorways had framed a kind of expectancy of her; some trees in the distance, the stairs, a part of the garden seemed always to have been lying secretly at the back of her mind.

It was, also, on the first and only other visit, that she had made friends with Myra – that in itself was memorable. Myra was 'interesting', cultivated, sketched beautifully, knew about books and music. She had been to Germany, Italy, everywhere that one visits acquisitively. It had been a bond to discover that Francie and Myra must have been in Germany at the same time, the summer of '92, though without meeting. Myra was the same age as Francie – they had been presented the same year, though not at the same Drawing-room – and thought of Hugo as quite a boy: she could not help showing it. Sometimes, guessing what she had shown, she would laugh and say something clever and quite irrelevant to cover the awkwardness. For Hugo was ten years younger than both of them, Francie's husband.

Francie and Myra had had long remarkable talks about almost everything, confidential if not alarmingly intimate – walking, driving, on the seat by the caroline allspice tree, and at the head of the stairs at night – while their candle-flames stooped from their vehemence.

When at the end of that visit the Montmorencys left Danielstown this had seemed to Francie more of a pause than a break in the continuity. 'Next spring,' they all four promised each other, shaking hands and kissing at the foot of the steps – it was then autumn, the bronze trees were sifted through by the wind and shivered along the outlines – 'Next summer, Hugo,' Myra exclaimed, '*at latest!*' and the last view they had of her was as standing bright and imperative. Only as they drove away did the trees run, watery, into the sky and Francie's lids prick: she slipped her hand into Hugo's under the rug. And, pressing it, he had alone to continue the business of turning, yearning and waving back till a bend in the avenue.

She had felt, perhaps, a chilly breath from the future. Between their smart turning out, with a roll of carriage wheels, through the gates with their clipped laurels, and their swerving in with a grind of motor brakes twelve years afterwards, nothing large was to intervene. Their life, through which they went forward uncertainly, without the compulsion of tragedy, was a net of small complications. There was the drag of his indecisions, the fine snapping now and then of her minor relinquishments. Her health, his temperament, their varying poverty – they were delayed, deflected. She was ordered abroad for successive winters, to places he could not expect to endure. He came and went without her; going for consolation, of course, to Danielstown. The Naylors sent her out wails, injunctions and declarations. They would never, *never* be happy till she was with them also.

So at last Hugo and Francie returned together. And today something – that break in the trees on the avenue, something unremembered about the face of the house, some intensification of the silence surrounding it, or perhaps simply Lois' figure standing there on the steps – made the place different.

Lady Naylor and Mrs Montmorency now went upstairs together. Francie looked down at the top step to see if the marks were still there – becoming much excited in the course of an argument about Robert Hugh Benson she had waved her candle and scattered a rain of hot grease. But there was a new stair carpet. Myra looked down also, but in surprise; she did not remember. She had argued with so many people in twelve years – nowadays she argued about Galsworthy.

'I shouldn't be surprised,' she said, lowering her voice as they approached the ante-room, 'if we found Laurence up here – my nephew. He is with us a good deal, between Oxford. Though I expect it is dull for him. He is not out of doors very much; he is very intellectual. Though, of course, he plays tennis.'

Francie was much relieved, on entering the ante-room, to find that Laurence had gone. 'It's so nice,' she said, 'the way you have the house full of young people.' She turned to the right instinctively, to her old door.

'No, this way, Francie, the Blue Room. The rooks on that side of the house disturbed so many people; we've changed the rooms round and put Lois in there; she prefers them.'

As they came into the Blue Room, Francie saw their two faces reflected in the tall dressing-table glass, the door swinging behind. 'Myra's aged!' she thought with a shock. Her own face never seemed to have changed at all.

She said: 'You look wonderful, you know. I couldn't think when I was ever to see you again, or Richard either.'

Myra kissed her – a compact, sudden pursing and placing of the lips. It was as though they were meeting again only now. The door swung to with a rush. 'It's been too bad, too bad – not even as if you had been in Canada!'

The linen of Myra's sleeve was cool to the touch of the dusty Francie. Myra wore a grey linen dress with embroidered panels, a lace scarf twice round the throat and a green hat dipping in front and trimmed with clover. Her bright grey eyes, with very black, urgent pupils, continued in a deep crease at each outside corner. High on the curve of her cheeks, like petals, bright mauve-pink colour became, within kissing distance, a net of fine delicate veins. Her eyebrows, drawn in a pointed arch, suggested tragic surprise till one saw the arch never flattened, the face beneath never changed from its placid eagerness, its happy dissatisfaction. '*Has* she aged?' Francie thought, glancing closely and shyly again as they parted. Yes, she felt something set now in Myra; she was happier, harder.

Myra receded now that the kiss was over. There was life to go on with, the duty of love and pleasure fully discharged. She moved round the Blue Room, nodded out of a window to someone distant coming out from some trees – she could never learn how one vanishes in the dark of a house. She glanced intently along the books in the book-trough. 'Lois has not changed the books!' she exclaimed. 'You know how I like them to be appropriate. Here's a technical book on rubber a man left behind last summer – it looks ridiculous. She's a girl who never forgets the same thing twice; always something different . . .'

'She looks sweet, I think. And surely the image of Laura?'

'She's not so much like Laura in character. There's a good deal, I sometimes think, of poor Walter.'

'Wasn't it terribly sad about Walter?'

'To tell you the truth, it was what we always expected,' said Lady Naylor.

When Francie was left alone she went to the window and shook the dust out of her motor veil. Then – she was so very tired from motoring, everything seemed to rush past – she sat down on the sofa and put her hands over her eyes. Her mind lay back in the silence, but there was a kind of sentinel in her waiting for Hugo. She did not know what she should say if he noticed the drive from Carlow really had been too much for her. She had said beforehand she was afraid it might be too much, and he had said: nonsense, that she was fit for anything nowadays. Flattered by this, she gave in. She was so tired – just for these few moments when she let herself go – she could not bear to realize Danielstown. Her thoughts ached. When she looked out there were some intolerable trees and a strip of gold field on the skyline.

When she heard steps coming she fled to the washstand. Her skin was dry, her hair felt laden and limp, it was so dusty. But that was the fine, the phenomenal weather for which, in this country, one could not be thankful enough. When Hugo came through from his dressing-room she was washing her hands – they turned in the water like gentle porpoises in a slaver of violet soap.

'Well,' he said, looking round the room.

'Well, Hugo . . . isn't it lovely?'

'Richard's in great form – I thought I'd never get up at all to you . . . Not tired?'

'Indeed, no . . . Doesn't it all seem the same as ever?'

'I tell you one thing: Myra's ageing. Didn't you notice?'

'Oh,' said Francie vaguely. She stooped her face to the basin, the rain-water comforted, creeping into the pores. '*Oh!*' She dried her face in damask, among stiff roses. 'But then, we all are.'

'She's got into a terrible habit of shutting doors.'

'Times have been worse down here. Yes, I thought, you know, she had a rather strained look. What does Richard think of the situation? . . . Oh, and had you any idea that Lois was so grown up? I had imagined her quite a schoolgirl. She's so pretty, such a . . . a frank little face.'

'She's self-conscious,' said Hugo, 'but I dare say most girls of that age are . . . I should lie down now for a bit, it will freshen you up – though you don't need it. Then would you like me to brush your hair?'

Francie got her dressing-gown out of a trunk and lay down on the sofa. She had just relaxed there when Hugo said that the sofa did not look comfortable and she had better lie on the bed. He made a valley for her head between the two pillows – he did not believe it rested anybody to lie with their head high – and she lay down on the bed with her head in the valley. 'Oh, but I don't think I ought to lie on this lovely quilt,' she soon protested.

'They're not fussy here,' returned Hugo; 'do lie and be still.'

So she lay and watched him begin to unpack her two boxes, carry dresses over his arms and lay them along the shelves of the 'gentleman's wardrobe'. She wondered: whatever would Richard and Myra think? – 'Uxorious' they would be bound to declare; Richard who could hardly handle a jug without dropping it, and Myra who would not have him otherwise.

'What a disgusting noise,' said Hugo, pausing and listening.

'Somebody playing a gramophone –'

They might well say she had taken the brilliant young man he'd once been and taught him to watch her, to nurse her and shake out her dresses. And she knew she could, now, never explain to Myra what she had failed to explain twelve years ago – when there had been so much less to explain and to justify – how Hugo was too much for her altogether. How she had tried, but had not been able, to keep him – first from marrying her, then from giving up Canada, leaving his friends when she had to go to the south of France, or from brushing her hair in the evenings.

'Hugo, you might leave that blue dress out; I think I'll wear it . . . *When* was it you were in love with Laura?'

'When I was twenty-two – I was in a sort of way. She was lovely then – though indeed she was always lovely. But she was never happy at all, even here. She never knew what she wanted – she was very vital.'

He hesitated over two pairs of evening shoes. 'Leave the bronze ones out,' she suggested. 'They go with the blue.' She lay with her eyes shut a moment, then asked, 'But why wouldn't she marry you?'

Francie's delicacy, her absences from him, her long queer relapses into silence gave her the right to ask curious things, as from a death-bed. Hugo, wandering at the end of the bed, looked at her feet thoughtfully.

'She wanted her mind made up,' he said at last, 'and I couldn't do that – why should I? I had enough to do with my own mind. And she was Richard's own sister – talk and talk and you'd never know where you had her. And if she thought you had her, she'd start a crying-fit. Then she went up North and met Farquar, and I imagine that that was all fixed up before she knew where she was or had time to get out of it. After that of course she really *had* got something to be unhappy about. Yet I don't believe things ever really mattered to Laura. Nothing got close to her: she was very remote.'

'I wonder if Lois is remote?'

'What I think I felt about Laura,' pursued Hugo, interested, 'was, she was never real in the way I wanted. Nobody was before you, as you know . . . If you get up now, I can brush your hair.'

'It is very dusty,' said Mrs Montmorency.

She had met Laura in England and been very shy of her. Laura was a success in England, and so quite brilliant – she was too Irish altogether for her own country. Lois had been at school as usual and did not come home because Laura had forgotten which day the Montmorencys were coming. Six months afterwards, without giving anyone notice of her intention, Laura had died.

'It still seems odd,' remarked Mrs Montmorency, 'that I shouldn't have met Lois.' Seating herself in front of the glass she took out the pins one by one, then shook down her hair round her face – bright bronze threads went in and out, crisply, over the light-grey waves – she ran it through her finger-tips, shaking her head ruefully. But the dust seemed to have gone, perhaps

19

because she was happier, less tired; or perhaps she had left a drift of it between the two pillows. Her husband, selecting a brush, knocked over the vase of geraniums. 'The darlings!' she cried out, mopping with her kimono-sleeve.

'Confusion,' said Hugo, shaking water out of the brush, 'on all who put vases on dressing-tables!'

3

Lois, dressed for dinner, was tidying her writing-table; two stamped letters, her handiwork, leaned on the clock. She shook out her pink suède blotter and started to sort its contents, but had to re-read everything. Gerald, who had written about a tournament, concluded: 'You have the loveliest soft eyes.' She was perplexed, thought: 'But what can I do?' and snapped the letter, with the others, under a rubber band. Then she pulled out a drawer called 'general' and swept the rest into it. She had a waste-paper basket, but only for envelopes. Strokes of the gong, brass bubbles, came bouncing up from the hall. She ran to the glass, changed a necklace, had an apprehensive interchange with her own reflection. What of the night?

Mrs Montmorency and Laurence were in the drawing-room. They looked anxious, nothing showed the trend of the conversation. The pale room rose to a height only mirrors followed above the level of occupation; this disproportionate zone of emptiness dwarfed at all times figures and furniture. The distant ceiling imposed on consciousness its blank white oblong, and a pellucid silence, distilled from a hundred and fifty years of conversation, waited beneath the ceiling. Into this silence, voices went up in stately attenuation. Now there were no voices; Mrs Montmorency and Laurence sat looking away from each other.

As Lois came in Laurence slapped his pockets over and saying something about a pipe left the room quickly, leaving Lois in the grip of a *tête-à-tête*. Mrs Montmorency, seated in a window, held by a corner a copy of the *Spectator*, that had slipped down against the silk of her dress, as though she must be sure to retain this constant refuge from conversation. Vague presence, barely a silhouette, the west light sifting into her fluffy hair and lace wrappings so that she half melted, she gave so little answer to one's inquiry that one did not know how to approach. So Lois stood staring, full in the light.

'Oh, you do look sweet!' exclaimed the visitor. 'Black is so striking. No, you are not like Laura – I don't know who you're like.'

'Aunt Myra isn't sure about black for girls,' said Lois, sweeping forward for admiration the folds of her dress. 'But a white slip lightens it.'

'And I expect you are having a wonderful time now you've grown up?'

'Oh, well . . .' said Lois. She went across to the fire-place and rose on her tiptoes, leaning her shoulders against the marble. She tried not to look conscious. She still felt a distinct pride at having grown up at all; it seemed an achievement, like marriage or fame. Having a wonderful time, she knew, meant being attractive to a number of young men. If she said, 'Yes, I do,' it implied 'Yes, I am, very –' and she was not certain. She was not certain, either, how much she enjoyed herself. 'Well, yes, I do,' she said finally.

'Tell me,' continued Mrs Montmorency, 'wasn't that your cousin Laurence?'

'As a matter of fact I am Uncle Richard's niece and he Aunt Myra's nephew.'

'And isn't he very intellectual?'

'I suppose he is, really.'

'I'm afraid,' said Mrs Montmorency, 'I had no idea how to talk to him. I suppose *you*'d never find that difficult. I expect now, Lois, you're very modern.'

'Oh, well, not really,' said Lois, pleased. Mrs Montmorency's expression, condensing now from her outline, was of such affection and interest that Lois was moved to go on: 'You could talk to him really about almost anything except about politics. He isn't allowed any here because the ones he brings over from Oxford are all wrong.'

'*Wrong?*' cried the visitor, with a startled flush, putting up a hand to her face as though to press back the mounting colour. 'Wrong – which way? How do you mean, "wrong"?'

'Inconvenient.'

'Oh,' said Mrs Montmorency. And upon a recurrence of the puzzled silence that had been the note of Lois's entrance, Sir Richard came in. Sir Richard was very much worried by visitors who came down early for dinner: evidently he had not expected this of Francie. 'Oh!' he exclaimed reproachfully, 'this is too bad; I had no idea you were down. Myra's been delayed – you know yourself what happens.'

'Indeed, yes,' said Francie warmly. She would never have been in time herself if she had had a home of her own. Only the little blanks and rifts in her life accounted for her punctuality.

Sir Richard, touching his tie vaguely, wandered about the room, displacing with some irritation the little tables that seemed to spring up in his path, in the pent-up silence of a powerful talker not yet in gear.

'Very fine weather,' he said at last, 'warm at nights – or would you like me to shut that window?' He was bothered; he could not remember how well he had once known Francie, or decide at just what degree of intimacy he was expected to pick her up again. 'Lois has grown up, hasn't she?' he continued, pointing out his niece with an air of inspiration. 'She seems to me to have grown up very fast. Now how long is it since you saw her over in England?'

'But I never did see her.'

'That was extraordinary,' said Sir Richard, looking from one to the other. 'Didn't you meet poor Laura?'

'I did, but Lois was out.'

'That was too bad.' Sir Richard's bother increased, with a suspicion of something somewhere. He observed rather flatly: 'Then it can hardly be such a surprise to you that she's grown up.'

'Not in the same way.'

'We can all sit on the steps tonight,' said Lois, determined to check the couple in their career of inanity. She went across to a window and folded her arms on the sill.

The screen of trees that reached like an arm from behind the house – embracing the lawns, banks and terraces in mild ascent – had darkened, deepening into a forest. Like splintered darkness, branches pierced the faltering dusk of leaves. Evening drenched the trees; the beeches were soundless cataracts. Behind the trees, pressing in from the open and empty country like an invasion, the orange bright sky crept and smouldered. Firs, bearing up to pierce, melted against the brightness. Somewhere, there was a sunset in which the mountains lay like glass.

Dark had so gained the trees that Lois, turning back from the window, was surprised at how light the room was. Day, still coming in from the fields by the south windows, was stored in the mirrors, in the sheen of the wallpaper, so that the room still shone. Mr Montmorency had come in and was standing where she had stood, his shoulders against the mantelpiece.

'We can sit out on the steps tonight, can't we?' persisted Lois. And because no one answered or cared and a conversation went on without her, she felt profoundly lonely, suspecting once more for herself a particular doom of exclusion. Something of the trees in their intimacy of shadow was shared by the husband and wife and their host in the tree-shadowed room. She thought of love with its gift of importance. 'I must break in on all this,' she thought as she looked round the room.

'Do you still go to sleep after dinner?' she asked Mr Montmorency.

'It's a thing that I n ver have done,' he said, annoyed.

'But it's what I chiefly remember about you.'

'I'm afraid,' he said, tolerant, 'you are mixing me up with someone else.'

'Listen, Richard,' said Francie; 'are you sure we will not be shot at if we sit out late on the steps?'

Sir Richard laughed and they all shared his amusement. 'We never have yet, not even with soldiers here and Lois dancing with officers up and down the avenue. You're getting very English, Francie! Isn't Francie getting very English? Do you think maybe we ought to put sandbags behind the shutters when we shut up at nights?'

'No, but Richard, seriously –' began Francie, then, as they all stared, laughed and had to give up and go on laughing. Now in County Carlow they had said things were bad round here, that she made a grave mistake in coming at all. But then, as Richard would certainly say, that was County Carlow all over.

Lady Naylor came in arm-in-arm with Laurence and said they were all very punctual. 'The gong's only gone three minutes, also I could be certain I never heard any of you go down. But I was delayed, as I told Richard to tell you. Shall we go in?'

'Francie wants to know,' said Sir Richard, offering Francie his arm, 'if we haven't got a machine-gun?'

'Ah, you're too bad!'

'*Do* you dance on the avenue?' said Mr Montmorency to Lois.

'Only once, for a bet. I and a man called Mr Lesworth danced

23

to the white gate, and the man that we had the bet with walked after us carrying the gramophone. But naturally, I don't as a rule.'

'It would come hard on your shoes, I expect,' said Mr Montmorency distantly.

'And the men we know can't get over here in the evening, now.'

'Still, I expect you have a very gay time,' said Mr Montmorency, and turned away.

In the dining-room, the little party sat down under the crowd of portraits. Under that constant interchange from the high-up faces staring across – now fading each to a wedge of fawn-colour, and each looking out from a square of darkness tunnelled into the wall – Sir Richard and Lady Naylor, their nephew, niece and old friends had a thin, over-bright look, seemed on the air of the room unconvincingly painted, startled, transitory. Spaced out accurately round the enormous table – whereon, in what was left of the light, damask birds and roses had an unearthly shimmer – each so enisled and distant that a remark at random, falling short of a neighbour, seemed a cry of appeal, the six, in spite of an emphasis of speech and gesture they unconsciously heightened, dwindled personally. While above, the immutable figures, shedding on to the wash of dusk smiles, frowns, every vestige of personality, kept only attitude – an out-moded modestness, a quirk or a flare, hand slipped under a ruffle or spread airily over the cleft of a bosom – cancelled time, negatived personality and made of the lower cheerfulness, dining and talking, the faintest exterior friction.

In Laurence's plate of clear soup six peas floated. Six accurate spoonfuls, each with a pea in it, finished the soup. He glanced right in his aunt's direction, left in Mrs Montmorency's: both were talking. Mr Montmorency, listening to Lady Naylor, seemed to be looking across at Laurence, but he sat with his back to the light so that Laurence, short-sighted, could not be sure – he preferred uncertainty.

Lady Naylor spoke of the way things were, with her pointed spoon poised over her plate. She noticed the others were waiting, and with a last bright emphatic look in Hugo's direction bent to finish her soup. He said at once to Laurence: 'And what do *you* think of things?'

'Things? Over here?'

'Yes – yes.'

'Seem to be closing in,' said Laurence, crumbling his bread detachedly; 'rolling up rather.'

'Ssh!' exclaimed Lady Naylor, running out a hand at both of them over the cloth. She frowned, with a glance at the parlour-maid. 'Now you mustn't make Laurence exaggerate. All young men from Oxford exaggerate. All Laurence's friends exaggerate: I have met them.'

'If you have noticed it,' said her nephew, 'it is probably so.'

Lois, on his other side, leant eagerly to Mr Montmorency. 'If you are interested, would you care to come and dig for guns in the plantation? Or if I dig, will you come as a witness? Three of the men on the place here swear there are guns buried in the lower plantation. Michael Keelan swears he was going through there, late, and saw men digging. I asked him, "What were they like?" and he said, "The way they would be," and I said, why didn't he ask them what they were doing, and he said, "Sure, why would I; didn't I see them digging, and they with spades?" So it appears he fled back the way he had come.'

'– Ah, that's nonsense now!' Sir Richard exploded. 'Michael would see anything: he is known to have seen a ghost. I will not have the men talking, and at all accounts I won't have them listened to.'

'All the same,' pursued Lois, 'I feel that one ought to dig. If there is nothing there I can confound Michael for the good of his soul, and if there should be guns, Uncle Richard, just think of finding them! And surely we ought to know.'

'And why would we want to know? You'll have the place full of soldiers, trampling the young trees. There's been enough damage in that plantation with the people coming to sightsee: all Michael's friends. Now I won't have digging at all: do you understand?' said Sir Richard, flushed.

Francie felt torn in herself, dividedly sympathetic. 'I expect one can't be too careful ... The poor young little trees ... and besides,' she added to Lois, 'one might blow oneself up.'

'This country,' continued Sir Richard, 'is altogether too full of soldiers, with nothing to do but dance and poke old women out of their beds to look for guns. It's unsettling the people, naturally. The fact is, the Army's got into the habit of fighting and doesn't know what else to do with itself, and also the Army isn't at all what it used to be. I was held up yesterday for I wouldn't like to say how long, driving over to Ballyhinch, by a

thing like a coffee-pot backing in and out of a gate, with a little
brute of a fellow bobbing in and out at me from under a lid at
the top. I kept my temper, but I couldn't help telling him *I*
didn't know what the country was coming to – and just when
we'd got the horses accustomed to motors. "You'll do no good,"
I told him, "in this unfortunate country by running about in a
thing like a coffee-pot." And those patrols in lorries run you into
a ditch as soon as look at you. They tell me there's a great deal of
socialism now in the British Army.'

'Well, it's difficult for them all,' said his wife, pacific, 'and
they're doing their best, I think. The ones who come over here
seem quite pleasant.'

'What regiment have you now at Clonmore?'

'The 1st Rutlands.'

'And there are some Field Gunners and Garrison Gunners too,'
added Lois. 'Most people seem to prefer the Garrison Gunners.'

'The Garrison Gunners dance better,' said Laurence to Mrs
Montmorency. 'It would be the greatest pity if we were to become
a republic and all these lovely troops were taken away.'

'Fool,' said Lois across the flowers. Mr Montmorency looked
at her in surprise.

Lady Naylor continued: 'From all the talk, you might think
almost anything was going to happen, but we never listen. I have
made it a rule not to talk, either. In fact, if you want rumours,
we must send you over to Castle Trent. And I'm afraid also the
Careys are incorrigible . . . Oh yes, Hugo, it's all very well to talk
of disintegration; of course there is a great deal of disintegration
in England and on the Continent. But one does wonder sometimes
whether there's really much there to disintegrate . . . I dare say
there may have been . . . And if you talk to the people they'll tell
you the whole thing's nonsense: and after all what is a country if
it isn't the people? For instance, I had a long conversation this
morning with Mrs Pat Gegan, who came down about the apples –
you remember her, Hugo, don't you, she always asks after you:
she was really delighted to hear you were coming back – "It is
the way the young ones do be a bit wild," she said, and I really
agreed with her. She said young people were always the same,
and wasn't it the great pity. She is a most interesting woman:
she thinks a great deal. But then our people do think. Now have
you ever noticed the English? I remember a year ago when I
was staying with Anna Partridge in Bedfordshire – she is always

so full of doing things in the village, little meetings and so on. Well, I went to one of her meetings, and really – those village women sitting round in hats and so obviously despising her! And not a move on their faces. I said to her afterwards: "I do think you're splendid, Anna, the way you throw yourself into things – but really what can you do with people with so little brain –" She seemed quite annoyed and said that at least they were loyal. I said they hadn't got any alternative, and if they had an alternative I didn't suppose they'd see it. She said they had hearts of gold if they didn't wear them on their sleeves, and I said I thought it was a pity they didn't – it would have brightened them up a bit. She said that at least one knew where one was with them, and I said I wouldn't live among people who weren't human. Then I thought it seemed a shame to unsettle her, if she really likes living in England ... Oh, and I said to Mrs Gegan this morning: "Some of your friends would like us to go, you know," and she got so indignant she nearly wept. And the Trents were telling me – Oh, Hugo, the Trents are coming to tennis tomorrow, specially for you and Francie. And the Thompsons are coming, and I believe the Hartigans. The Hartigan girls are still all there, you'll be surprised to hear. Nobody seems to marry them – and oh, a Colonel and Mrs Boatley are coming, and three or four of the Rutlands –'

'Five,' said Lois.

'Anyhow, several Rutlands. Everyone's so delighted to hear that you and Francie are back.'

'The Trents,' said Lois to Mr Montmorency, with indignation, 'swear that you and they are related. But you are not, surely? It is a perfect obsession of theirs.'

When he said he supposed that he was, through an aunt's marriage, she became pensive. It seemed odd that even the Trents should have a closer claim than she had. Though it was she who had been humming with agitation the whole morning. The sweet-peas in the urn before them bore evidence to her agitation: they all slanted to the west like a falling haystack. It was true she now hoped nothing more of him, but he still was in shadow, faintly, from the kindly monolith of her childhood. What he might have been, what he persisted in being, met in her mind with a jar, with a grate of disparity. The face she had watched sleeping – wiped clear of complexity, quiet but so communicative in stillness that, watching, she seemed to have shared in some kind

27

of suspense, stayed – like the bright blur from looking too long at a lamp – over the face now turned to her, intelligent, dulled, with its sub-acid smile. She was likely to think of him now as a limitation, Mrs Montmorency's limitation; something about Mrs Montmorency that was a pity. The Trents could have him.

'I expect,' she said slightingly, 'you are related to every one.'

'The longer one lives in this country,' he all too agreeably said, 'the more likely that seems.'

Yet she had been certain she felt him looking at her while she argued with Uncle Richard about the guns. Seeking a likeness, perhaps. It was this consciousness that had lent her particular fervour – though she was interested in the guns. Though when she turned round his profile was turned away – in, it seemed, the most scornful repudiation.

He had, as a matter of fact, been looking at her, but without intention and with purely surface observation of detail. When she turned away, light from behind her ran a finger round the curve of her jaw. When she turned his way, light took the uncertain, dinted cheek-line where, under the eyes, flesh was patted on delicately over the rise of the bone. Her eyes, long and soft-coloured, had the intense brimming wandering look of a puppy's; in repose her lips met doubtfully, in a never-determined line, so that she never seemed to have quite finished speaking. Her face was long, her nose modelled down from the bridge, then finished off softly and bluntly as by an upward flick of the sculptor's thumb. Her chin had emphasis, seemed ready for determination. He supposed that unformed, anxious to make an effort, she would marry early.

'Danielstown can't have been so exciting when you were here before,' said Lois to Mrs Montmorency.

But Mrs Montmorency, in an absence of mind amounting to exaltation, had soared over the company. She could perform at any moment, discomfitingly, these acts of levitation. She was staring into one of the portraits.

4

Lois was sent upstairs for the shawls; it appeared that a touch of dew on the bare skin might be fatal to Lady Naylor or Mrs Montmorency. On the stairs, her feet found their evening echoes; she dawdled, listening. When she came down everybody was on the steps – at the top, on the wide stone plateau – the parlourmaid looking for somewhere to put the coffee tray. Mrs Montmorency sat in the long chair; her husband was tucking a carriage rug round her knees. 'If you do that,' Lois could not help saying, 'she won't be able to walk about, which is the best part of sitting out.'

No one took any notice: Mr Montmorency went on tucking.

'Haven't you got a wrap for yourself?' said Lady Naylor. Lois took a cushion and sat on the top step with her arms crossed, stroking her elbows. 'I shouldn't sit there,' her aunt continued; 'at this time of night stone will strike up through anything.'

'If you don't get rheumatism now,' added Francie, 'you will be storing up rheumatism.'

'It will be my rheumatism,' said Lois as gently as possible, but added inwardly: 'After you're both dead.' A thought that fifty years hence she might well, if she wished, be sitting here on the steps – with or without rheumatism – having penetrated thirty years deeper ahead into Time than they could, gave her a feeling of mysteriousness and destination. And she was fitted for this by being twice as complex as their generation – for she must be: double as many people having gone to the making of her.

Laurence, looking resentfully round for somewhere to sit – she had taken the only cushion – said: 'I suppose you think ants cannot run up your legs if you cannot see them?'

Mr Montmorency surprised her by offering a cigarette. He had a theory, he said, that ants did not like cigarette smoke. The air was quiet now, the flame ran up his match without a tremble. 'The ants are asleep,' she said, 'they disappear into the cracks of the steps. They don't bite, either; but the idea is horrid.'

'Don't you want a chair?' When she said she didn't, he settled back in his own. Creaks ran through the wicker, discussing him, then all was quiet. He was not due to leave the ship in which they were all rushing out into Time till ten years after the others, though it was to the others that he belonged. Turning half round, she watched light breathe at the tips of the cigarettes; it seemed as though everybody were waiting. Night now held the trees with a toneless finality. The sky shone, whiter than glass, fainting down to the fretted leaf-line, but was being steadily drained by the dark below, to which the grey of the lawns, like smoke, as steadily mounted. The house was highest of all with toppling immanence, like a cliff.

'I don't think,' said Francie, 'I remember anything so – so quiet as evenings here.'

'Trees,' said Laurence, shifting his pipe. His shirt-front was high above them, he stood by the door with his foot on the scraper.

'This time tomorrow,' said Lady Naylor, 'we shall want to be quiet – after the tennis party.' She let out a sigh that hung in the silence, like breath in cold air.

'Oh yes, the party! The tennis party . . .'

'Francie, did I tell you who were coming?'

'You told her,' said Laurence. 'I heard you.'

'It is the people who don't play tennis who make it so tiring.'

Something about the way, the resigned way, Francie's hands lay out on the rug gave her the look of an invalid. 'It is a good thing,' said Sir Richard, 'you two never went out to Canada. I never liked the idea myself; I was very much against it at the time, if you remember.'

'I was divided about it myself,' said Hugo. 'It seemed worth trying, and yet there was so much against it. I don't know that I should have done very much good – I wonder.'

They wondered with him, with degrees of indifference. Lois stroked her dress – the feel of the stuff was like cobwebs, sticky and damp. There must be a dew falling.

'Oh!' cried Francie. '*Listen!*'

She had so given herself to the silence that the birth of sound, after which the others were still straining, had shocked her nerves like a blow. They looked, from the steps, over a bay of fields, between the plantations, that gave on a sea of space. Far east, beyond the demesne: a motor, straining cautiously out of the silence. A grind, an anguish of sound as it took the hill.

'Patrols,' said Laurence.

Hugo reached out and pressed a hand on to Francie's rug. 'Patrols,' he told her, translating the information.

Sir Richard explained severely: 'Out every night – not always in this direction.'

'They're early; it's half-past nine. Now I wonder . . .'

The sound paused, for a moment a pale light showed up the sky in the darkness. Then behind the screen of trees at the skyline, demesne boundary, the sound moved shakily, stoopingly, like someone running and crouching behind a hedge. The jarring echoed down the spines of the listeners. They heard with a sense of complicity.

'A furtive lorry is a sinister thing.'

'Laurence, it isn't furtive!' said Lady Naylor. 'Can't you be ordinary? If it wouldn't be taken in some absurd kind of way as a demonstration, I should ask the poor fellows in to have coffee.'

'They're careful enough,' said Hugo impatiently. It seemed that the lorry took pleasure in crawling with such a menace along the boundary, marking the scope of peace of this silly island, undermining solitude. In the still night sound had a breathlessness, as of intention.

'The roads are so rough,' said Lois: she could see the wary load lurching into the hedges. 'I wonder now,' she added, 'who is with the patrol tonight?'

'Someone you know?' cried Francie. But Sir Richard, who did not like his friends to be distracted from him by lorries any more than by introspection or headaches or the observation of nature, bore this down with one of his major chords:

'The lower tennis court, Hugo' – waving sideways into the darkness – 'is not what it used to be. Some cattle got on to it after the rain and destroyed it. It's had rolling enough to level a mountain, but it won't be the same for a long time. D'you remember the fours we had on that court that summer – wasn't it nineteen-six – you and I and O'Donnell and poor John Trent?'

'I do. Now was it James O'Donnell or Peter that went to Ceylon?'

'That was a great summer; I never remember a summer like it. We had the hay in by the end of June.'

The lorry ground off east towards Ballyhinch; silence sifting down on its tracks like sand. Their world was clear of it and a pressure lightened. Once more they could have heard a leaf turn in the trees or a bird shifting along a branch. But they found it was now very dark. Francie shivered, and Lady Naylor, rising formally, said she thought they should go in. 'Poor John Trent,' she added, gathering up her cushions, 'never got over that trouble he had with the Sheehans over the Madder fishing. It went into court, you know, and of course he lost. We always told him to keep it out of court. He was very obstinate.'

'He was indeed,' said Sir Richard. 'He made an enemy of Sheehan and it's not a good thing to have made an enemy. Though of course he's dead nowadays, so it may not matter.'

'It may to the Archie Trents ... Laurence, help Uncle Richard in with the long chair, and remember to bring in your own chair afterwards.'

'I never had a chair.'

'Oh, they haven't lighted the lamp in the hall. That is too bad! I am lost without Sarah – do you remember Sarah, Francie? She died, you know.'

Lois, sitting still among rising, passing and vaguely searching figures, cried: 'But it's only just beginning! You're missing the whole point. I shall walk up the avenue.'

Francie went in, groping; trailing her rug. The three men, carrying wicker chairs, converged at the door: the chairs jostled. They all put them down and apologized. Lois repeated: '*I* shall walk up the avenue.' But having arranged an order of procedure they all passed on into the house, creaking and bumping. She walked down the steps alone: she wanted to be alone, but to be regretted.

'Mind you don't get locked out!' her uncle shouted after her. The glass doors shut with a rattle.

Lois walked alone up the avenue, where she had danced with Gerald. She thought what a happy night that had been, and how foolish Mr Montmorency now thought them. He had seemed annoyed at her being young when he wasn't. She could not hope to explain that her youth seemed to her also rather theatrical and that she was only young in that way because people expected it. She had never refused a role. She could not forgo that intensification, that kindling of her personality at being considered very happy and reckless, even if she were not. She could not hope to assure him she was not enjoying anything he had missed, that she was now unconvinced and anxious but intended to be quite certain, by the time she was his age, that she had once been happy. For to explain this – were explanation possible to so courteous, ironical and unfriendly a listener – would, she felt, be disloyal to herself, to Gerald, to an illusion both were called upon to maintain.

Just by the lime, in that dancing night, she had missed a step and sagged on his arm, which tightened. His hand slid up between her shoulders; then, as she steadied back to the rhythm, down again. They had set out laughing, noisy and conscious, but soon had to save their breath. Gerald's cheek, within an inch of her own, was too near to see. All the way up, he had not missed a step; he was most dependable. And remembering how the family had just now gone into the house – so flatly, so unregrettingly, slamming the glass doors – she felt *that* was what she now wanted most – his eagerness and constancy. She felt, like a steady look from him, the perfectness of their being together.

'Oh, I do want you!'

But he was very musical, he conducted a jazz band they had at the barracks: while reaching out in her thoughts she remembered, the band would be practising now. She was disappointed. To a line of tune the thought flung her, she danced on the avenue.

A shrubbery path was solid with darkness, she pressed down it. Laurels breathed coldly and close: on her bare arms the tips of leaves were timid and dank, like tongues of dead animals. Her fear of the shrubberies tugged at its chain, fear behind reason, fear before her birth; fear like the earliest germ of her life that had stirred in Laura. She went forward eagerly, daring a snap of the chain, singing; a hand to the thump of her heart, dramatic with terror. She thought of herself as forcing a pass. In her life – deprived as she saw it – there was no occasion for courage, which like an unused muscle slackened and slept.

High up a bird shrieked and stumbled down through dark, tearing the leaves. Silence healed, but kept a scar of horror. The shuttered-in drawing-room, the family sealed in lamplight, secure and bright like flowers in a paperweight – were desirable, worth much of this to regain. Fear curled back from the carpet-border ... Now, on the path: grey patches worse than the dark: they slipped up her dress knee-high. The laurels deserted her groping arm. She had come to the holly, where two paths crossed.

First, she did not hear footsteps coming, and as she began to notice the displaced darkness thought what she dreaded was coming, was there within her – she was indeed clairvoyant, exposed to horror and going to see a ghost. Then steps, hard on the smooth earth; branches slipping against a trench-coat. The trench-coat rustled across the path ahead, to the swing of a steady walker. She stood by the holly immovable, blotted out in her black, and there passed within reach of her hand, with the rise and fall of a stride, a resolute profile, powerful as a thought. In gratitude for its fleshliness, she felt prompted to make some contact: not to be known seemed like a doom: extinction.

'It's a fine night,' she would have liked to observe; or, to engage his sympathies: 'Up Dublin!' or even – since it was in her uncle's demesne she was straining under a holly – boldly – 'What do you want?'

It must be because of Ireland he was in such a hurry; down from the mountains, making a short cut through their demesne. Here was something else that she could not share. She could not conceive of her country emotionally: it was a way of living, an abstract of several landscapes, or an oblique frayed island, moored at the north but with an air of being detached and washed out west from the British coast.

Quite still, she let him go past in contemptuous unawareness. His intentions burnt on the dark an almost visible trail; he might well have been a murderer he seemed so inspired. The crowd of trees, straining up from passive disputed earth, each sucking up and exhaling the country's essence – swallowed him finally. She thought: 'Has he come for the guns?' A man in a trench-coat had passed without seeing her: that was what it amounted to.

She ran back to tell, in excitement. Below, the house waited; vast on its west side, with thin yellow lines round the downstairs shutters. It had that excluded, sad, irrelevant look outsides of houses take in the dark. Inside, they would all be drawing up closer to one another, tricked by the half-revelation of lamplight. 'Compassed about,' thought Lois, 'by so great a cloud of witnesses . . .' Chairs standing round dejectedly; upstairs, the confidently waiting beds; mirrors vacant and startling; books read and forgotten, contributing no more to life; dinner-table certain of its regular compulsion; the procession of elephants that throughout uncertain years had not broken file.

But as Lois went up the steps breathlessly, her adventure began to diminish. It held ground for a moment as she saw the rug dropped in the hall by Mrs Montmorency sprawl like a body across the polish. Then confidence disappeared, in a waver of shadow, among the furniture. Conceivably, she had just surprised life at a significant angle in the shrubbery. But it was impossible to speak of this. At a touch from Aunt Myra adventure became literary, to Uncle Richard it suggested an inconvenience; a glance from Mr Montmorency or Laurence would make her encounter sterile.

But what seemed most probable was that they would not listen . . . She lighted her candle and went up to bed – uncivilly, without saying good night to anyone. Her Uncle Richard, she afterwards heard, was obliged to sit up till twelve o'clock. He had not been told she was in, so did not think it right to lock up the house.

5

Gerald walked across the lawn to the lower tennis court, swinging his racquet. Once he put up a hand and touched the back of his head, but with assurance: it was perfectly smooth and round. His flannels were gold-white in the sun; he almost shone. He smiled everywhere. It was nonsense for him to pretend he did not care for parties; he went everywhere, he liked to go out every day.

Everybody was sitting or standing about where the green slatted seats were, at the edge of the shade. No one was playing yet; there were two courts and eighteen players; they were discussing who was to play first, their voices sharp with renunciation. Lois was nowhere; Laurence sat on the ground smoking and taking no part in the argument. Lady Naylor talked eagerly to a number of guests who, holding up parasols very straight in the unusual sunshine and wearing an air of vague happiness, were waiting for play to begin before settling down to conversation. Livvy Thompson was organizing: as Lois's friend she felt this devolved upon her in Lois's absence; also, she liked organizing. 'You and you,' she said shrilly, stabbing the air within an inch of each player's chest with a sharp forefinger, 'and why not *you* and *you*?' But before she had ever finished arranging the second four, the first would become involved again.

'Oh, Mr Lesworth,' cried Lady Naylor, and waited for him to approach, 'if you really are coming out, would you bring some more rugs for some more of the people to sit on?'

He turned and went back to the house. It seemed very odd about Lois – now where could she be?

Livvy Thompson looked after him anxiously. Had not Mr

Armstrong come also? During this temporary absence of her attention two fours arranged themselves and walked hurriedly out to take possession of the courts.

The hall, very dark after sunshine, was full of wraps and racquet presses; shoes had wandered away from each other under the chairs. The rest of Gerald's party – they had all driven out from Clonmore in a hired motor – were still there, waiting for Mrs Vermont. Captain Vermont and David Armstrong stood holding her things while she powdered her nose with difficulty before an antique mirror.

'Aren't women awful?' she cried gaily, as Gerald rejoined them. She knew the subalterns hated going about without her. 'My dears, I do wish I knew if we really were asked. Lois is so – I mean, well, you know – vague, isn't she?'

'Well, they wouldn't mind, anyhow,' said David, and tried not to sound proprietary.

'Aren't they hospitable!' Betty Vermont was not disappointed in Ireland after all. She had never before been to so many large houses with so small a sense of her smallness. Of course, they were all very shabby and not artistic at all. Mrs Vermont used to say she longed to be turned loose in any one of them with a paint-pot – white – and a few hundred yards of some really nice cretonne from Barker's.

'Half Ireland is here,' said David, looking out at the crowd of cars on the gravel-sweep. 'I doubt if we get any tennis.'

'Ah, well, David, there's plenty of that at the club. Now, Gerald, don't stand there glaring! You *do* disapprove of powder, you unkind wretch!'

'Rather not,' said Gerald, beaming. But all the same he did like girls to have natural complexions – he was perfectly certain Lois's was. He was carrying all the rugs he could find slung over his shoulder and looked, she informed him, just like a Bedouin. This was not a thing she could have said to every man, because really the East had become so very suggestive. But he was the dearest boy, so absolutely nice-minded. They all went out.

'There seem to be many more people here than I thought we'd asked,' Lady Naylor was saying to Mrs Carey of Mount Isabel. 'Lois asks people she meets at the Clonmore Club, and then forgets. I have been rather wondering about the raspberries; I've sent her out to the garden to see about getting in some more. Colonel and Mrs Boatley are coming – she was a Vere Scott, a

Fermanagh Vere Scott ... Why is it that the Hartigans never will talk to men? I never think they give themselves a chance, do you? Oh, Mr Lesworth, how kind to think of bringing the rugs out! And now there doesn't seem anyone left to sit on them ... Look, would you break up that party of girls on the bank; I don't think they seem to be sitting on anything, and anyhow they look dull and would like to talk. And I am sure they'd be glad if you'd smoke – the midges are terrible. Who is that girl in pale blue who's just coming out?'

'Mrs Vermont. She – er – I think Miss Farquar –'

'Oh, well, never mind; it's a pleasant surprise.' She went over to Mrs Vermont with enthusiasm. 'I'm so glad you could come; it's delightful.'

Gerald looked round everybody again, carefully. Then he respectfully displaced the Miss Hartigans, spread out a rug on the bank and sat down between them. He was at a disadvantage, he could not remember if he had ever been introduced to them, whereas they were perfectly certain he had been. They were pleased at his coming, though on the other hand they were suffering so terribly from the midges that what they wanted most at the moment was to scratch their legs peacefully.

'I call this a frightfully good party,' said Gerald, breezily.

'Yes, it's most enjoyable,' agreed Norah Hartigan.

'I don't think there's anything like these tennis parties you have in Ireland.'

'We have been to tennis parties in England,' replied Doreen.

'Oh, you must certainly come over.'

'I dare say we should feel strange,' said Norah, and her sister agreed with her. Gerald smiled from one to the other so encouragingly that they told him how a sister of theirs, who was not here today, had once stayed for quite a long time near London, and had been taken by an aunt, who was rather what they would call a London Society sort of person, to a very fashionable party – in South Kensington it had been. But their sister had not cared for the party, she thought the English unnatural and said it was extraordinary how their voices sounded when they were all shut up in the one room. 'But excuse me,' concluded the elder Miss Hartigan, turning away because she was afraid the talk was becoming personal and scratching her ankle as discreetly as possible, 'we should not say this to you.'

'It was splendid of you to forget I was English. Well, we shall

37

all be leaving you soon, I dare say; all we jolly old army of occupation.'

'Oh, one wouldn't like to call you *that*,' said Miss Hartigan, deprecatingly.

'– As soon as we've lost this jolly old war.'

'Oh, but one wouldn't call it a *war*.'

'If anyone would, we could clean these beggars out in a week.'

'We think it would be a great pity to have a war,' said the Hartigans firmly. 'There's been enough unpleasantness already, hasn't there? ... And it would be a shame for you all to go,' added Doreen warmly, but not too warmly because they were all men. In fact, it was all rather embarrassing, they fixed their eyes on the players firmly and wished that the set would finish. They thought how daring it was of Mr Lesworth to come so far to a party at all, and only hoped he would not be shot on the way home; though they couldn't help thinking how, if he should be, they would both feel so interesting afterwards. 'Poor young fellow,' they thought with particular tenderness because he was so good-looking, and neither of them, with this tenderness in their eyes, dared to look at him.

Livvy was walking along the top of the bank with David Armstrong. She smiled, with a small tooth over her lower lip; the tip of her nose quivered downward with feminine sensibility. 'It is really a long time since I have seen you, Mr Armstrong.'

David was the nicest of all the subalterns; so agreeable. 'Why, yes,' he agreed, 'I suppose it really must be.' He glanced at the brim of her hat and added: 'It has certainly seemed an awful long time to me.'

'Oh, you mustn't say that,' cried Livvy; she blushed to the chin and laughed.

'*I* don't see why I shouldn't,' said David, alarmed but gratified.

'Well, I mean, you oughtn't to say it *like* that!'

'But I can't help saying what I mean.' His manliness increased with confusion. 'I suppose I am that kind of fellow.'

'You *are* awful!' Livvy laughed so much from the shock of David's behaviour that people sitting along the foot of the bank looked up expectantly. She would not share him, she hurried him off at an angle and then continued: 'Why were you not at the Mount Isabel bicycle gymkhana? I understood you to say that you would be. It was the greatest pity you couldn't be there, it was a grand gymkhana, and they had a putting competition too.

And they had sentries armed in the avenue and made twenty-four pounds for the hospital. And the priest's niece from Kilnagowan fell off and cut her lip; she bled too dreadfully, but Doreen Hartigan has her V.A.D. certificate. And two hundred people sat down to tea – how was it now that you couldn't be there?'

'On duty,' said David, and took on a mystic and obstinate look. 'I was up with some of the men and an N.C.O. in those mountains the other side of the Madder.'

Livvy felt in her spine, running down it from under her waistband, a sharp little thrill. She felt all the soldiers' woman, and said in a glow: 'Well, I call that too awfully dangerous.' He told her: 'It's what we are here for.' They glanced at each other, then both were embarrassed – and showed it – at what they had seen. She stooped, and her hat was an elegant mushroom. From David's complexion blushes cleared slowly away – the last having never quite vanished into his hair before another came after it from his well-fitting collar.

'I can't think what Lois can be doing.' She peered through gaps in the shrubbery towards the gate of the garden. This concern for her friend she put up and twirled like a parasol between them. She sighed: the expansion of her thin little frame, the rise and fall of her two little points of bosom were clearly visible under her white silk jersey. Her panama hat turned down and light tufts of hair came out in fluttering commas against her cheek-bones. From under the brim her eyes looked, slanting slightly up at the corners, with a veiled preoccupied kind of inquisitiveness. She was inquisitive as to so many things her friend Lois hoped one might not have to bother about. David watched her watch the shrubbery for her friend and thought, with a shock, that this really did seem a girl he was to be in love with. He had the fatalism of a recurrent sufferer.

'It will be too bad,' continued Livvy, 'if she doesn't come soon. You would think she might be picking those raspberries herself. You see, all the people she asked from Clonmore have come and were not expected. If she doesn't come soon I must go – yes, indeed I must, Mr Armstrong – and see about the two next fours. You see, her cousin Laurence is no good for that, he is so intellectual, and Lady Naylor doesn't much notice the tennis so long as the party goes off all right. But it seems too bad she shouldn't see Mr Lesworth. I expect Mr Lesworth often speaks to you of her, doesn't he, Mr Armstrong?'

'Er – I don't remember, really.'

'I think it's wonderful to see a man so much in love. I must say I often wonder what love feels like. I always seem to feel so natural about the men I know. But I suppose that's because I am so young – or perhaps I was born platonic. Do you believe in platonics, Mr Armstrong?'

'Plato? Jolly old Grecian – what?'

'No, but listen – do you?'

'Well, what I think,' said David, looking carefully at his racquet and turning it over and over – 'of course it is awfully difficult to express, but I think the right kind of girl and the right kind of fellow can be almost anything to each other, if you know what I mean?'

'*I* think,' said Livvy, 'you put it rather wonderfully.' She suddenly waved her racquet. 'Ah – there's Lois!'

Lois came down the shrubbery path from the garden startled, as if at her own great speed, flushed and visibly breathless. A pink unbuttoned cardigan slipped away at the shoulders, she had a hand in both the pockets to keep it on. Her hat flapped back, it rose above her face in surprise, like a wave. Behind her the bushes stirred in an almost visible backwash. Over the laurels, cropped knee-high at the back of the tennis court, her body rose and dipped with her long steps.

'Ah, here she is!' exclaimed several people, and all looked up the bank uncritically and kindly. The dark air of the shrubbery glittered with midges; she jerked her hands from her pockets and waved her way through. Chinks of sunlight darted up her like mice and hesitated away like butterflies. She had been looking down at the party, deployed in all its promise, with greed and eagerness as at a box of chocolates; eyes like a thumb and finger hovering to selection. Now, engaged by its look, she became all profile; her step flattened, she would have liked to crawl. She was, as Mr Montmorency had noticed, very self-conscious.

The Hartigans said to Gerald: 'Here comes Lois; isn't she very sweet-looking!' They smiled at each other across him.

He said 'Rather!' pocketing their tribute gratefully, with simplicity, as a small boy pockets a tip. His directness baffled them, they were shocked – but he thought how nice they were. In his world affections were rare and square – four-square – occurring like houses in a landscape, unrelated and positive, though with sometimes a large bright looming – as of the sunned west face of Danielstown over the tennis courts. He did not conceive of love as a nervous interchange but as something absolute, out of the scope of thought, beyond himself, matter for a confident outward rather than anxious inward looking. He had sought and was satisfied with a few – he thought final – repositories for his emotions: his mother, country, dog, school, a friend or two, now – crowningly – Lois. Of these he asked only that they should be quiet and positive, not impinged upon, not breaking boundaries from their generous allotment. His life was a succession of practical adjustments, into which the factor of personality did not enter at all. His reserve – to which one was apt to accord a too sensitive reverence – was an affair of convenience rather than protection. Pressed for a statement, he could have said, 'I love her,' to the Hartigans, Mrs Carey, anyone there, without uneasiness, without a sense of the words' vibrations or alarm at a loud impact on something hollow. So he looked up the bank at Lois, while the Hartigans watched him.

Mr Montmorency sat on the ground with his knees apart, holding his ankles limply. His grey flannel coat-collar was turned up over his white shirt, as though a strong wind were blowing. He was being talked to by ladies who sat above him on high green chairs, and though he looked up to answer, it was never higher than their knees. He had more than ever his waxen blinking look, as though exposed unnaturally to the sunshine. His nostrils contracted slightly, as though the smell drawn up from the roots of the grass in a perpetual hot shimmer were more offensive than he cared to explain. He was to play in the next set, and Laurence looked forward to a melancholy exhibition of departed proficiency. A wiry tenseness and setting of teeth there would be, Laurence anticipated, then balls going straight and cleanly into the net. He would be the magnificent player of ten years ago, with little painful grunts as point after point was given away. Laurence guessed that Mr Montmorency hated parties and conversation as much as he himself did, but being less adept at evasion or honouring less fiercely the virginity of his intelligence, could not escape from talking and being talked to.

Laurence achieved this escape by sitting always with a social alert expression between two groups; when one tried to claim him he could affect to be engaged by the other.

A net had been carefully stretched behind the seats to prevent balls going through to the shrubbery. But it was full of rents, and these the balls, driven with force from the further back line, discovered unerringly. To meet these deficiencies children up from the lodge were on duty in the shrubbery; they stared and rambled, pushing among the laurels. They got their teas, an excellent view of the party and a halfpenny for every ball they recovered. Those who did not find any balls and seemed disappointed were given halfpennies also. So why, as Lady Naylor said, bother? She hated to see her guests go round the net, smearing their nice white flannels.

But now, as three balls in succession fled through the leaves, she broke off a conversation and cried: This was too much! Would some kind person – she looked at Laurence – go round and help? He rose, reluctant: simultaneously Mr Montmorency went gratefully round the net at the other end. He was followed by an anxious little boy called Hercules, the only child among the guests and gravely *de trop*. They all three met in the middle.

Laurence said – beating the bushes vaguely – 'Imagine, sir, a small resurrection day, an intimate thing-y one, when the woods should give up their tennis balls and the bundles of hay their needles: the beaches all their engagement rings and the rivers their cigarette cases and some watches. The sea's too general, an affair of furniture and large boilers, it could wait with the graves for the big day . . . Yes, Hercules, that is a tennis ball, but it is pre-war. Put it back in the rabbit hole for the children to find; it is worth a halfpenny to them . . . Last term I dropped a cigarette case into the Cher, from the bridge at Parson's Pleasure. It was a gold one, flat and thin and curved, for a not excessive smoker, left over from an uncle. It was from the days when they wore opera cloaks and mashed, and killed ladies. It was very period, very virginal; I called it Henry James; I loved it. I want to see it rush up out of the Cher, very pale, with eyeballs, like in the Tate Gallery. It wants a woman to be interested in a day like that, to organize; perhaps the Virgin Mary? Don't you think, sir?'

Mr Montmorency, startled at this address, replied: 'I have never been to the Tate Gallery.'

'Talking of being virginal, do you ever notice this country? Doesn't sex seem irrelevant?'

'There certainly are a great many unmarried women,' said Mr Montmorency, looking doubtfully through the net at the Miss Hartigans.

'It is: "Ah, why should we?" And indeed why should they? There is no reason why one should not, so one never does. It applies to everything. And children seem in every sense of the word to be inconceivable.'

'My mother has five,' said Hercules. 'I am the youngest. Hercules is a family name because I am the only boy, but when I go to school I shall be called Richard after my godfather, as everybody says that Hercules even as an initial would be such a disadvantage to me, though not nearly so bad as being afraid of bats.'

'I wonder you aren't at school now,' said Mr Montmorency.

'It would be holidays now anyhow, so I should be bound to be here. That is my eldest sister, playing tennis. They do not see how I can possibly go to school till I have got over being afraid of bats. Besides, I am using up the end of my sisters' governess.'

'Nobody could possibly be sorrier for you than I am, Hercules,' said Laurence. 'This is an unreal party.'

'Well, nobody brought you, I suppose,' said Hercules.

The strong and dreadful smell of laurels made them all irritable. Hercules tore off the tips of bland leaves which kept slapping against his forehead. Laurence came with a ball on his racquet to Mr Montmorency and said: 'I am sure this is one that you lost with Uncle Richard and poor John Trent and the man who did not go to Ceylon in the summer of '06.'

'Whereas, I did not go to Canada.'

'No, you never did, did you?'

Lady Naylor came and looked at them through the netting. 'If between you you cannot find any balls,' she said, 'Laurence, you had better please fetch that other box from the back hall. They are beginning a new set with only three.'

'I have two here that seem quite clean, but they haven't much bounce,' said Hercules.

'Oh, that is splendid, you are a good little boy!' She took the balls from him through a hole. 'Here are a nice lot to go on with,' she called out hopefully, rolling them to the court. Mr Montmorency and Laurence went on searching.

'Now take Aunt Myra; what does she think she's doing?'

'If it comes to that,' said Mr Montmorency, nettled, 'what do you think *you*'re doing? Why are you here at all if you don't like it – as Hercules said? I was happy here at your age, I was full of the place, I asked nothing better. I ask nothing better now.'

'Oh,' said Laurence.

'However, I have no doubt you are right in being dissatisfied; I dare say it is progress,' said Mr Montmorency angrily. 'I dare say it is good for the race.'

Laurence, who did not consider that he had anything to do with the race, replied with some indignation: 'I have no money; where do you expect me to get any money from? I was to have gone to Spain this month with a man and last year I should have gone to Italy with another man, but what do you expect me to go on? I have to eat somewhere, don't I, and here it is simply a matter of family feeling.'

'This is one of the balls; I shall throw it over . . . I had no idea that you were such a materialist.'

'I can't help my stomach. Besides, I like eating, it is so real. But I should like something else to happen, some crude intrusion of the actual. I feel all gassy inside from yawning. I should like to be here when this house burns.'

'Quite impossible; quite unthinkable. Why don't you fish or something? . . . Nonsense!' he added, looking warningly at the house.

'Of course it will, though. And we shall all be so careful not to notice.'

'Are you the undergraduate of today?'

'I should love to be quite, quite abstract.'

Mr Montmorency, offended by all this clever conversation, felt more than ever his isolation, his homelessness. Life was to him an affair of discomfort, but that discomfort should be made articulate seemed to him shocking. The overfine machinery of his mind ceaselessly strained and caught and was agonizingly jerked over details. His refuge was manly talk: he suspected Laurence. He said: 'You are fortunate. There was never a time when I had not other people to think about.'

Laurence, who immediately thought this womanish, said: 'Oh yes, love.' He flicked out and studied the word indifferently – coin of uncertain value.

'Not entirely. One had a certain debt . . .'

'Oh, yes, yes.'

Laurence became more formal, very much better mannered. He recalled that the man was married, had given away his integrity, had not even a bed to himself. The husband, glancing a last time through and under the bushes, was negligible, diffused even a certain staleness. Laurence sheered away mentally, moved further off through the shrubbery. He had been talking foolishly, in his vein of the third or fourth quality, and regretted now having talked still. He felt there had been something morbid about his intrusion, as in a visit to a prison.

'I was to have played in that second set,' said Mr Montmorency. 'It seems to be nearly over: perhaps I shall play in the third.'

'Tea will be coming, never forget tea.' Indeed, a move was being made to the house already. Tea was too grave an affair to be carried outside; besides, one wasn't accustomed to stability in the weather.

'Oh, Hugo, come out now, dear,' cried Francie, walking past with Mrs Hartigan. 'I am sure it doesn't matter about the balls. And the Trents have come – don't you see them? We are just going back to the house to meet them now.'

'Archie? Splendid!' He burst from the shrubbery at the other side, gained the path and hurried towards the house. At a turn of the path, in an arch cut under some holly, he saw Gerald and Lois standing; talking, looking down earnestly at their racquets. With her head bent, Lois was like her mother. He started, then passed them quickly.

But Lois did not notice him going by. She was saying: 'I feel certain you have illusions about me; I don't believe you know what I'm like a bit.' And while she spoke she counted the crimson strings in her racquet: three down, six across.

6

Mrs Vermont ate more hot cakes than she cared to remember because they were so good and nobody seemed to notice. She went on to chocolate cake, then to orange layer cake, to which she returned again and again. An idea she had had, that one should not eat very much when invited out, languished; she finished up with a plate of raspberries. She put all thought of her figure resolutely behind her. Mother, of course, had filled out terribly, but oneself mightn't.

'Nummy-nummy,' she said, pointing out the raspberries to David Armstrong who sat beside her. 'David have some!'

Livvy Thompson, sitting beyond David, deplored these women who talked baby-talk. She felt that her own appeal to men was more serious. 'Mr Armstrong has got to play in the next set,' she said warningly.

'Hoity-toity!' thought Betty Vermont (she never used the expression aloud, as she was not certain how one pronounced it: it was one of her inner luxuries). Turning to Mrs Carey (the Honourable Mrs Carey), who sat on her other side, she said frankly:

'Your scrumptious Irish teas make a perfect piggy-wig of me. And dining-room tea, of course, makes me a kiddy again.'

'Does it really?' said Mrs Carey, and helped herself placidly to another slice of the chocolate cake. She thought of Mrs Vermont as 'a little person' and feared she detected in her a tendency, common to most English people, to talk about her inside. She often wondered if the War had not made everybody from England a little commoner. She added pleasantly: 'This chocolate cake is a speciality of Danielstown's. I believe it's a charm that they make it by, not a recipe.'

'Things do run in families, don't they? Now I am sure you've all got ghosts.'

'I can't think of any,' said Mrs Carey, accepting another cup of tea. She smiled and nodded across the table to Mrs Archie Trent, who had just come in. 'We have been much more worried lately by people taking away our car. Of course it is always brought back again, but one doesn't like to think of its being used for nefarious purposes. That is the worst of a Ford.'

Mrs Vermont opened her mouth to tell Mrs Carey the latest Ford story, then checked herself because in Ireland they seemed to take Fords so seriously. She observed instead: 'All this is terrible for you all, isn't it? I do think you're so sporting the way you just stay where you are and keep going on. Who would ever have thought the Irish would turn out so disloyal – I mean, of course, the lower classes! I remember Mother saying in 1916 – you know, when that dreadful rebellion broke out – she said: "This *has* been a shock to me, I never shall feel the same about the Irish again." You see, she had brought us all up as kiddies to be so keen on the Irish, and Irish songs. I still have a little bog-oak pig she brought me back from an exhibition. She always said they were the most humorous people in the world, and with hearts of gold. Though of course we had none of us ever been in Ireland.'

'Well, I hope you are pleased with us now you have come,' said Mrs Carey hospitably. 'I expect you have all been enjoying this lovely weather?'

'Oh, *well* – you see, we didn't come over to enjoy ourselves, did we? We came to take care of all of you – and, of course, we are ever so glad to be able to do it. Not that I don't like the country; it's so picturesque with those darling mountains and the hens running in and out of the cottages just the way Mother always said. But, you see, one can't help worrying all the time about Timmie – my husband – and all the boys: out all night sometimes with the patrols or else off in the mountains.'

'Terrible. And do you find this a tiring climate?'

A word attracted Mrs Trent's attention across the table. 'Terrible what?' she said. 'Terrible who?' She was youngish, brusque and dominant; the high pink colour over her face as from riding hard in the wind, gave her a look of zestfulness alarming to Mrs Vermont. 'I shouldn't worry,' she said to Mrs Vermont.

Mrs Vermont replied with a shade of asperity that it was *they* who were in a position to worry and therefore must not. ''Cause *we*'re here to take care of you!' The remark, caught in a momentary silence around the table, was received with civility and attention. 'That's splendid!' said Mrs Trent heartily. She got up, having finished her tea rapidly and went to smoke outside. Her husband was M.F.H. and really, thought Mrs Vermont, they did not seem to worry about anything but wire. Mrs Vermont turned for support to David; his ears were scarlet, he rapidly stirred his tea.

Five days ago, an R.I.C. barracks at Ballydrum had been attacked and burnt out after a long defence. Two of the defenders were burnt inside it, the others shot coming out. The wires were cut, the roads blocked; there had been no one to send for help, so there was no help for them. It was this they had all been discussing, at tea, between tennis: 'the horrible thing.' No one could quite understand why Captain Vermont and the subalterns did not seem more appalled and interested. It was not apparent how the subject rasped on their sensibilities. These things happened, were deplored and accepted, and still no one seemed to look on David or Gerald, Smith, Carmichael or Mrs Vermont's Timmie as a possible remedy. Here they all were, playing tennis, and every one seemed delighted. 'If they'd just let us out for a week –' felt the young men. David could not look up as he stirred his tea. What was the good of them? This, he felt, every one should be wondering. But the party would indeed have been dull without them, there would have been no young men. Nobody wished them elsewhere.

Lois had been worried chiefly because Gerald had illusions about her, also, as to whether Aunt Myra noticed the raspberries still would not go round. The guests for which she was responsible were not only unexpected but ravenous. And while she sat watching Aunt Myra, Gerald sat watching herself as though she were an entirely different person, not the sort of person one could describe at all. After tea she played on the upper court with Captain Vermont, against Gerald and Nona Carey. She played well, all her strokes came off; it seemed that worry agreed with her. It could not agree with Gerald, who played badly. Then it occurred to her: he was not worried; she had not the power to worry him. Some idea he had formed of herself remained inaccessible to her; she could not affect it.

By now the upper court was in shadow, they all flickered against the dark screen of the trees like figures cut out of light green velvet. Below, where hot banks of light still blinded the players, there was a suggestion of strain and violence. Whenever she looked down, Mr Montmorency seemed to be handing balls to his partner in silent anger. She guessed it must be himself who was playing badly, so that while she could not resist looking down, she had to keep looking away from him just as fast.

'You were splendid,' said Captain Vermont when their set finished.

'Oh no, I wasn't,' said Lois by reflex action, and wished all the other things to which she was always replying, 'Oh no, I didn't,' or 'Oh no, I'm not,' were half as true. And she thought what a pity it was that Mr Montmorency, instead of exerting himself so fruitlessly, had not been sitting there at the edge of the court to watch her.

She walked down the slope from the court with Gerald beside her. Conscious of many people's attention, she did not know if she seemed enviable or foolish. 'I wish you wouldn't keep looking so pleased the whole time,' she said to Gerald.

'Oh? . . . but I am.'

'What at?'

'Well, I love coming over here. I think you have such awfully nice parties.'

'Oh, the party ... But David enjoys them, and he hasn't got the same expression as you have. In fact, he looks rather sick. What can be the matter?'

'Well, we all feel a little rotten about that barrack.'

'*Don't!* Do you know that while that was going on, eight miles off, I was cutting a dress out, a voile that I didn't even need, and playing the gramophone? ... How is it that in this country that ought to be full of such violent realness, there seems nothing for me but clothes and what people say? I might just as well be in some kind of cocoon.'

'But what could you have done? You, you –'

'I might at least have felt something.'

'But you do; you've got the most wonderful power of feeling.'

'But you never take in a word I say. You're not interested when I tell you about myself.'

'You know I could listen all day to you talking.'

She thought: 'As though you could make me talk all day!' To cover the thought she said earnestly:

'You think we don't understand your not being there in time and not doing anything afterwards? We're not all such idiots. We know it's most terribly difficult for you and that you must obey orders. It's bad luck the orders are silly. It's all this dreadful idea about self-control. When *we* do nothing it is out of politeness, but England is so moral, so dreadfully keen on not losing her temper, or being for half a moment not a great deal more noble than anyone else. Can you wonder this country gets irritated? It's as bad for it as being a woman. I never can see why women shouldn't be hit, or should be saved from wrecks when everybody complains they're superfluous.'

'You don't understand: it would be ghastly if those things went.'

'Why? I don't see – and *I* am a woman.'

Which was, of course, exactly why it wasn't to be expected or desired she *should* understand. He smiled, too happy to answer, and tore out a handful of leaves from the privet hedge. She had this one limitation, his darling Lois; she couldn't look on her own eyes, had no idea what she was, resented almost his attention being so constantly fixed on something she wasn't aware of. A

fellow did not expect to be to a girl what a girl was to a fellow –
this wasn't modesty, specially, it was an affair of function – so
that the girl must be excused for a possible failure in harmony, a
sometimes discordant irreverence. When he said: 'You will never
know what you mean to me,' he made plain his belief in her
perfection as a woman. She wasn't made to know, she was not
fit for it. She was his integrity, of which he might speak to
strangers but of which to her he would never speak.

He tore out another handful of leaves from the hedge and
scattered them carefully over the grass. They both laughed.

She was thinking: 'When next I write to Viola, can I describe
him?' Viola flashed off her men in a phrase, with a sweep of her
red quill pen. The red pen had leaned from the Chinese inkpot,
against the window, like a thin flame, a leaning flamingo on that
day's sunny mist in the Westminster street. It remained a picture
of their intercourse. They had said goodbye in December, a slight
day, anxious between the enormous past and future. The parting
was hardly real, they had barely kissed. They were impatient,
nervous, waiting for the curtain to rise. They had just left school.

They had left school the day before. Yet the new life had been
impatient for Viola, drawing her away from Lois in the taxi,
appropriating her with certainty. She had stepped from their taxi
toppling with school trunks with a kind of solemnity, as on to a
carpet stretched for her festal approach from the kerb to the doors
of her home. Next day, when they said goodbye, her hair was in
place already, woven into her personality. Her pigtail had been
the one loose end there was of her, an extension of her that had
independence, a puppyish walloping thing with nerves of its own.
Now the hair was woven in bright sleek circles over her ears, each
strand round like an eel's body. The effect completed her; Lois
knew she had been missing or else discounting something all these
years. Viola must have played at being a schoolgirl just as Lois
would have to play at being a woman. Two expensive young
men's photographs had risen like suns on her mantelpiece; these
young men had loved since last Easter holidays; their position
was now regularized magically by the putting up of Viola's hair.
For only little commonalities, she declared, had affairs while still
at school. And Lois, after that goodbye so distinct and distant, as
at the little end of a telescope, had left her with the composed,
knowing photographs and the red pen leaning against the sunshine. She had wondered, going out to a day of shopping and the

night mail to be caught at Euston, whether life was to hold her, too, a man's passion; and if so, when? And she had bought a dozen pairs of silk stockings and the black georgette Aunt Myra said was 'old'.

But a man's passion was not at all the thing. My dear, too Dell-ish! Viola went to what she supposed one would call her first ball; in tulle she went, smoke blue, with a close gold-leaf round the hair – not bright gold, dull gold. Various people had seemed intrigued, were in fact intrigued rather definitely. There was So-and-so, an absurd person (flash of the red pen), and the aloof, rather mask-like So-and-so – who might intrigue Lois. But when it came to *So-and-so* (a most brilliant flash of the pen) Viola would admit to Lois she *was* affected: it really had been affecting. But enough of Viola. 'Now, Lois darling, you must tell me about them all: I must know everybody.'

And there arose, recurrently, the difficulty in describing Gerald. Who else had been intrigued, Lois was not certain. How much was somebody intrigued when they wished to sit out in a car in the barrack square for four dances? Might not Viola consider sitting out in a car at all rather Dell-ish? When someone tried to kiss you with whisky-ish breath, how much were they intrigued and how much was whisky? She thought a major proposed to her, though he seemed rather old, but he was so much confused and had such a mumbly moustache she could not be certain. And later on at the Clonmore Club a lady was pointed out to her as, she was almost certain, that major's wife. David had seemed intrigued, but then he himself intrigued Livvy so very definitely, and did not a young man under these conditions become slightly sordid? So Lois became so very general in her references that Viola was suspicious: she asked, was there really anyone? Then she began to write in a married-womanish tone of encouragement, which, considering she *could* be married at any moment, was really justified. Lois was forced to state, there *was* a man in the Rutlands, a Gerald Lesworth, whom she found affecting. She supposed there was no question as to his being intrigued; people seemed to notice. So Viola wrote back, she must hear all about him, should have heard before: her Lol was really the final Sphinx. She wanted to know, to see, to hear him, even to smell him – because all the nicest men did smell, didn't they, indefinably but divinely. One noticed it when one was dancing or, sometimes, sitting out. So now, please, everything; by return.

Viola did not like moustaches, but some men did qualify their moustaches, surely? Gerald's lay like a fine dark shadow, so that his lips seemed to curl up more than it did. It answered his eyebrows somehow – that had a way of drawing together while he spoke – and some soft edgeless darkness about his eyes. If one mentioned his teeth so white that his smile seemed a long slow flash in the tanned face, didn't it make him sound like Fairbanks? For he was *not*, at all. He had a way of looking down while he spoke, as though his thoughts were under his eyelids. From his look she had sometimes turned in impatience, never in discomfort. There was emotion there unclothed in the demi-decency of thought; nakedness, not a suggestive deshabille. If he was looking away and one spoke, his eyes returned with an extraordinary look of welcome. He had a good chin, cut sharply away underneath with a strong shadow. His head was pleasant with bumps, that made planes of light and shadow over his polished hair. And she knew she liked something about the back of his neck: it was a personal neck – not just a connection, an isthmus – with skin fitting closely over the muscles.

As she stood looking at Gerald by the privet hedge, he emerged from the mist of familiarity, clear to her mental eye. She saw him as though for the first time, with a quick response to his beauty; she saw him as though he were dead, as though she had lost him, with the pang of an evocation. While she could hold him thus – before he receded or came too closely forward – she wanted to run indoors and write to Viola. Viola would be certain to tell her she loved him, and by that declaration, to be expressed with vigour, Lois was too certain to be affected. She was afraid at the thought of it.

She would have loved to love him; she felt some kind of wistfulness, some deprivation. If there could only be some change, some movement – in her, outside of her, somewhere between them – some incalculable shifting of perspectives that would bring him wholly into focus, mind and spirit, as she had been bodily in focus now – she could love him. Something must be transmuted . . . Or else, possibly, if he would not love her so, could give her air to grow in, not stifle imagination.

He said: 'What's the matter? Bothered?'

'Thinking – about you, in a kind of way.'

'Good.'

'I was describing you. How would you describe me?'

He was surprised, he needed time to think of this; he did not know. 'I must just go in,' she said – 'do you mind? – and write a letter. It's so important. Will you post it for me at Clonmore?'

But meanwhile, they had been irritating Lady Naylor, who seeing Lois stand so vaguely down by the privet hedge, disclaiming implicitly the party given for her amusement, was goaded to the point of an interruption. Now she called: 'Lois – Lois!'

Lois sighed and went to her.

'I want you to take the Trents and Maguires and Boatleys round the garden,' she said as her niece approached. 'I shall be coming later' – she murmured: 'when some more of the people have gone. Mrs Trent wants a cutting of the allspice and would like to see if there's anything else she would like. Tell Donovan.' She murmured again: 'And don't let Mrs Boatley get with Mrs Maguire, she is a Christian Scientist and will talk of it, and you know the Maguires' little nephew died of that. And if the Boatleys like the peaches give them some; let Donovan pack them.' She added in a still lower tone of reproach: 'Because I don't believe there were raspberries for them at tea.'

7

Francie was finding Laurence not so difficult after all, if one just ran on quite naturally. They sat at the top of the steps together, after everybody had gone. The fields looked wider, the sky more gracious and distant seen through the clearing smoke of social activity. The Trents left last but one, the Hartigans and their aunt Mrs Foxe-O'Connor had just gone jogging away up the avenue, knee to knee in their little trap. The gravel at the foot of the steps was all scored up and flung into spirals by the turning of wheels. Early tomorrow, there would be a busy sound of gardeners raking it smooth again. At present, there was the busy sound of rooks: it heightened Mrs Montmorency's and Laurence's peaceful lassitude to reflect that rooks still had to talk, to flock and mix in intricate sociability. Men and women had, since seven o'clock, been released from this obligation.

There was nothing to say, they did not have to say anything: they exclaimed their thoughts casually, not answering one another's, on the retreat towards silence. All the afternoon they had been asking questions, and ignoring the answers as far as possible. Laurence knew he could not be asked by his aunt to bring the chairs in or see whether Lois had locked up the garden while he sat here, so apparently entertaining Mrs Montmorency.

Francie had not wanted to know how anyone was; health played too large a part in her life already. She had not wanted to know if they thought the garden lovely – the supremacy of Danielstown garden made opinion irrelevant – whether they preferred winter to summer because of the hunting, or summer to winter because of the tennis. Neither had it seemed to Laurence important whether anyone wanted more tea or had had really enough, whether they feared to be driven into the ditch by Black and Tans on the way home, or whether they knew Oxford. They both felt themselves coming to life again slowly, now that the party was over, and putting off a sort of antagonism. At an up-stairs window they could hear Lady Naylor and Lois discussing the guests, agreeing that it had been a successful day.

Francie said: 'I do wonder now whether this weather will last.' This gold weather had all the delights of a new perception, it made Danielstown real as a memory.

'I suppose they don't really feel like that inside,' said Laurence.

'I wonder at them bringing a child like Hercules. I found him walking about the house when I went up for my air-cushion. The poor little fellow . . . I let him blow up my air-cushion and then I took him and showed him photographs of the Carnival that I brought back from Nice. We talked quite a time; he tells me he is afraid of bats. I wonder now why they called him Hercules.'

'Wouldn't it be terrible to be in the Army . . .'

'Isn't that young Mr Lesworth devoted to Lois? I wonder does she feel it at all?'

'I always wonder what one does in the Army when one's not doing something particular, very particularly.'

'I wonder if they would marry?'

'Marry?' said Lawrence, surprised into attention. 'I don't see why. Though I don't see why not. As Lois never does anything or seems to want to, I suppose she must be expecting to marry someone. And Lesworth is pleasant, I think, and rather pretty. He is like a photograph of a man in an advertisement putting on the right kind of collar. Doesn't advertising develop – I sometimes wonder if one might not think of taking it up.'

'But doesn't she draw very nicely?'

'Well, she could draw people in the Army doing things, like Lady Butler.'

'She is so sweet; I love to watch her.'

'Her consumption of tennis is something enormous. There's tennis tomorrow at Castle Trent and I've got to drive her over. I often wonder whether she really *would* get assaulted by Black and Tans if she went alone, or by sinister patriots, or whether she might not be old enough now to look after herself.'

'I'm afraid at *her* age,' said Francie, blushing; 'her age isn't any protection.'

'I cannot imagine wanting to assault anybody. But then I never can conceive of anybody else's mentality – or isn't that mentality? Why is it so much worse for a young girl to miss tennis than for a young man to miss Spain? I suppose it is something to do with the life force and that one must not trace the connection.'

'I wonder why she's so fond of that Livvy Thompson – she seems to be managing.'

'She's not fond – it's contiguity. Why should they chop up the rather beautiful name of Olivia into something that sounds like cat's meat?'

This Francie well understood, she herself did not care to be called Frances, it sounded formal. She sighed, and gathered together the folds of her grey-and-blue 'mottledy' foulard. She had been wondering – watching Hugo so happy with Mrs Trent, and now the speculation recurred to her – whether the woman Hugo had really needed would not have worn coats and skirts, snapped her fingers at dogs and recrossed her legs with decision. Mrs Trent was an amusing good sort; she so radiated the quality that Francie, after a minute or two's conversation, had felt quite a good sort also. Was she, though, perfectly understanding? But then did Hugo perhaps feel a little smothered in one's own understanding, a little reduced by it? For instance: Francie thought, honestly, Hugo had played magnificently this afternoon; several people had said to her: 'It's a delight to see your husband play on these courts again'; they would not have said that, surely, if he had not been playing magnificently! But even so armed, she would not be able to combat Hugo's conviction that his tennis was going off, because it was something he never mentioned and he would be furious at hearing it put into words. So still she would have to feel his pride suffer – as though he were growing old, when there wasn't a shadow of age on him. She remembered how he had shown up today, playing, sitting or walking, among the young men. She liked the young men, but they seemed all limbs and faces, not yet related. She wondered what Hugo thought of the young men.

She thought of their room upstairs with quiet light in the ceiling; of ghostly roses that still showed faintly when one drew the curtains over the daylight. She supposed she ought to be lying down; she got up, murmuring something, and went indoors. Laurence stood up, vacillating. He wondered if they would meet him and make him do things if he were to venture up for his book.

Francie, crossing the ante-room, was waylaid by Lady Naylor coming out of Lois's room. 'Ah, there you are, Francie, good! Now I'm longing to know what you thought of them all. To tell you the truth, I am thankful it's safely over. I hope they enjoyed themselves really: they *looked* all right.'

'Indeed they must have! It was a great success.' They sat down on two of the crimson chairs, stepping-stones over a lake of floor, to discuss the party.

Francie declared how pleasant she had found Mrs Archie Trent, and how nice it had been to see Mrs Carey again, and how handsome Nona was growing up. And what a pity it was, she said, about the Hartigans; they had been grown-up girls when she had seen them last, and it did seem hard! 'And oh,' she cried, in a glow of pleasure and sympathy, 'isn't that young Mr Lesworth very devoted?'

'Yes, he has charming manners; he comes over here a good deal. He's so helpful with chairs and rugs: I do wish he were Laurence!'

'But so devoted to Lois – and really one can't be surprised. The way he follows her round with his eyes – and his feet too –'

'*Sssh!*' exclaimed Lady Naylor. 'She's in her room! I wouldn't like her to pick up ideas like Livvy's. Are you sure, by the way, you're not thinking of Mr Armstrong? There's a very great case of devotion there. He follows Lois and Livvy follows him. I expect in the general confusion, with so many people, you mixed up the young men. They are all alike – it's a pity, I always think. It's a pity, too, about Lois and Livvy; it isn't a friendship I like. But poor Livvy's motherless and she's always riding over to meals and of course Lois needs girls of her own age. She made very nice friends at her school in England, but it's so unlucky, they're never allowed to come over. Something said in the English press has apparently given rise to an idea that this country's unsafe. It's unlucky for Lois. *I* should never go by the papers about England ... No, Francie, if you didn't mix up the young men, I really don't know what you mean.'

'Oh, it's been very stupid of me,' cried Francie, flushing with agitation. 'Of course I should never have said if I hadn't thought – if I hadn't been led to think ... No, I see now that I oughtn't to have. But I thought from what everyone said ...'

'But I am still quite in the dark, dear,' said Lady Naylor, flushed also and smiling with irritation. 'I suppose, however, you must have gathered that as I *don't* understand what you *do* mean, what you mean cannot really be so.'

'Oh, of course,' agreed Francie, ruffling the silk on her lap with light, feathery touches. 'All the same, I do think you ought to know, Myra, that everyone said ...'

'One cannot help what people say, though it is always annoying. Not that I ever do know what they say: I make a point of not knowing. You know how I've always turned my face against gossip, especially these days: it's annoying to hear of it everywhere, even at one's own parties. It's a very great danger, I think, to the life of this country.'

'Well, but really, you couldn't say this was political. It seems to me natural that people should take an interest – they're all so fond of her. If young Mr Lesworth and Lois *are* really –'

Lady Naylor was forced into open country. 'Oh, is that it?' she exclaimed in enlightenment. 'But really, my dear Francie, what a fuss about nothing! No, not you, dear; I never meant you made the fuss, but really with all these hints: "People are saying," you might have meant almost anything. One's friends do excel themselves, really! Just because they've played tennis together and danced once or twice! Really, you would think they wanted one to divide one's tennis parties up like a Quaker meeting, and turn ballrooms into that horrible kind of country dancing they have in England – Anna Partridge's people do it – women hopping one way, waving things, men all hopping the other way, stamping. "Really," as I said to Anna Partridge, "if this is what you call getting in touch with the people, give me what you call feudalism!"'

'Yes. But really, Myra, is it so very improbable? They're both so young, and so –'

'Why yes, of course; exactly!' Lady Naylor sat up in her chair with a heightening of colour, an incisive gesture; her eyes threatened a falcon-swoop on her friend's rash flank. 'Ex-*actly*! Which is one of the many things that do make it so impossible.'

'I said "Improbable!"' Francie spoke with a funny zest. She hated arguments as she hated rain; once caught in the rain she could hear it crashing on her umbrella, feel it spill on her shoulders with exhilaration. She knew so little excitement. She now felt for the first time Myra's equal in vigour and personality; she felt this opposition to Myra must at last increase their confidence in each other.

'In the first place,' said Lady Naylor, 'he's a subaltern. Subalterns can't marry – not of course that they're like priests, but they might just as well be until they are captains and thirty. Colonel Boatley feels very strongly ... Of course, he's a thoroughly nice boy, so much liked in the Regiment. But then, what are the Rutlands nowadays? Of course they did magnificently in the War. But now they seem to be full of people like that extraordinary little Mrs Vermont, who turned up perfectly pleased with herself this afternoon, in spite of Lois's having quite forgotten that she'd asked her. No, *he* of course is charming, but he seems to have no relations. One cannot trace him. His mother, he says, lives in Surrey, and of course you do know, don't you, what Surrey *is*? It says nothing, absolutely; part of it is opposite the Thames Embankment. Practically nobody who lives in Surrey ever seems to have been heard of, and if one does hear of them they have never heard of anybody else who lives in Surrey. Really altogether, I think all English people very difficult to trace. They are so pleasant and civil, but I do often wonder if they are not a little shallow: for no reason at all they will pack up everything and move across six counties ... Of course, I don't say Gerald Lesworth's people are in *trade* – I should never say a thing like that without foundation. Besides, if they were in trade there would be money; money on English people shows so much and he quite evidently hasn't any. No, I should say they were just villa-ry.'

'But there are so many villas in England,' said Francie, 'that some of the people who live in them are bound to be nice. I often think so, looking out of the train.'

'Very nice in their way, I am sure – but that's not the immediate point, dear. There is *no* question at all – you understand? – of anything between Mr Lesworth and Lois. And of course naturally *they* haven't thought of it – if they had, don't you see, they'd be much more careful to make it appear there wasn't. Of course I agree that Lois ought to be more careful. I was careful at her age; I was careful by instinct, which is a thing that girls nowadays seem to lack. There seems nothing to do between putting ideas in a girl's head and letting her behave like an absolute donkey. It is all very difficult, really. If she were my own niece I should speak to her – I should certainly speak to Laurence if he were going on like that – but as she's Richard's niece I don't very well see that I can. There's so little to go on. And I really cannot have Richard bothered, it makes him so difficult. When he feels he ought to do something and isn't sure what, there's no saying at all what he may do. One does dislike awkwardness. And it doesn't seem kind to ask the young man his intentions when if he *should* have any they would have to be quashed immediately ... No, one must leave it at this. I rely on you, Francie, to contradict any more of this gossip that comes your way, and you might ask Hugo to also – if he has heard any – Perhaps on the whole better not put the idea into his head; he might forget and discuss it with Richard ... Meanwhile, I shall talk to Lois seriously about her future. She draws very nicely; I often think that she might take that up. I must tell her to show you and Hugo some of her drawings.'

'But I don't know anything about drawing.'

'Oh, all she needs is a little encouragement.'

'Just one thing, Myra – I think you're so wise, you're so perfectly right, as you know. I do always in general believe in letting things like this take their course. But . . . as this thing can't *have* a course, really mustn't: is it quite fair to the young man? Because Lois is so very –'

Here she broke off, scared by a terrible clatter in Lois's room. A pail had been kicked and some furniture violently shifted.

'Oh, Francie!' exclaimed Lady Naylor reproachfully. 'You ought to remember she's there! One can't be too careful! In fact, if you don't mind, I expect we had better not talk any more. You must go and lie down – you're looking as fresh as a rose, but I know how Hugo insists upon it.'

They got up, she took Francie's arm and led her as far as her door. Francie felt like something being put back in its box. Lady Naylor went down, calling, to look for Laurence and ask him to bring the chairs in and lock up the garden.

For Lois, this had all been exceedingly difficult. There she was, caught in her bedroom, she had not the face to come out. The door went paper-thin as they raised their voices. At first it had seemed all right: Aunt Myra knew she was in here, having just left her. But soon their tones changed, a keen hunting note came into them; they were on a topic. Carried away, Aunt Myra had forgotten. She heard 'Lois ... Lois ... Lois ...' She hummed and sang: they were too intent. To one's sense of honour such things were agonizing. She leaned right out of a window into the cooling air, into the hush of limes on the avenue; she watched Uncle Richard and Mr Montmorency walk to the white gate. Their heads nodded down from their shoulders like old men's, happily; they spoke of Archie and Mrs Archie and poor John. But from the room behind the other voices, flooding in through the door, came after her. She flung herself on her bed with a squawk from the springs and pressed her ear shut till the lobes and her finger-tips ached: also she pulled the pillows over her head. It was hot thus and still the voices penetrated. They came on steadily, like the Hound of Heaven. It was hard, really, the way they both kept at it.

The voices spoke of love; they were full of protest. Love, she had learnt to assume, was the mainspring of woman's grievances. Illnesses all arose from it, the having of children, the illnesses children had; servants also, since the regular practice of love involved a home; by money it was confined, propped and moulded. Lois flung off the pillows and walked round the room quickly. She was angry; she strained to hear now, she quite frankly listened. But when Mrs Montmorency came to: 'Lois is very –' she was afraid suddenly. She had a panic. She didn't want to know what she was, she couldn't bear to: knowledge of this would stop, seal, finish one. Was she now to be clapped down under an adjective, to crawl round lifelong inside some quality like a fly in a tumbler? Mrs Montmorency should not!

She lifted her water jug and banged it down in the basin: she kicked the slop-pail and pushed the washstand about. .... It was victory. Later on, she noticed a crack in the basin, running between a sheaf and a cornucopia: a harvest richness to which she each day bent down her face. Every time, before the water clouded, she would see the crack: every time she would wonder: what Lois *was* – She would never know.

8

Sir Richard, to whom the idea about Lois and Gerald percolated in time through the family conversation, declared the idea was preposterous. What chiefly worried him was, might she not have mentioned to Gerald those guns in the lower plantations? He had charged her not to, but she was just like Laura, poor Laura's own child in fact; she would talk and talk and you never knew where you had her. He announced, he had been thinking for some time subalterns should be fewer and more infrequent. He was delighted when he heard from the postman, and was able to pass on, how three young women in the Clonmore direction had had their hair cut off by masked men for walking out with the soldiers. And indeed they got no sympathy from the priest either, the postman said, for the priest knew that English soldiers were most immoral.

'And how would you like it,' Sir Richard said to his niece indignantly, 'if a thing like that were to happen to you?'

'I should be bobbed,' said Lois. 'I should take it as a sign. But I have never walked an inch with anyone, not what you would call *out*, Uncle Richard.'

'But masked men,' said Lady Naylor, 'would be a very nasty experience for a girl of your age.' Lois said she would prefer the men to be masked; she would be less embarrassed in the event of meeting them afterwards.

'I wonder what they do with the hair,' she added. She thought inwardly: 'If they're going to take this attitude, I could not be blamed for falling in love with a married man.' She searched her heart anxiously. She wrote to Viola that she feared she might be falling in love with a married man. But when she looked at Mr Montmorency next morning at breakfast, and still more when she had to drive him back from Mount Isabel, the idea seemed shocking. She regretted having sent her letter to post in such a hurry.

Scandalized by the memory, she drove home briskly. On the bright sky, opposite, Mr Montmorency's pale face hung like an apparition's. She took the curves of Mount Isabel drive with a rattle: the trap swung on its axle, the traces creaked. Beyond the gates, light lay flat and yellow along the hedges where brambles showered; hard red blackberries knocked on the spokes and swung back, shining. She took the short way, over a shoulder of mountain; the light-pink road crunched under the wheels like sugar. Coming up out from the lanes they bathed an hour or so in the glare of space. Height had the quality of depth: as they mounted they seemed to be striking deeper into the large mild crystal of an inverted sea. Out of the distance everywhere, pointless and unrelated, space came like water between them, slipping and widening. They receded from one another into the vacancy. On yellow furze-dust, light was hard and physical; over parching heather shadow faded and folded tone on tone, and was drawn to the sky on delicate brittle peaks.

The road bent over a ridge, the trap ran down on the pony's rump; he and she shifted back on their seats. They stared with unfocussed intensity over each other's shoulders. Gorse, they said, was never out of bloom (he commented). Nor kissing, they said (she supplied), out of season – yet she supposed this untrue; she supposed that they both sometimes must be. 'And so much bitterness,' he exclaimed, 'over this empty country!'

'What is it exactly,' she asked, 'that they mean by freedom? What does it affect? What is it besides an excuse for war?'

'I suppose,' he said in his faint voice, as at the pit of a yawn, 'some kind of a final peace – stability.'

'Then to fight's absurd; the more one keeps on, the further from it one is. It's a hopeless kind of beginning.' She looked at him earnestly, lucidly, like a puppy.

'You are very reasonable . . . Do you read the papers?'

'Well . . . I do hate things that have just happened.'

'– I don't follow.'

'They're so raw.'

The road was steep and the pony determined to trot; it stumbled; she pulled it up sharply. She was inclined to forget she was driving at all. He started and put out a hand, to steady himself, along the back of the seat. He hated things to be done badly; he was old-maidish. They were silent in a mutual criticism. As they came down and the mountains, drawn behind, were once more scenic, as hedges ran up at the sides of the road, the illusion of distance between them faded; they obtruded upon each other; a time when they could have talked was gone. They might have said, she felt now, anything; but what had remained unsaid, never conceived in thought, would exercise now a stronger compulsion upon their attitude. She was to believe they had approached each other in the unintimacy of silence. Shy with retrospective emotion, she fidgeted in the trap, irked by his look, his manner, all his presence physically. Whenever she stretched a foot it touched his, always she seemed to be retreating, apologizing, having to shift her position. When she sat well forward to give her attention to driving, their knees touched.

'This trap's too small,' she said finally. Mr Montmorency – face dull on the bright sky – replied: 'Oh, I don't know – depends on how one arranges oneself.' If he only would not smile – but he smiled constrainedly. Next to Laura, she was the most fidgety person from whom he had suffered. But Laura's unrepose had been an irradiation, a quiver of personality. She was indefinite definitely, like a tree shining, shaking away outlines; a bay, a poplar in wind and sunshine. Her impulses – those incalculable springings-out of mind through the body – had had, like movements of branches, a wild kind of certainty. He had been half aware of some kind of design in her being of which she was unaware wholly.

Whereas, here still was Lois (now Laura's tree had fallen), twisted away from him on the opposite seat of the trap, outraging tone in her pink jersey – a shade or two nearer than Laura, perhaps, to the accuracy passing for beauty. She looked gênée, dispirited; some failure, no doubt, in his company: he must be an old man to her. She glanced back once or twice at the mountains, from which a light peaty breath still came after them down the descending road.

She laughed suddenly, parted the reins, and jerking a rein in each hand, with wide elbows, chirruped and clucked to the pony. 'This,' she said, 'is how my governess used to drive. She used to say it came natural because all her people were horsey. She said her father had been a colonel and she used to plait hats out of crinkled paper and wear them. She loved my mother embarrassingly, and she was always embroidering things. My mother hated it – do you remember?'

'I don't remember your governess. Hated what?'

'Being loved like that, and given embroidery. Miss Part used to laugh and say, "I'm afraid I'm terribly whimsical, Mrs Farquar," and Mother used to say, "Oh no, I don't expect you are really" – was it unkind?'

'Well, it sounds unkind.'

'I wonder if she would have liked being loved at my age – do you remember?'

'I don't suppose she had made up her mind.'

Lois turned and looked at him so intently that he was uneasy suddenly: the bottom dropped out of the past, spilling all its security. He would never know how much Laura had said to her daughter those last ten years – years locked away from him: Lois had got the key. He said with acidity: 'If she and I had married –'

'Oh, *yes* . . .'

'My dear child, you wouldn't be there.'

'Oh, but half of me would be. And I dare say,' she said charmingly, 'the other half of me would have been much nicer.' The turning away of her look was more confidential than any directness.

'Thank you – don't run over the little pigs!'

Michael Connor's farm first announced itself by some pink little silky pigs running along the roadside. A sow got up, like a very maternal battleship. Connor children looked, shrieked, fell from a gate and fled to the farmhouse, skirting a pool of liquid manure in the front yard. It was a nice farm, Lois pointed out, it had the door and window-frames painted blue, the colour of all the cart-wheels. The Connors were darling people; she drove past slowly, leaning over the side of the trap to see if the family were about. The house was one storey high, with a slate roof. Mr Montmorency sat frowning; he could not remember if this were a Michael Connor he ought to remember.

Michael Connor came out from a furze-thatched shed at the side. He took off his wide straw hat and shook hands with them both. His hand was bony, nervous and dry as earth.

'It's a grand evening,' said he with a melancholy smile.

'It is indeed. And how,' she asked, apprehensive, 'is Mrs Connor?'

'Ah, the poor woman . . . the poor woman!' Michael looked away from them, nobody spoke. Lois at last said: 'Give her my love.'

'I will,' said Michael, 'and proud she will be. And yourself's looking lovely, Miss Lois; a fine strong lady, glory be to God.'

'You remember Mr Montmorency?'

'Sure indeed I do!' exclaimed Michael, and shook hands with Mr Montmorency again with greater particularity. 'And very well I remember his poor father. You are looking grand, sir, fine and stout; I known you all these years and I declare I never seen you looking stouter. And welcome back to Danielstown, Mr Montmorency, welcome back, sir!'

'Are your grandchildren well?'

'They are,' said Connor gloomily, 'but they're very bashful. And they do be stravaging about always and not contented at all. They are a great distress to herself, and she unable to come out after them.'

'But is Mrs Peter Connor not with you?'

'She is, Miss Lois. But she is desthroyed with it all and disheartened. Indeed, miss, she is in great distress; and she always looking and starting and craning up the boreen. It is torn in herself she is; distracted for Peter and dhreading he'll come. It would dishearten yous to be with her daily and nightly the way she is, the poor woman. And the military Carveen have the hearts torn out of us nightly, and we stretched for sleep, chasing and charging about in the lorries they have. Sure you cannot go a step above in the mountains without them ones lepping out from your feet like rabbits. Isn't it the great pity they didn't finish their German war once they had it started?'

'And no news at all of Peter?' Lois asked, diffident.

'We have not,' said Michael, expressionless. His face resumed its repose. The sum of detachment and sadness was this special kind of nobility. 'And I don't know what is to be the end of it,' resumed Michael, with a return to his conversational manner. 'I couldn't tell you what will be the outcome at all. These surely are times that would take the heart from you. And thank you, Miss Lois, and you too yourself, your honour.'

They once more shook hands, complimented each other again on the beauty of the evening, and Lois drove on. Michael stood at the gate till they turned the corner. The mountain farm, its wind-bitten firs dragged east, its furze-thatched byres, sank slowly under the curve of a hill. Looking longest after them, like an eye, a window glittered. Some grey geese that had gaped and straggled behind the trap relinquished the chase abruptly, stumbled round in a flock and went straining off in the other direction. Their backs were more than oblivious; they made the trap, the couple in it, an illusion. And indeed Lois and Hugo both felt that their pause, their talk, their passing had been less than a shadow.

'That is not,' said Hugo, after reflection, 'the Michael Connor that I remember. He was a foxy man with a chin. Has that one a son Peter?'

'He has. I expect you guessed – he is on the run – "Proscribed" don't they call it? He could be shot at sight. He is wanted over an ambush in County Clare; they got him once, but he escaped again – I was so glad. I shouldn't wonder if he was up the boreen at the moment. I know he is home, for Clancey saw him three days ago. But don't speak of it – one cannot be too careful. Poor Mrs Peter must be in a dreadful state, wherever he is. Mrs Michael is dying, you know: she has been dying a long time. The last time I went up they wouldn't let me see her, because of the pain . . . There are young men gone from three of the farms up here – Captain Carmichael told me; he is Intelligence Officer. And I know it is true, because Clancey told me too – I say, supposing Gerald had happened to be with us and Peter Connor had come down the boreen, would Gerald have had to have shot him, or would he have been off duty?'

'Peter might have shot Gerald.'

'Oh no, not when he was with me. Besides,' she added, 'Gerald is so matter of fact. Nothing could make him into a tragedy.'

Hugo debating if she were subtle or very stupid, Lois busy with melodrama, they drove home briskly. To the south, below them, the demesne trees of Danielstown made a dark formal square like a rug on the green country. In their heart, like a dropped pin, the grey glazed roof reflecting the sky lightly glinted. Looking down, it seemed to Lois they lived in a forest; space of lawns blotted out in the pressure and dusk of trees. She wondered they were not smothered; then wondered still more that they were not afraid. Far from here too, their isolation became apparent. The house seemed to be pressing down low in apprehension, hiding its face, as though it had her vision of where it was. It seemed to gather its trees close in fright and amazement at the wide, light, lovely unloving country, the unwilling bosom whereon it was set. From the slope's foot, where Danielstown trees began, the land stretched out in a plain flat as water, basin of the Madder and Darra and their fine wandering tributaries, till the far hills, faint and brittle, straining against the inrush of vaster distance, cut the droop of the sky like a glass blade. Fields gave back light to the sky – the hedges netting them over thinly and penetrably – as though the sheen of grass were a shadow on water, a breath of colour clouding the face of light. Rivers, profound in brightness, flowed over beds of glass. The cabins lifting their pointed white ends, the pink and yellow farms were but half opaque; cast doubtfully on their fields the shadow of living. Square cattle moved in the fields like saints, with a mindless certainty. Single trees, on a rath, at the turn of a road, drew up light at their roots. Only the massed trees – spread like a rug to dull some keenness, break some contact between self and senses perilous to the routine of living – only the trees of the demesne were dark, exhaling darkness. Down among them, dusk would stream up the paths ahead, lie stagnant over the lawns, would mount in the tank of garden, heightening the walls, dulling the borders like a rain of ashes. Dusk would lie where one looked as though it were in one's eyes, as though the fountain of darkness were in one's own perception. Seen from above, the house in its pit of trees seemed a very reservoir of obscurity; from the doors one must come out stained with it. And the kitchen smoke, lying over the vague trees doubtfully, seemed the very fume of living.

But as they drove down the home-sense quickened; the pony, knowing these hedges, rocketed hopefully in the shafts. The house became a magnet to their dependence. And indeed it was nice, they felt in this evening air, to be driving home, with all they would have to tell of the Mount Isabel party, to all they would have to hear of Sir Richard's day in Cork. Friendly women smiled at them over half-doors of cabins. And they both felt approached, friendlier, turning in up the avenue under the arch of the trees; he accepting her with philosophy as though she were his daughter, she comforted in her fancy, as though he had wept coming over the mountains and told her his life was empty because she could never be his wife.

She said: 'I hope we shan't have to wait for dinner; I couldn't bear it.' He said: 'Really?' shocked to discover that he also had been thinking of dinner.

Livvy Thompson had ridden over; she sat on the steps with her habit over her knee, waving as they approached. She had sent a message round to the yard when she heard the trap, so that a man immediately came to take the pony. 'Listen now –' she began. But Lois only gave her a brush of the hand; she couldn't speak till she had rushed past her into the hall to look for the post, because of a tearing feeling of expectation. There was Viola's square blue temperate envelope on the table. There was nothing

67

more but some gloves Lady Naylor had worn in Cork, some English papers, a box of tennis balls. She had again that conclusive feeling of disappointment. 'They're back,' she said to Hugo.

'Listen now,' resumed Livvy, coming in after her. Lois slipped Viola's letter into her pocket and buttoned the flap over it. For what Viola would think of Livvy she did not like to imagine.

Livvy was anxious to know if Lois had seen Mr Lesworth lately, and if so, whether he had happened to mention Mr Armstrong. Because it did seem strange, she thought, about Mr Armstrong; she almost feared that he must be ill. When she heard Mr Lesworth had not appeared either, she was amazed, she said, that Lois was not more worried. It was now too evident something must be the matter. She pointed out it was her duty and Lois's to find out if they were ill, or indeed if worse hadn't happened, as worse might, to the two young Englishmen in a hostile country. Lois, thumbing Viola's envelope, said she was quite certain they would have heard. Livvy suspected something was hushed up for fear of the English papers: nothing was ever allowed in the English papers that could be mortifying for the English people to read.

'If they should only be ill,' she said, 'there would be so many little things we could do for them. It does seem in a kind of way an opportunity. I often think it is only when a man is ill that he understands what a woman means in his life.'

Lois said that her own impression of a man ill was one of extreme crossness and of inability to find the nicest woman attractive at all. She pointed out that there was an excellent military hospital at Clonmore, so that they need not imagine David and Gerald tossing feverish and untended. She did not suppose they would be allowed a visit, and confessed that, for her part, she found people lying down while she stood up embarrassing; so curiously bumpy and extremely difficult to talk to.

'But if he seemed at all unlikely to recover,' said Livvy, 'there would be several things I should like to say to Mr Armstrong. If he should recover after all, he would be gentlemanly enough to forget them, though there would be no harm in their leaving a pleasant impression. To tell you the truth, Lois, I have often wondered if he does not think me a little reserved and cold. Does it ever seem to you that he looks discouraged? You see, he is accustomed to English girls who are very free; I believe there is almost nothing they will not let a man say and that they get kissed before they get engaged. Now I should not like him to think I had no heart at all. You know Irish girls in books are always made out so fascinating and heartless; I should not like him to think that of me. And if he does recover, he might go back to England and get engaged to a girl simply out of his lower nature. I should not like to feel I had spoilt a man's life.'

'I expect,' said Lois, 'it is their week for extra duty.' She thought: 'If only I weren't so certain there'd be a letter from Gerald tomorrow! If only he'd let me wonder! He is so terribly *there* . . .' If only his coming or writing could have some touch of the miracle, heal a doubt.

'Will you not stay to dinner?' she said to Livvy. 'You could borrow one of my frocks.'

'I'd like that yellow taffeta, though I should have to reef it in. It's a great inconvenience, Lois, being so slight as I am, though it does seem to be admired. Are you sure your aunt will not mind? . . . But no, thank you, I couldn't; my father'd kill me for riding home after dark. In fact, I should go now,' – looking up at the sky – 'one never knows, does one? Isn't that too bad?'

'*Too* bad,' agreed Lois, touching her letter. She walked round to the yard with Livvy to get her horse. 'But listen,' said Livvy, mounting, 'there's one thing that we had better do. We can drive in to Clonmore, Wednesday, to do some shopping: I really do need wool for a jumper. And if we should meet Mr Smith or Captain Carmichael, I should just mention, laughingly, we hadn't seen any of them for a long time. And then it might all come out. Or if the worst came to the worst, we could drop in to tea at the Fogartys'; if there was nobody else, there'd be bound to be Mrs Vermont. I don't think she's trustworthy, but if there were anything definite she'd be bound to say – like illness or an ambush they were not supposed to mention. Or it might all come right and the first we would meet might be Mr Lesworth or Mr Armstrong . . . I certainly think, Lois, that is what we should do. If you can't get your uncle's trap, I will take my father's.'

She rode away. Lois listened until the romantic horse-hoofs had died on the avenue, smothered in trees. This manner of Livvy's of coming and going gave her a setting – picaresque, historical somehow. She would have been much worse if she had ridden away on a bicycle – Then she took Viola's letter out of her pocket and read it out there in the yard. Gnats danced in the underneath gloom of the chestnuts.

Viola did think Lois took feeling rather too earnestly. Lois must not grow less interesting. She admitted the little Gerald might be affecting; he was permitted to happen once. Gerald assimilated, she should be more of a woman. Only don't lose detachment, darling; do not lose distance. Viola would be delighted if Lois would give her 'Trivia'. She confessed it did startle her to be reminded that up to now she had been only eighteen by this talk of a nineteenth birthday. She felt, she said, older than the rocks among which she sat – she wrote from a rock-garden. Maurice Evans, a really ridiculous person, sat on a pink tuft of something valuable, apparently painting her. By the way, did Laurence read Pater? Maurice did not – did really anyone nowadays? Did Lois think that Viola might intrigue Laurence? Laurence continued a subject for speculation for three paragraphs. She only referred to Mr Montmorency indirectly, and at the very end. She warned against introspection. 'For introspection, darling, does make us the prey of the nice-middle-aged.' She complained there was too much introspection and tennis in Lois's letters. 'Don't talk of yourself to that elderly man.'

Lois, relieved but chagrined by the omission, wondered if Viola really did read one's letters at all thoroughly. She always noticed the split infinitives – one could not be sure. Lois turned in at the back door and pulled herself up to dress by the back-stairs banisters. She sniffed – duck for dinner again: it seemed the end of a cycle. This morning she had renewed the roses in Mrs Montmorency's room.

Crossing the ante-room, a spring in some board from her step made an unlatched door swing open. She saw Mr Montmorency in shirt-sleeves brushing his wife's hair. And Francie, facing the glass, saw Lois reflected, standing still in alarm on the shining floor. They smiled at each other. Mr Montmorency, thoughtfully and heavily brushing, did not observe the interchange.

The Visit of Miss Norton

9

Livvy's afternoon in Clonmore was such a great success that she forgot the wool for her jumper. At first there had been uneasiness; she let Lois drive while she looked carefully round the Square, went into the Imperial Hotel to see if her father had left a stick and searched both pavements of Cork Street, down which they drove from end to end. In despair, she had just suggested going up to the tennis club to see was there anyone there, when the rain came down – it had been threatening all day, the mountains looked moist and close on their drive in. They had to turn in to the Fogartys'. And there, to them anxiously awaiting tea and social developments in Mrs Fogarty's artistic drawing-room, entered severally all whom they wished to meet: Captain Carmichael, Smith with Mrs Vermont, finally Mr Armstrong himself. Mr Lesworth did not appear (which, as Livvy whispered to friends, would be a disappointment for Lois): it turned out that he was on extra duty. Mrs Fogarty had one of the narrow houses looking out on the Square; her windows were screened from outside observation by cubes of evergreen; between the pane and the evergreens rain fell darkly. Mrs Fogarty's drawing-room was thronged with photographs; all the dear boys who for years back had been garrisoned at Clonmore, many of whom, alas! had been killed in that dreadful War. You could not stoop to put down a cup on one of the little tables without a twinge of regret and embarrassment, meeting the candid eyes of some dead young man. The room was crowded with cushions that slid from the narrow seats of the chairs and tumbled over the back of the sofa; cushions with pen-painted sprays, with poker-worked kittens; very futurist cushions with bunches of fruit appliqués, dear old cushions with associations and feathers bursting out at the seams. And there were cushions with Union Jacks that she wouldn't, she said, put away – not if They came at night and stood in her room with pistols. And this was all the more noble in Mrs Fogarty in that she was a Catholic, with relations whose politics were not above reproach at all. Mr Fogarty was a retired solicitor; he had no politics; he became very cross and reproachful when they were discussed at the Club and said he supposed he could not help being a philosopher. But he drank, which shows that nobody can be perfect. He never appeared at tea.

As more and more people dropped in and the chairs gave out, the subalterns pulled the cushions on to the floor and sat on them. Mrs Fogarty was delighted. The room warmed up, there was just enough air left not to make one aware of discomfort in breathing. There was a smell of wallpaper, tea and tea-cakes, polished Sam Brownes and the *Nuit d'Amour* on Mrs Vermont's handkerchief which she pulled out frequently to wipe honey from her fingers. They all felt very easy and very Irish – the qualities radiated, perhaps, from Mrs Fogarty, who sat flushed with pleasure and hospitality, taking up rather more than half of her own sofa. She wore a brown lace blouse and a tweed skirt, with a green shell rope that swung and clinked on the teapot. Indeed, it was all very harmonious; she did not know how she would have lived at all without the military at Clonmore.

After tea, cigarettes went round, there was a kick and splutter of patent lighters. Livvy said she would *not* smoke, she would not indeed: they might laugh but she was an old-fashioned girl. Her continued protests attracted a good deal of attention, till she noticed that old-fashioned girls were after all in the majority. The rector's daughters and Doreen Hartigan all sat looking approving and rather unfinished about the mouth. So she accepted a strong cigarette of Captain Carmichael's and Smith broke into a howl and said she had sacrificed his ideal of womanhood. Mrs Fogarty suggested music: they helped her move the bowls and photographs off the grand piano which, undraped and opened, gave out to Mrs Vermont's fingers some damp chords. It was too bad, declared Mrs Fogarty, listening doubtfully, that their tuner had died in Cork and she hadn't the heart to look for another since. She said they must have real music, not just the piano. Real talent was present, she added, and looked round compellingly. There was a scuffle from which Mr Smith was forced up. He stood with his weight on one leg, stroking his hair detachedly, while Mrs Vermont looked through the music.

Mrs Vermont remarked to Captain Carmichael in passing that this was a country where the most extraordinary people died. 'Well, I mean,' she said, 'who would have expected that of

a piano-tuner? There was a house where I went for tennis; they
had had a parlourmaid there who died. And last week I went for
some little cakes to Fitzgerald's and they were all plain ones. I
asked for some fancies and they said the woman who did the icing
had been taken, God rest her soul! Really, there's something
grizzly about that cake shop.'

'In the midst of life we are in death, if you know what I mean,'
said Captain Carmichael.

Mr Smith said he didn't mind what he did sing: they all
wanted 'The Green Eye of the Little Yellow God'. The piece was
very tragic and sinister, they all sat wrapt and Livvy did not
notice that Mr Armstrong was pressing her arm till she felt
Doreen Hartigan notice. She moved away from him, closer to
Lois.

'There's a b-r-r-roken-hearted woman tends the grave of Mad Carewe
    And the Yellow God sits smiling up above.'

Lois blushed and let Livvy squeeze her hand. They both
wondered: 'How should I feel under the circumstances?' The
subalterns round all looked dogged, clasping their knees, and
thought of what one would do for a woman. There was a stagger
of emotional clapping. Then Mrs Vermont cried they were too
ridiculous, the boys were sillies, she couldn't sing at all really, but
if she must she would. So she sang 'Melisande', which sent every
girl there into a trance of self-pity; it was so clearly written about
oneself.

'With your eyes for fear and your mouth for love
    And your youth for Pity's grace
    – All alone, Mel-lisande, all alone.'

The subalterns thought it pretty, high-class but rather dull,
and clapped with abandon when it was over. They cast up David
Armstrong, blushing and looking very much surprised at himself
and all of them. He blushed till half-way through 'The Shooting
of Dan McGrew', when he became carried away and carried his
audience with him.

'A woman came between us,
    She was beautiful as Venus,'

brought a momentary return to consciousness. He looked at the
ceiling to avoid seeing Livvy and Lois. The atmosphere strained

with cramp, there was a creak of leather as subalterns readjusted their attitudes. Mrs Fogarty sent round a plate of chocolate biscuits. What a pity it was, she said, that they did not get up some pierrots. When David returned to his place Livvy was rose-pink; she fluttered at him her remarkably long lashes.

'Indeed,' declared Mrs Fogarty, looking from David to Smith (who had no Christian name), 'I never heard anything like the two of you. No, not in Dublin in Horse Show week, nor in London nor Liverpool either. You're remarkably gifted. Isn't it a pity they were all so sad? Shall we all have a song now, something rousing, you know, that you sang in the Great War?'

'Oh, do you know,' cried Mrs Vermont, 'I never knew Tipperary was really a place till I came to Ireland.'

'Listen to her!' shouted Mrs Fogarty, sweeping some more of the cushions on to the floor. They were all delighted. Mrs Vermont spread her fingers over her face. Under cover of all this excitement Lois rose and said they would have to go. She was sorry, because the party seemed slightly insulted; also, Livvy was so happy. If David should die now, she did not think Livvy would have to reproach herself. Also Captain Carmichael had seemed intrigued; he had spoken mysteriously of the adventures he had in the mountains and of the disguises he sometimes put on. She knew he must feel like the Scarlet Pimpernel; she could not help sympathizing. When she arose, he said they must meet again. He and David came out to help them into their trap in the Imperial yard, tucked them up in their rugs, relinquished them disapprovingly to the exposures of the journey and stood looking after them with rain dripping down their bronzed and military noses.

They drove home very much flushed and excited. The rain came down in a curtain and hid the mountains; brown shining puddles were linked along the road. They agreed about almost every one – especially Mrs Vermont and the D.I.'s niece – they laughed at each other over their mackintosh collars, eyes bright with comprehension and sympathy, while the strong rain stung their noses, then numbed them. Only when Livvy said, 'Melisande' was a beautiful poem, wasn't it, something stiffened in Lois: she said she thought it was sentimental.

'All that fuss, if you know what I mean, about just somebody.'

'Well, love is that, if you come to think,' said Livvy, 'and myself, I think it is very satisfying.' There was something so very experienced about the tip of her nose that Lois went flat. She felt that she herself must be like a cake in which the flour had been forgotten.

She complained: 'I wish we were not being late just this evening. Miss Norton, you know, is arriving and I did so want to look nice. My nose will not have thawed till half through dinner.'

'Oh, who is she? Is she pretty? How old is she? Is she engaged?'

'Never met her – though she often seems to have come to Danielstown. But I feel she may be a person one wants to look pretty at. She annoys Aunt Myra by being unfortunate in ways that are far more trying for other people than for herself. When she was little she came over to Danielstown to a children's party: she fell down at once on the scraper and cut her knee and there was a good deal of fuss and bloodiness. And another time when there were people to tea she started an argument about Kimberley: they all stayed till past eight o'clock in the library taking down the *Encyclopædia Britannica* while other people who were coming to dinner kept arriving. And another time she lost her engagement ring at a tennis party and they were all very much upset. She wrote afterwards to say it didn't matter because she had broken off her engagement anyhow and the man said he didn't want the ring, he said he wished it were at the bottom of the sea. I always thought people breaking off an engagement went all noble, but that sounds to me vindictive. Aunt Myra stayed put out ... She is twenty-nine.'

'It seems to me odd,' said Livvy, 'that she shouldn't have brought anything off by this time. But I dare say,' she added, 'that there has been a disappointment.'

At this point they heard a lorry coming. Black and Tans, fortified inwardly against the weather, were shouting and singing and now and then firing shots. The voices, kept low by the rain, the grind of wheels on the rocky road, tunnelled through the close air with a particular horror. To meet in this narrow way would be worse than a dream; before the half-obscured lorry appeared Livvy had turned the pony hurriedly up a boreen. They went up some way and waited under a dripping thornbush: if Black and Tans saw one hiding they were sarcastic. They heard the lorry grind past the mouth of the boreen with apprehension, feeling exposed and hunted. Lois recalled with surprise that she had cried for a whole afternoon before the War because she was not someone in a historical novel: it had begun, she thought, because they told her to go and practise. The road clear again, they discovered they could not turn the trap; they had to back the pony out. 'My!' said Livvy, glaring at the horizon. 'I wish I were driving a lorry! I should like to crash those fellows head on!'

Just before eight, Livvy dropped Lois at Danielstown gates and drove off, beating her pony into a gallop. Her father would kill her, certainly! Lois raced up the avenue till she had no breath, then had to crawl the rest of the way, recovering. Apprehensive, she strained for the throb of the dinner-gong, a shriek of reproach from a window. But her unpunctuality passed unnoticed: Miss Norton herself had only just arrived. The hall was full of suitcases, a fur coat sprawled on a chair, there was a tennis racquet, a bag of golf-clubs.

'Though where the poor female is going to play golf ... !' thought Lois. 'A nice coat ... Good, she has brought the *Tatler*!'

No one had even gone up to dress, from the library voices exclaimed in excitement; voices complained insistently through the drawing-room door. Lois undid the top buttons of her mackintosh and stepped out of it, leaving a damp ring. Absently she wrung the water out of her hat. She listened.

'She is certain she has left it in the train,' her aunt was saying; 'she says she would swear it was put in with her at Kingsbridge and that she saw it after leaving Darramore. I do not believe myself in travelling with suitcases, one is always counting – I believe in one good trunk.'

'Looking at it from the porters' point of view –' said Mrs Montmorency.

The library door clicked open and Laurence, looking quite enthusiastic, shot into the hall. 'She thinks telephoning will do it,' he said to Lois. 'I cannot make her understand about the Bally-hinch telephone.' He disappeared, shouting, into the back part of the house. Evidently there need be no hurry for anything. Lois sat on the hall table to look at the *Tatler*. Early autumn fashions reminded her – this was an opportunity to try on the fur coat. She hoped for the proper agony, finding a coat she could not live without ... Her arms slipped silkily through; her hands appeared, almost tiny, out of the huge cuffs. 'Oh, the escape!' she thought, pressing her chin down, fading, dying into the rich heaviness. 'Oh, the *escape* in other people's clothes!' And she paced round the hall with new movements: a dark, rare, rather wistful woman, elusive with jasmine. 'No?' she said on an upward note: the voice startled her, experience was behind it. She touched the fur lightly, touched the edge of a cabinet – her finger-tips drummed with a foreign sensitiveness. And the blurred panes, the steaming changing trees, the lonely cave of the hall no longer had her consciousness in a clamp. *How* she could live, she felt. She would not need anyone, she would be like an orchestra playing all to itself. 'Is it mink?' she wondered.

'You look so nice!' said Miss Norton, from the door of the library.

Lois went quite blank. 'Oh,' she said.

'Where is that unfortunate Lady Naylor?'

'I can't *think* – Well, she is in the drawing-room.'

'Anyhow,' said Miss Norton, 'I will go up now. When she sees me looking less arrived she may forget about the suitcase.' She looked at Lois earnestly. 'I don't lose things except coming here; I am efficient really. But there seems a kind of fatality . . .'

'I *know*.'

'Do you?' she said with interest, a keen disconcerting flash. 'How odd that you should!'

An approach seemed possible, imminent. Lois, feeling herself smiled at, unwrapped herself from the coat without embarrassment. Miss Norton, who did not seem surprised by the disappearance of the family, asked to be shown where she was. They went upstairs together; she was on the top floor opposite Laurence.

'Who was the capable person? Who wouldn't let me telephone – the young man?'

'Laurence.'

'Oh, Laurence. And the other people: I couldn't hear their names. They seemed very much here – faintly resentful: I expect I must be horrible for them. He at once accused me of having cut my knee on a scraper – when I was three or four. Who did you say?'

'The Montmorencys.'

'Oh, Hugo and Francie? Of course I have heard of them. Isn't she his mother – practically?' Miss Norton took off her hat and looked at herself in the glass dispassionately and closely. 'God!' she remarked.

'He brushes her hair,' said Lois, laughing – in the sharp unshadowy atmosphere produced by Miss Norton it sounded more of a giggle – and swinging with her back against the edge of the door.

'Oh, then it is mutual.'

'I knew him best when I was a child.'

'Yes, he looks like that. Thank you so much; I think I have got everything. Yes, heaps of hot water. Wouldn't you like to go now: I mean, won't there be dinner? . . . Oh, Lois!'

Lois, from over the threshold, came back willingly. 'Mm?' she said.

'I mean, you are Lois, aren't you? I've heard so much . . . No, don't be late: I should hate you to help me.' Miss Norton had taken her coat off and stood in a frilled shirt looking round distastefully at her suitcases. 'Go,' she said, 'do really.'

Lois, half-way down the gallery, met Laurence coming up. 'Mm?' said Laurence.

'I think she seems quite mad,' said Lois doubtfully.

'You would,' replied Laurence and went past her coldly.

10

One did not lightly telephone. There was a telephone six miles away, at Ballyhinch, but its use made excessive demands upon the sympathy and attention of the post-mistress. Marda could not understand – as Sir Richard said, one would think she had come from America. From all their angles she seemed to them very modern. They sat on the steps after breakfast, waiting for post to come, discussing what they should do. There was something agonizing to Sir Richard in the thought of that suitcase. Marda said, it would not have mattered at all but that her tennis shoes seemed to be in it. It was quite a relief when the postman settled the matter by saying there had been another raid last night in the Brittas direction and that all the wires were down again. It had been a great raid, the postman said; if the boys had not fled it would have been almost a battle. What times, said Francie, looking at Marda doubtfully, they did live in! But other times, said Marda, other disadvantages. Nobody hurt, they hoped? Well, said the postman, the Black and Tans had been fired on, but why would they not be, they themselves firing to the left and right continually? It seems two of them ones had pitched from the lorry the way you would think they'd be killed and the boys had bolted, leaving the two lying.

'How do you know?' said Marda. The postman, looking austerely at her, asked how would one help hearing? Though it was not for him to say what was true and what was what you would hear. Sir Richard agreed with this hastily and with some warmth: he did not want to have the postman discouraged.

Marda received her six letters as a matter of course and glanced them through sceptically. Lois watched her. Putting the letters away Marda suggested that, since Laurence was so practical, he should drive her into Clonmore or Ballydarra to buy more tennis shoes. Laurence feared he did not drive the car nicely: he could avoid things but he was inclined to wobble.

Sir Richard had disappeared on his morning round; how much of his corn had been 'laid' by the rain last night he did not like to imagine; it was better to know. The rain had ceased before break-fast; loud drops still drummed through the leaves; the trees with their rainy smell were a wall of moisture. Thin vapours trailed on the sky over an intermittent brightness; distances showed up thinly, as though painted. 'The end of our weather,' said poor Francie.

'But I feel,' persisted Marda, 'I must have tennis shoes. I don't mind wobbling.'

'Laurence is more of the intellectual type,' explained Francie.

'I don't think that matters.'

'It does with a car,' said Lois.

'I have never consciously driven *you*,' said her cousin coldly.

Marda laughed; she got up and stood on the steps. Fixed in their row, the others all looked up at her. She was tall; her back, as she stood looking over the fields, was like a young man's in its vigorous slightness. She escaped the feminine pear-shape, her shoulders were square, legs long from the knee down. Her light-brown dress slipped and fitted with careless accuracy, defining spareness negatively under its slack folds. Sophistication opened further horizons to Lois. Marda gathered her strung cornelians in one hand into a bunch at her throat; they slipped down the nape of her neck. Standing vaguely she had still that quality of directed-ness – from which they all swerved off in their different ways. A hardy unawareness of self in her heightened one's own conscious-ness. Her lightest look watched, her casual listening assessed, her speech was a lightning attack on one's integrity out of the strong-hold of her indifference.

They remained sitting behind her with a vague sensation of

having been abandoned. Hugo came out, shut the glass door with precision and blinked at the sky. 'Clearing,' he said, then asked Marda to come for a turn. Exercise seemed the order of the morning; Lois and Laurence were later to go to the village with messages. Francie was waiting to go to the garden with Lady Naylor.

'Am I or am I not to drive her?' wondered Laurence aloud, with fatalism, looking after Miss Norton.

'She'll certainly let you know.' Francie's little ironical smile sent her cheeks up, their faint flush wavering, under her eyes. She was not so simple. Her diffidence, her inquiring softness, an outward 'laciness' of her personality – into which impressions seemingly filtered like light, diffusedly, making no impact – covered a structure of delicate hardness. She was in spirit insistent, tenacious and quick in antagonisms; complexity tightened, as had been her delicate body's, by constant resistance to pain. She gave hospitality to the ever-living Laura, she invited claims from Mrs Archie Trent, she would have endowed Lois, but she watched Marda turn beside Hugo into the beech walk with raised brows, a cat's blank unsparing lucidity.

'She's very positive,' said Laurence, still looking after them.

'Positive about what?' asked Lois eagerly. Laurence held his breath with annoyance and pulled up a sock.

Marda wanted nothing of Mr Montmorency but entertainment. She was an experienced fellow-visitor. He interested her; his negativeness was startling. She had heard of him, and of it, in all parts of the country, had arrived at several houses into a loud reaction, a kind of indignant excitement following his departure. Her acquiescence in finding him so exactly as he had been described was tempered by incredulity, almost shock. And she could define in him qualities which her friends in the rush of discussion had slurred or had overshot: one, a kind of drawn-back apprehension in his approaches, as though something bright were being brandished before his eyes. His look, coming wavering round this interruption, had, in regard to herself, a peculiar intensity. She was already real to him as a woman.

He now swung his blackthorn, slashing the air widely. 'I remember this walk,' she said. 'I seem to have been here yesterday. But I thought it was somewhere in Kerry, at Castle Reagh.'

'Oh no, it is here,' he said wisely. They laughed. Down the walk, brightening air slipped like gauze round the beech trunks;

great pewter limbs went turning and straining up with the sheen of muscles. Drops, infrequent and startling, loudly fell on his hat brim, icily on her shoulders through the mesh of her dress. The path's perspective was a tunnel of glass. Her companion's lameness of thought, the faltering silence produced a kind of vacuum in her; she covered a yawn.

'This is not a good morning,' he suggested, 'to walk under trees.'

'Really the worst possible.'

'Oh . . . had we better – ?' However, they walked on.

'I always come here,' he said in extenuation. 'My turn to the right's mechanical. I was here as a boy, you know.'

'Were you here when I bled so much at that children's party?'

'Not actually, but I have always heard of it. Didn't you lose a ring?'

'At another party, at a more suitable age. It was the most lovely ring I have ever had – Regent Street. The jeweller said it must be emeralds because the lady was Irish and Timothy fully agreed with him. I had had no idea I had such an expensive nationality.'

'What a pity!'

'Yes, those things are always a pity.'

He was not sure how much she included. 'Did your – did Timothy mind?'

'Not so much as the Naylors. Later, he was killed on the Somme. But he had two sons first, so it all came right – I mean he married.'

'Oh yes . . . I suppose you are often here? I have often heard of you. And at Johnstown and Ballyduff and up in the North I have heard you expected. But I was always going. Once, I believe, we crossed at an avenue gate.'

The fact was, she acknowledged with a laugh, that they both visited incorrigibly. She knew also, she told him, that he not only visited but travelled; he had been almost everywhere but Canada.

'But I really should not have come back here,' she said. 'There is something in Lady Naylor's eye: a despairing optimism. I feel that suitcase won't be the end of me here. There will be a raid and I shall be shot on the avenue, not even fatally, or Laurence will take me out and upset that car. Then really she will never forgive me, though the efforts she makes will follow me over

Europe . . . How far do you think this war is going to go? Will there ever be anything we can all do except not notice?'

'Don't ask *me*,' he said, but sighed sharply as though beneath the pressure of omniscience. 'A few more hundred deaths, I suppose, on our side – which is no side – rather scared, rather isolated, not expressing anything except tenacity to something that isn't there – that never was there. And deprived of heroism by this wet kind of smother of commiseration. What's the matter with this country is the matter with the lot of us individually – our sense of personality is a sense of outrage and we'll never get outside of it.'

But the hold of the country *was* that, she considered, it could be thought of in terms of oneself, so interpreted. Or seemed so – 'Like Shakespeare,' she added more vaguely, 'or isn't it? . . . But now tell me,' she said, 'about Lois?'

'Lois?' He was guiltily startled, thinking of Laura's daughter.

'Lois – haven't you noticed her? She sat beside you at dinner.'

He feared he was no good at people, he was preparing to say -- but the remark, tried over critically, seemed a kind of echo: he reminded himself of Laurence. He was confused by her cool watching, her eyebrows drawn up and together in ironical friendly despair at him. Her face – like a Dutch doll's, he defensively told himself, in its accurate clear disposition of red-and-white colour – was, at this sudden pull-up to her interest, like a mask in its halt of expression. Her features, the dark line of hair springing over the white square of forehead, were in their special relation like something almost too clearly written that he still could not read; to be learnt now and puzzled over in retrospect.

She was, in fact, repelled by his lack of sympathy. 'Lois,' she said, 'is nice. She is in such a hurry, so concentrated upon her hurry, so helpless. She is like someone being driven against time in a taxi to catch a train, jerking and jerking to help the taxi and looking wildly out of the window at things going slowly past. She keeps hearing that final train go out without her. How I should hate to be young again! But, I had no ambitions.'

He watched her unguarded profile. 'Oh yes,' he said, 'ambition?'

'I've never met any woman so determined to love well, so anxious to love soon, so certain of her ability. She really prays for somebody to be fatal; she eyes doors. And you are all disappointments.'

'To begin with,' said Hugo, nettled. 'She's not a woman –'

'Awful if nothing happens to her! She reminds me, too, of a little girl I remember at school sports; in a team race, one of those things with bean-bags. Hopping at the end of the line, working up to the front slowly, simply sick with eagerness. Her turn comes, she is the whole world: her eyes shoot out of her head – she drops the bean-bag. They all groan . . . It makes me go dry inside to think of it now.'

'There is a young man – Harold – Gerald. They dance on the avenue.'

'Like rabbits!'

'They have a gramophone.'

'Is he supposed to love her?'

'My wife thinks so. Laurence considers he suitably might. Her aunt does not think it suitable at all and won't hear a word of it, so he officially doesn't.'

'Anyhow, to be loved is not her affair at all, it is quite irrelevant. She does not love him, poor little thing: he is useless.'

'I can't think it necessary for a young girl, at her age, to love anybody.'

'Oh, it is not,' she said impatiently, 'at any age. But one has those ideas.'

This dismissal, this lightness vexed him. Let her speak for herself. She had, then, her whole sex's limitations: a teachable shallowness, a hundred little abilities. But he, prey to a constant self-reproach, was a born lover, conscious of cycles in him, springs and autumns of desire and disenchantment, and of the intermediate pausing seasons, bland and frigid, eaten at either margin by past or coming shadows of change.

'I have not these ideas,' he said coldly.

They turned at the end of the walk through a gateway, into a fir plantation. Here they walked between walls of dusk, to be released to an airy green space, tree-pillared. The green strip, measureless on ahead but narrow, slanted down on their left to the open meadows, on their right was bounded by an uneven wall. Below the wall an unseen swift stream flowed, tinkling and knocking. The path hesitated ahead of them, faint on the bright green turf. Here the few beeches stood, unrelated, lovely, desultory; between their trunks – the tall mountains, vivid in a suffusion of distant light. The scene glittered. 'More rain coming,' said Mr Montmorency.

But she stared ahead. A trench-coat flickered between the trees, approaching. Her look focussed; there was an interchange. Coming to them, the young man almost hurried. After consideration: 'Hullo!' said Mr Montmorency.

'Hal-*lo*!' cried Gerald, flushing with expectation. Never had they been so acclaimed. He was out this way, he explained, coming into ear-shot, and was proposing to take advantage of something rash that Lady Naylor had once said about dropping in to lunch any time. 'They're not *out*?' he asked suddenly with, Marda noticed, a queer haggardness. They were not? That was splendid, marvellous. Early about? – he had been out all night, he told them. Oh yes – feeling Mr Montmorency glance at his chin interrogatively – he had shaved by the road; he had brought his tackle with him, he often did. Here – no, that was his pistol: the other pocket. Marda extolled his foresight. Mr Montmorency had forgotten to introduce them; they stood socially grouped round a beech and exchanged cigarettes.

'Very busy now?' said Marda, bending down to the match Gerald sheltered.

'Off and on – generally on, but we don't know.' She really seemed most remarkable, he looked intently, just lightly enough to avoid a stare. He liked talk like this, square and facty, compact with assumptions. Pleasant that she should be here at the house for lunch. Light slipped back over the dints of her hair as she looked up again. Lunch seemed a torch in the future; between now and lunch-time he would have come on Lois, somewhere, somehow, and amazingly kissed her amazed hands. There would be, till the kiss, no speaking – there she eluded him. He had thought this out.

He had thought this out, seen ahead to this climax rather – as though a flower's centre had been revealed by an impetuous opening out of lovely confused petals – on the lorry, breasting the darkness. Watching the morning skylines form and creep out like enemies from the cold night, he had burned at her nearness under the insistent groping of the wind. Rushing under his eyes the hedge-tops shivered; he had laughed and shivered, hand in his pistol pocket, hand on his razor. And now, as looking at Marda he once more kissed Lois's hands, he knew once more, assured by her eyes, that keen truth of the first showing of daylight. He was fortified in assurance. Leaning with her elbow against the tree, returning casually his directness of look, she recalled some profound and certain excitement, as of his first approach to the War. Now he meant to go past the hands, to kiss the curve of Lois's cheek as she strained away, then stamp her uncertain mouth with his own certainty. Naïvely, he looked at his wrist-watch.

'Yes, go on,' she said, looking up through trees where a bright breath disturbed the closeness. He looked past her, the path led to Lois. This green open path spaced out with trees was (he afterwards thought) like something in heaven.

'It will rain by lunch-time,' said Mr Montmorency. And indeed the sky was already creeping together and fading, and the mountains' sharpness seemed a kind of anxiety.

'I wish,' said Gerald to Marda, 'you'd been out up there this morning. You wouldn't know where you were, with the light coming.'

'Is there a smell of daylight? I once heard a man say –'

'Well, that is just like me – I was smoking.'

'Look, you must go on.'

'Yes, perhaps –' He went on. She was left only half protected by irony from an inrush of desolation. His look and smile clung to her memory with the tenacity of irrelevance: his steps on the grass died out quickly. There was silence: a cold apprehension of rain in the beeches, the tinkling and knocking of water beyond the wall. Hugo, having walked a short way ahead, looked back at her sharply. She was startled. 'Bother!' she thought. For there was bother behind the look.

'Do we go on?' They walked on, but were oppressed by their lack of objective. They met the white stare of a cottage, stared and turned.

'Dannie Regan lives there: he shot out an eye shooting rabbits and now he's losing the sight of the other. I used to go out with him when I was a boy – so high. His mother lives with him – or should still; I haven't heard that she's gone. She must be a hundred and four.'

'Do you know the man I am going to marry, Leslie Lawe? He's a stockbroker; he fishes a good deal. His people are in Meath.'

'Meath? . . . I didn't know you –'

'I am really. I haven't told the Naylors. They think my engagements fantastic; you see, they have all come to nothing. But I ought to have told the Naylors; it ought to have come at once, but there was that wretched suitcase. I will say something at dinner, not lunch: please do something to lessen the atmosphere of surprise.'

'When?'

'Oh, we think this winter.'

He looked from one window of the cottage to the other. 'It will make a break in the winter,' he said at last. 'I dare say you will go somewhere sunny. Algiers perhaps – Morocco, if you are able.'

'Yes, he is quite rich.'

'I shouldn't go to the Riviera ... But I thought you didn't believe in this sort of thing?'

'I? Oh, I never said so.'

Now he came to think of it, she had not explicitly said so. 'I hope you will be happy.'

'I don't expect I shall be much different.'

'I think,' he said, 'I must go in and talk to Dannie. He will have heard I'm back. It seems a good time now – do you mind?'

'I'll talk to Mrs Regan.'

'She's deaf.'

'Then we'll smile at each other – she's not blind.'

They approached the doorway that yearned up the path like an eye-socket. A breath of peat smoke, of cold trodden earth, of the ghostly dark of white walls came out from the cottage. Dannie took form on the darkness, searching with his one eye. He stood with his white beard, helpless and eager. 'Well!' exclaimed Hugo. Then Dannie broke out: this was young Mr Hugo, wasn't he the lovely gentleman, as fine and upstanding as ever. And here was his wife he'd brought with him, the beautiful lady. And, trembling and searching, he took Marda's hand. He declared that she brought back the sight of youth to his eyes.

11

It rained before lunch-time. Gerald heard loud drops come after him as he went up the beech walk. Under every beech he expected to see Lois looking round in surprise. When he heard a dog in the undergrowth he turned, laughing with expectation. But it was the *louche* yellow dog from the lodge, intent on rabbiting. Soon a square black eye of the house – three – four – looked down at him through the branches; he came out under the whole cold shell of it, streaked with rain and hollow-looking from an interior darkness. The yellow dog passed him, looked back scornfully from the steps and pattered in at the door with an air of possession. 'Hallo!' called Gerald, looking about him.

But she was nowhere; the place was cold with her absence and seemed forgotten. The tennis party became a dream – parasols with their coloured sunshine, rugs spread, shimmer of midges, amiable competition of voices. Something had now been wiped from the place with implied finality. Gerald told himself it was all very queer, quiet; that it was disappointing about Lois. He tugged the bell, a maid appeared in surprise, did her back hair hastily, encouraged him in with a smile and left him. The hall with staring portraits contracted round a glove on the table – a grey suede gauntlet strapped at the wrist – he picked up the glove and kissed it. But the house was full of ladies, the glove might as well be Marda's – he dropped it doubtfully.

A lovely mystery of feminine life: what did a young girl do with herself in the mornings? Vaguely he pictured keyboards and pink ambling fingers. He recollected those sage-green sexless covers of intellectual books. He recalled the musty smell of work-boxes, the blush through transparent paper of shell-pink needlework wrapped away hastily. You never asked a girl what she was making.

He listened, took off his trench-coat, stepped to the drawing-room door. The five tall windows stood open on rain and the sound of leaves, rain stuttered along the sills, the grey of the mirrors shivered. Polished tables were cold little lakes of light. The smell of sandalwood boxes, a kind of glaze on the air from all the chintzes numbed his earthy vitality, he became all ribs and uniform. He was aware of intrusion. But he dared not go in unasked to the library, where Sir Richard might well look up from writing, sharp with pince-nez. He could not again face the hall – he was shy of the glove.

He took up the *Spectator*, read an article on Unrest and thought of the Empire. Mechanically his hand went up to his tie. He looked ahead to a time when it all should be accurately, finally fenced about and all raked over. Then there should be a fixed leisured glow, and relaxation, as on coming in to tea from an afternoon's gardening with his mother in autumn. He turned in thought to confident English country, days like the look in a dog's eyes, rooms small in the scope of firelight, neighbourly lights through trees. He thought of a woman, kind and palpable, who should never produce this ache, this absence . . . A door dragged forward its portière; Lois came in from the dining-room, brushing rain from her frieze coat. He stood for a moment in a kind of despair at her agitation, as though he were trying to take her photograph. Then he stepped forward and kissed her, his hands on her wet shoulders.

'– Oh, but look here –' cried Lois.

But she was his lovely woman: kissed. He shone at her, she helpless. She looked out at the hopeless rain.

'I love –' he said eagerly.

'Oh, but look here –'

'But I love –'

'What are you doing in the drawing-room?'

'I've come to lunch.'

'Do they know?'

'I haven't seen anyone.'

'*I* don't know who to tell,' she said distractedly. 'They have all disappeared; they always are disappearing. You'd think this was the emptiest house in Ireland – we have no family life. It's no good my telling Brigid because she forgets, and the parlourmaid is always dressing. I suppose I had better lay you a place myself – but I don't know where the knives are kept. I can't think why you are being so sudden all of a sudden, in every way: you never used to be. I haven't even done the flowers yet. I do wish you wouldn't, Gerald – I mean, be so *actual*. And do be natural at lunch, or I shall look such a goat. You really might have asked me, I never mind talking things over. But now the gong will go at any moment. And how do you know I'm not in love with a married man?'

'You wouldn't be so neurotic; I mean, like a novel. I mean: do be natural, Lois.'

'Don't look so, so inflamed . . . Miss Norton is here; she's a girl – at least a kind of a girl. She's awfully attractive.'

'I think I met her. She's awfully – well, not beautiful, but . . . Oh, Lois . . .'

'Do be normal: do play the piano.'

'I can't start playing the piano before I've even told them I've come to lunch. I may be musical, Lois, but I'm not artistic.'

'All right,' she said, and walked away from him round the room. So that was being kissed: just an impact, with inside blankness. She was lonely, and saw there was no future. She shut her eyes and tried – as sometimes when she was seasick, locked in misery between Holyhead and Kingstown – to be enclosed in nonentity, in some ideal no-place, perfect and clear as a bubble. Or she was at a party, unreal and vivid, or running on hard sands. 'It wouldn't have mattered so much at the seaside,' she said to Gerald.

'But we never are at the seaside.'

She opened a sandalwood box and looked in: three blue beads and a receipt of her own from Switzers: three-and-eleven for yellow velvet pansies, worn at a dance and spoilt. 'It's not even as though we were at a dance,' she added.

'Lois, I've been thinking about you all night, up in the mountains – right up there when you were asleep. You were wonderful.'

'Haven't you been to bed at all?'

'No, you know I –'

'Oh, Gerald – Oh . . . darling – But you did have breakfast?'

The gong sounded: great brass balls went bouncing about the empty rooms. The parlourmaid looked in perfunctorily. 'Lunch?' said Gerald to Lois.

'No one is in – and I don't suppose lunch is even ready. Gerald, *did* you have breakfast?'

'An enormous breakfast at Ballydarra . . . What were you saying, Lois? what did you call me *then* . . . before the gong?'

But now she flushed and answered: 'I'm sopping wet; I'm steaming, I smell like a dog. I should have thought you would want me to go and change. I should have thought you'd be – protecting.'

'You know I'd die for you.'

They looked at each other. The words had a solemn echo, as though among high dark arches in a church where they were standing and being married. She thought of death and glanced at his body, quick, lovely, present and yet destructible. Something passed sensation and touched her consciousness with a kind of weight and warmth; she glimpsed a quiet beyond experience, as though for many nights he had been sleeping beside her.

'What *did* I say then? Say it.'

' "Darling" . . .'

But she turned away from some approach in his look.

Lady Naylor and Mrs Montmorency passed, in profile, under the three west windows, pressed very close together under a green en-tout-cas, discussing the vice-regency of the Aberdeens. Simultaneously, Mr Montmorency and Miss Norton were heard coming up the steps rather breathlessly, talking about money. They must both have been conscious of being a little vulgar, a little English, for as Sir Richard rattled open the glass door and went out to meet them, they broke off flatly.

'You must have got very wet,' said Sir Richard. 'Marda, about that suitcase of yours. I have been thinking it over –'

'Sir Richard, I can't bear you to –'

'My dear girl, a suitcase is a suitcase – I was just saying to Marda, Myra, that I have been thinking over that suitcase of hers –'

'We had better have lunch at once,' said Lady Naylor imperatively.

'Miss Norton will have to change.'

'Hugo, how *could* you let her get so wet!'

'My dear, I am not an umbrella.'

'Marda, how could you go out without a mackintosh!'

In the drawing-room Gerald walked to a window and stared at the rain in perplexity, stroking the back of his head, looking rather an ordinary kind of subaltern. Lois looked at herself in a mirror, then went out to the hall to tell them about Gerald. Everyone stared, she put up a hand to her face. 'Mr Lesworth has come to lunch,' she said deprecatingly. 'You told him he could whenever he wanted, so I suppose he thought he might.'

'Of *course*,' said Lady Naylor; 'I suppose you have told Sarah?'

'Well, I don't know where to find her: she is always dressing.'

'Of course she is not always dressing; should I keep a parlour-maid who was? She only changes once a day, but you always go and look for her at the wrong times. Where is Mr Lesworth?'

'In the drawing-room.'

'How extraordinary! Wouldn't he rather be in the library? Richard, why didn't you ask Mr Lesworth into the library? I expect now he had better wash.'

Lois went upstairs: Marda came up after her and took her arm; Lois started. She could not think of anything to say, Marda was not even trying; they went up silently. 'Some time,' Lois said as they parted, 'can I show you my drawings? They're fearfully bad.'

'Come up to my room after tea.'

Throughout luncheon, Sir Richard talked to Gerald about the

South African War and the Cork Militia. He liked the young fellow. Laurence talked to Marda about whaling, Lady Naylor and Francie continued the Aberdeens, Lois tried to explain to Hugo about Augustus John. The rain stopped, they agreed that it had been only a shower. Lois and Gerald were side by side, but they did not have to speak, they simply passed things. The side of her next to Gerald felt numb.

'Raspberries?' she said towards the end of the meal, constrainedly.

'Please.' *He* was not nervous at all. Queer, she confusedly thought, how men throw off action without a quiver at severance from the self that goes into it. They remain complete, the action hangs in the air of the place, above the grass or furniture, crystallizing in memory; eternal, massive and edged to the touch of thought as, to the bodily touch, a grand piano. She herself felt bound to all she had done emotionally. But his kissing of her, his attack, were no longer part of him. He concentrated upon his raspberries, crushing them, on his cream with carmine beautifully folding through, on his flushing sugar. She watched the work on his plate. 'Magnificent,' he said to Sir Richard, agreeing about the Cork Militia.

Going out through the hall, Laurence offered Gerald a cigarette. 'American – extra mild.'

'Thanks – I –'

'How is your jazz band?'

'Very little practising; not much time, you see.'

'Do tell me: did you kill anybody?'

'How much?' said Gerald, startled.

'Anybody last night?'

'Oh, good Lord, no!'

'Isn't that why you go out?'

'We were looking for arms, really. And nights you find the most surprising people at home. We were after a fellow called Peter Connor: we got him.'

'He was at home, in bed. These blighters think we are greater fools than we are.'

'Very cynical of him ... Oh, I say, Uncle Richard, Lesworth has captured Peter Connor.'

'I'm sorry to hear that,' said Sir Richard, flushing severely. 'His mother is dying. However, I suppose you must do your duty. We must remember to send up now and inquire for Mrs Michael

Connor. We'll send some grapes. The poor woman – it seems too bad.' He went off, sighing, into the library.

Gerald was horrified. His duty, so bright and abstract, had come suddenly under the shadowy claw of the personal. 'I had no idea,' he exclaimed to Laurence, 'these people were friends of yours.'

'Can't be helped,' said Laurence. 'I dare say he was a dirty dog . . . If you hate that cigarette, Lesworth, have one of your own. It seems a long time since we have seen you. How is this war of yours really going? Do you realize I know nothing – this might all just as well be going on in the Balkans. I sometimes rather wish that I were a gunman. There are one or two things I should like to ask – but don't let me keep you if you want to talk to anyone else.'

'Rather not.'

The ladies were in the drawing-room laughing intimately, putting across the open door a barrier of exclusion. Laurence and Gerald wandered about the hall, taking note of each other indirectly and amicably. Laurence was by three years the younger, but imposed his own impression of seniority. Light hair tumbling, eyes startled open and limp grey flannels, he looked to Gerald as though he had slept through the morning. While Gerald circled, the grey glove lay on the table, its fingers crisped in derision. Outside, in an irresponsible burst of sunshine, the wet fields had a metallic brightness. Gerald thought of Lois's shoulders, their rounded squareness, the feel of wet frieze under his grip. He was flattered but uneasy under Laurence's interest, which had indeed, for the simple, the awkward menace of someone preparing to cast a net. He pursed his lips to a whistle and shrugged slightly.

'For instance, what do you, personally, think about all this?'

'Well, my opinion is –'

'Oh, but I don't want your opinion, I want your point of view.'

'Well, the situation's rotten. But right *is* right.'

'Why?'

'Well . . . from the point of view of civilization. Also, you see, they don't fight clean.'

'Oh, there's no public school spirit in Ireland. But do tell me – what do you mean by the point of view of civilization?'

'Oh – ours.'

Laurence smiled his appreciation: the conviction, stated without arrogance, had a ring of integrity. Gerald, embarrassed by this benevolence, had recourse again to the back of his head, so gratifyingly polished. 'If you come to think,' he explained, 'I mean, looking back on history – not that I'm intellectual – we *do* seem the only people.'

'Difficulty being to make them see it.'

'– And that we have what they really want ... though of course the more one thinks of it all, the smaller, personally, it makes one feel.'

'Oh? I don't feel small in that way. But I'm not English –'

'Oh, no – I beg your pardon.'

'– Thank God!'

'Don't understand.'

'God may. Shall we look for the others?'

Gerald, shocked, preceded Laurence into the drawing-room. Their conversation, torn off rough at this edge, seemed doomed from its very nature to incompletion. Gerald would have wished to explain that no one could have a sounder respect than himself and his country for the whole principle of nationality, and that it was with some awareness of misdirection, even of paradox, that he was out here to hunt and shoot the Irish. His alertness was blunted, while he approached the ladies, by a slight stupor of effort; he was groping for something Napoleon had once said, something remarkably neat and apposite that Gerald had once copied into a pocket-book. Laurence had not hoped to explain, but had wished that Gerald could infer, that there was a contrariety in the notions they each had of this thing, civilization. As a rather perplexing system of niceties, Laurence saw it; an exact and delicate interrelation of stresses between being and being, like crossing arches; an unemotioned kindness withering to assertion selfish or racial; silence cold with a comprehension in which the explaining clamour died away. He foresaw in it the end of art, of desire, as it would be the end of battle, but it was to this end, this faceless but beautiful negation that he had lifted a glass inwardly while he had said, 'Thank God!'

Gerald knew that no one who spoke of God in that family way could have any belief. He had heard that Oxford was full of Socialism of a wrongness that was the outcome of too much thinking, and in the light of this it did appear to him that Laurence's conversation had been decidedly Sinn Fein. But he liked and respected Lois's cousin, who made a man of one by that naïve curiosity as to bloodshed – curiosity to which Gerald had been a stranger since the days of the *Boys' Own Paper* spread on the nursery floor. Also, he could not have looked so consistently bored at parties if he had not been, as they all said, very intellectual.

Lois, watching Gerald approach with an absence of smile that was almost a shadow, was certain she must have done him injustice. His constraint (the pursuit of Napoleon) had a rather grave beauty. Their kiss under the high ceiling must be present and palpable to him also. Aware of some growth of manliness in him, she wanted the feel of his lips again, to capture what she had missed before. And a quick glance of Marda's from one to the other sealed their mood with a recognition.

'Can't we go out?' she said generally, for Gerald to take up.

'It will rain again in a minute,' said Lady Naylor, glancing cynically at the weather. And indeed a few drops already sparkled against the sunshine. 'Also I particularly want to talk to Mr Lesworth. When he comes he is always playing tennis, or I forget. But now there are some things I really want to ask him . . . I really want his point of view . . .'

She sat down in a faded bowery chair, settling herself with a rustle of expectation. Francie, attracted, trailed her skirts and her fancy work down the sofa; Marda, putting a new cigarette in her holder, leaned over the back. From the constellation of eager faces Lois wandered away. The three were no more her enemies than were her own irresolution or the bright vicious raindrops blotting the pane. Yet their unforeseen combination defeated her finally. She yawned at the outlook.

'Lois, don't yawn,' said her aunt. 'Now I want to know, Mr Lesworth, what Colonel Boatley really thinks of reprisals. Of course it will go no further, though you mustn't think I want you to be indiscreet . . . Laurence, just shut the door.'

Laurence shut himself out. And Gerald, sitting down with a sigh, said that of course it was all rather a problem. He caught Marda's eye, dark and bright with amusement, and read there the doom of his afternoon.

'Yes? Yes? Yes? This is so interesting – you were asking me, weren't you, Francie, and I said we would ask Mr Lesworth . . . Marda, do listen, dear, never mind, shake your ash on the carpet, you mustn't miss this. Because these days when so much nonsense is talked on both sides I do feel one owes it to speak on some good authority – unless Mr Lesworth would rather we didn't. Now please go on!'

And Gerald, half hypnotized, consciously barren and not in his Colonel's confidence, repeated to them what he had read in the *Morning Post*. As Lady Naylor said at the time, no one would dream of taking the *Morning Post* seriously, it was so anti-Irish, but an opinion on it from anyone so much 'in things' as Mr Lesworth was well worth hearing. And as she said afterwards, it was extraordinary how no amount of experience shook these young Englishmen up. Their minds remained cutting-books.

12

An armoured car called for Gerald at four o'clock and he was driven away through the rain. Towards the end of the afternoon he had become very dull, a kind of fog came over his personality; he confessed he was sleepy. Lady Naylor remarked what a pity it was he could not stay for his tea, that would have freshened him up again. There was still so much that she wanted to know. The drawing-room became to Gerald fantastic and thin like an ice-palace, and, reflected backwards and forwards in tall mirrors, seemed like a chain of galleries at Versailles down which, numbing with admiration, he had to advance wearily. He did not see Lois alone any more. She kept coming in, looking round vaguely, then going upstairs again. Upstairs, he could hear her playing the gramophone. She came out to the steps with Marda to see him off; they stood with arms linked, brushing the rain from their hair. The last they saw of him was a putteed leg being drawn in carefully. Something steel slid to; they waved, but never a hand came out. The machine seemed already to be digesting. He was swept from them with martial impersonality.

At half-past five Lois went to the top of the house with her drawing-books, paused for confidence, tickled a panel of Marda's door. Coming into the changed and vivid room, she tipped her drawing-books disengagedly on to a window-seat. Marda sat on the writing-table, engaged in manicure. Little pots, pads and bottles paraded; a chamois leather was spread on her knee. A sweet smell of varnish, like pear-drops, was in the air.

'The most I can do,' said Lois, intent, 'is to keep mine clean.'

'Quite enough. It's just this habit of making up every part of one that's exposed at all . . . Lois, have a cigarette?'

'Oh . . . thanks. You don't mind my coming?'

'My dear, why?'

'What lovely brushes! What a . . . what an uncommon photograph frame!'

'Yes, that's Leslie Lawe.'

'Oh? Oh yes,' Lois paused uncertainly. 'How good looking! Do – do you know him well?'

'Very. We're engaged.'

'Oh, how lovely!' Lois had a shock of flatness.

'Oh, yes; didn't you know?'

'Well, I thought you probably would be. Shall you live in London?'

'I suppose we shall. I suppose we shall have to.'

'Oh, how lovely!'

Marda laughed and began screwing on the lids of her little pots. In the light of her brilliant life, her deftness seemed to Lois inimitable. One would have had to have lived twenty-nine years as fast, as securely and wildly, to screw pink celluloid caps on to small white pots with just that lightness of finger-tip, just that degree of amusement, just that detachment in smile and absorption in attitude. And the pink smell of nail-varnish, dresses trickling over a chair, flash of swinging shoe-buckle, cloud of powder over the glass, the very room with its level stare on the tree-tops, took on awareness, smiled with secrecy, had the polish and depth of experience. The very birds on the frieze flew round in cognizant agitation.

'What a lovely dress!' said Lois, picking up the end of a red sleeve, so that she seemed to be standing hand in hand with the dress.

'Vienna.'

'And, oh, what a lovely green one! . . . Am I pawing things?'

'I like it. But haven't you got some drawings?'

'Drawings? Oh, my drawings! Oh – I'm afraid they'd bore you.'

'I don't expect so.'

'Well, I did just happen to bring them along.'

She had brought two drawing-books, cheerful in mottled bindings with tissue between the pages. She brought them across to Marda, then turned away. The drawings, in black ink, illustrated the Morte d'Arthur and Omar Khayyam. They remembered Beardsley. Lois, away at a window, heard Marda rustle the tissue paper: she watched the rain intently. Beyond the demesne trees, a farm cart rattled along the road. Marda, conscientious, turned back to the title-page. Here she paused, for Lois had printed out, in uncertain Gothic:

> 'I am a painter who cannot paint;
> In my life, a devil rather than a saint;
> In my brain, as poor a creature too:
> No end to all that I cannot do!
> But do one thing at least I can –
> Love a man or hate a man
> Supremely –'
>
> Lois Honoria Farquar: Her Book.

'Oh,' said Marda.

'Browning.'

'But can you really?'

'I don't see why not.'

'And are you sure that you can't paint? Have you ever tried?'

'I hated two of the girls at school and I really rather do hate Mr Montmorency. And I can't help getting involved with people. Personal relations make a perfect havoc of me; my headmistress said so. Of course I haven't had much scope here, so far. Being grown up seems trivial, somehow. I mean, dressing and writing notes instead of letters, and trying to make impressions. When you have to think so much of what other people feel about you there seems no time to think what you feel about them. Everybody is genial at one in a monotonous kind of way. I don't seem to find young men inspiring, somehow. I suppose I shall. Did you ever have any difficulty about beginning?'

'I can't remember. I never can see back to the other side of things that have happened.'

'I think I must cut that title page out. I wrote it when I was rather young. But surely love wouldn't get so much talked about if there were not something in it? I mean even soap, you know, however much they advertise . . .'

'Oh, there must be. Let me look at the drawings.'

Marda, still on the table with crossed knees, spread out the book briskly. But Lois, all in a glow, could not help remarking: 'Somebody told me I was neurotic.'

'I shouldn't worry.'

With a brutality of which she was unaware Marda returned to the drawings. Lois, thinking 'I do not interest her,' sat down on the floor with her back to the chest of drawers. Over the mottled carpet curled strange pink fronds: someone dead now, buying this carpet, had responded to an idea of beauty. Lois thought how in Marda's bedroom, when she was married, there might be a dark blue carpet with a bloom on it like a grape, and how this room, this hour would be forgotten. Already the room seemed full of the dusk of oblivion. And she hoped that instead of fading to dust in summers of empty sunshine, the carpet would burn with the house in a scarlet night to make one flaming call upon Marda's memory. Lois again realized that no one had come for her, after all. She thought, 'I must marry Gerald.'

But with a jump of the heart she heard every page turn over. She received the print of each look as though her sensibility were the paper. Reactions to Lois's drawings were as a rule momentary and staccato: 'My dear! . . . They're sinister . . . what a marvellous muezzin! . . . Aren't those the seven queens?' And indeed it had come to seem to herself that the drawings must really mean something. A glance at them, though she had lost the power to see them, gave her the kind of surprised assurance one might expect from motherhood.

Marda said nothing; once or twice she changed her attitude, shifting the book from knee to knee. Soot, dislodged by the rain, sifted sharply on to the paper fan in the grate, startling them to an exchange of glances. Then she said deliberately, closing the drawing-book:

'I think you're cleverer than you can draw, you know.'

'Oh –'

'You don't mind, do you? Look – have another cigarette. Why can't you write, or something?'

'That's so embarrassing. Even things like – like elephants get so personal.'

'I know. I give up reading – I'm sick of their personal elephants . . . Or act? But why do you stay here?'

'I can't think,' said Lois, startled.

'You like to be the pleasant young person?'

'I like to be in a pattern.' She traced a pink frond with her finger. 'I like to be related; to have to be what I am. Just to *be* is so intransitive, so lonely.'

'Then you will like to be a wife and mother.' Marda got off the writing-table and began to change her stockings. 'Jacob's ladder,' she explained. 'It's a good thing we can always be women.'

'I hate women. But I can't think how to begin to be anything else.'

'Climate.'

'But I would hate to be a man. So much fuss about doing things. Except Laurence – but he is such a hog. Ought I to go to London?'

'Ever been abroad?'

Of course she had not, she said, because of the War, and of course she would like to. There was Rome, and she would like to stay in a hotel by herself. There was just 'abroad': she always wondered how long the feeling lasted. And there was America, but one would have to have introductions or one would get a crick in one's neck from just always looking up at things. She would like to feel real in London. She had never come out through a pass and looked down on little distinct white cities with no smoke. She had never been in a tunnel for more than five minutes – she had heard there were tunnels in which you could nearly suffocate? She had never seen anything larger than she could imagine. She wanted, she said, to see backgrounds without bits taken out of them by Holy Families; small black trees running up and down white hills. She thought the little things would be important: trees with electric lights growing out of them, she had heard of; coloured syphons. She wanted to go wherever the War hadn't. She wanted to go somewhere nonchalant where politics bored them, where bands played out of doors in the hot nights and nobody wished to sleep. She wanted to go into cathedrals unadmonished and look up unprepared into the watery deep strangeness. There must be perfect towns where shadows were strong like buildings, towns secret without coldness, unaware without indifference. She liked mountains, but she did not care for views. She did not want adventures, but she would like just once to be nearly killed. She wanted to see something that only she would remember. Could one really float a stone in a glacier stream? She liked unmarried sorts of places. She did not want to see the Taj Mahal or the Eiffel Tower (could one avoid it?) or to go to Switzerland or Berlin or any of the Colonies. She would like to know people and go to dinner parties on terraces, and she thought it would be a pity to miss love. Could one travel alone? She did not mind being noticed because she was a female, she was tired of being not noticed because she was a lady. She could not imagine ever not wanting someone to talk to about tea-time. If she went to Cook's, could they look out all the trains for her, in Spain and everywhere? She had never been to Cook's. Was there any law about selling tickets to people under age?

Marda, smoothing the last wrinkle out of a stocking and fastening up a suspender, said she did not believe this was so.

'Of course anybody could do all that. But it would not be me.'

'But be interested in what happens to you for its own sake; don't expect to be touched or changed – or to be in anything that you do. One just watches. Pain is one's misunderstanding.'

The advice, fruit of her own relation to experience, unwisdom, lacking the sublimer banality, was – as she suspected while still speaking – to her young friend meaningless and without value. The infinite variance of that relation breaks the span of comprehension between being and being and makes an attempt at sympathy the merest fumbling for outlet along the boundaries of the self. Lois looked vaguely out at the sky, and thought how she could not possibly travel in Europe with a green canvas trunk with her school initials. She longed for three leather suitcases. She said sadly:

'The thought of places without one is so lonely.'

'Pull yourself together, my dear child.'

'Don't you think honeymoons are great waste of travelling?'

'That reminds – I must write a letter. Don't go – look, have another cigarette. What is the date?'

'I don't know. Does it matter?'

Evidently it did matter; Marda had to unpack the bottom of a suitcase and look the date up in a pocket-book. And from this Lois immediately concluded Leslie must be one of those keen square people who did not care for girls of nineteen, whose eyes slid past one's look impatiently, who had no enthusiasms and read the biographies of politicians other than Disraeli. She heard Marda writing with little pauses and gushes; her shoulders and the stoop of her head took on an appearance of obligation. Lois thought how anxious to marry Marda must really be, how anxious not to frighten Leslie away from her, and how all her distantness and her quick, rejecting air must be a false effect, accidental and transitory.

'I think,' she said, 'I must be a woman's woman.'

'Oh yes. *Where* are we going to tennis tomorrow?'

'Castle Trent – but we won't because of the rain. Is Mr Lawe very social?'

'Reasonably. Of course, he likes his people nice. *What* was the name of the man at lunch – surname?'

'Lesworth. Gerald is very social. He smiles all the time like a dog. Do you think that is good in a man?'

'I am telling Leslie he wants to marry you – may I?'

'Will it give Mr Lawe a good impression?'

'Well, it furnishes you rather. And I can't think what else to say.'

'Don't scratch it out,' said Lois after an interval, 'but as a matter of fact he didn't speak of marriage. He merely kissed me. The English have quite a different moral standard.'

'Besides, he had been up all night.'

'What are men one is engaged to like?'

'Very worried and kind,' said Marda, blotting a sheet of her letter. 'Business-like, passionate and accurate. When they press you against their chests a paper crackles, and when you sit up again to do your face and arrange your hair, they cough and pull out the paper, all folded, and say: "While I think of it, I just wanted to consult you about this." Dinner services come crashing through the air like in a harlequinade. You feel you have been kissed in a shop. I cannot be adequate. I suggested writing to those public schools for vacancies for our three little boys, but that was not nice apparently. When you are engaged you live in the future, and a large part of the future is improper till it has happened.'

'Oh . . . what would happen now if you lost your engagement ring?' asked Lois with enjoyment.

'I daren't wear it. Oh, look here, I am talking like a fool. I'm sorry, Lois, but you really must not talk to me when I am writing letters. I need Leslie. Dinner services don't matter. If you never need anyone as much you will be fortunate. I don't know for myself what is worth while. I'm sick of all this trial and error. Will you find a book or something? Don't go!'

Lois did not wish to go, but thought 'Why should she keep me here when she is thinking about Leslie?' She felt deprived and unhappy. She tried to imagine a situation in which Leslie would look ridiculous. She prayed that the three correct little boys might never be born. She hoped he would have five daughters, and all artistic. 'One thing more,' she said, 'how is it that men are so seldom photographed in profile? Do they have to look frank?'

Steps coming down the gallery, relentlessly, with intention, might have been Leslie's but were unmistakably Laurence's.

Laurence tapped and remarked through the door that his Aunt Myra wanted to know if the letters were ready. Timothy would be starting now; he could wait five minutes, but if he did would almost certainly miss the post.

'Damn!' said Marda.

'What d'you say?'

'Oh, come in. Why did I polish my nails?'

Laurence sat down on the window-sill. He was annoyed and surprised to find Lois present. He suspected that she had been bothering Marda, confiding, fidgeting, asking about love and wishing to try on her hats. Probably she had brought up a poetry book and kept coming across with a thumb on the margin to point out the bits she loved. He wished that Lois would marry and leave Danielstown; he could perfectly see her as a very pink bride, later as a girl wife in the Tchehov tradition in a pink blouse, sucking sweets audibly, prattling of girl friends' lovers, rustling papers endlessly. He only hoped that she might marry Gerald, who had no papers to rustle.

'I hope,' he said, 'that Lois has been amusing you?'

'Don't talk,' said Lois. 'I mean, she wants to finish her letter.'

'Evidently,' said Laurence.

'Explain Leslie,' said Marda, writing rapidly. 'It will help at dinner.'

'She is engaged,' said Lois, 'to a Mr Lawe. That is his photograph there. His name is Leslie.'

'Oh, yes,' said Laurence.

'He is not comic,' said Marda, leaning around and pushing the letter away. 'She makes him sound so – like "a Mr Wilkinson, a clergyman". Lady Naylor will like it all, but I haven't told her. Will you help Mr Montmorency and Lois form a public opinion and not be surprised when I talk about him at dinner? About the end of the fish, I thought . . . I cannot finish this letter; it will have to go tomorrow and I will wire.'

'And I have a piece of news for you. Castle Trent was raided for arms last night. Of course they didn't find any. They think the thing was entirely amateur, nothing to do with the I.R.A. at all. They took away some boots. The Trents think one of the raiders was a gardener's cousin from Ballydarra who hates the family. He left a quite unnecessary message behind with a skull and crossbones; he sounds to me rather a silly man. I am hoping perhaps they will come here tonight. We have two assegais and a stiletto that Uncle Richard uses for a paper-knife.'

'It is a paper-knife,' said Lois, 'only made so as to look like a stiletto. How perfectly thrilling; do let us all sit up.'

'I shall sit up, but you had better go to bed. You might be insulted.'

'Really, I am not so female as all that.'

Laurence shrugged his shoulders.

'At any rate, don't tell the others. Uncle Richard'll get fussy and spoil it, and if Aunt Myra meets them she will keep them talking all night.'

'It seems so odd,' said Laurence, 'that she should be my blood aunt and not yours.'

Marda looked at him thoughtfully over the back of her chair. She had not realized he could be so disagreeable. If he did not take care, he would grow up just like Mr Montmorency. She told him so, and added that she was surprised he did not appreciate Lois. 'She is very charming,' she said, 'and very intelligent. Think of all the cousins you might have had. It's not her fault that you're not in Tahiti or Valladolid or wherever it was you wanted to go this summer. If I were not going to marry I should ask her to come abroad with me. I have never been less bored.'

'It would be marvellous,' said Lois. Now that Laurence had come in she felt more alone with Marda, and nearer; she could think of all the things she had wanted to say. Intoxicated by being told she was charming and by Laurence's disapproval, she hitched herself up on to the end of the wooden bed, where she sat swinging her legs and smiling, all girlhood. She felt movement, a wind in her face as though she were on the prow of a ship. With a bound, life carried her forward again. She felt certain that Leslie would die or break off the engagement. 'Marvellous,' she repeated.

'At any rate,' Laurence said, 'you can ask her to be a brides-maid.' And there was Lois, forlorn in the aisle, with hot air coming up her legs from a grating and tears dripping off her nose into a bunch of chrysanthemums. She would keep the ribbon from her bouquet and show it to Gerald in confidence while she unpacked on their wedding night.

'I am thinking of going abroad quite soon,' she said to Laurence.

'Mr Montmorency has gone for a walk,' said Laurence. 'He had to take an umbrella. Apparently he does not usually take an umbrella, but when he was half-way down the avenue Mrs Montmorency suddenly said he must, because it had never rained like this before. So she took an umbrella and one for herself and started off down the avenue after him. Aunt Myra said she should not have done this because of her heart and looked round for me, but I had gone quickly into the dining-room, which is the last place anybody would look for one between meals. So she found Uncle Richard and he took another umbrella and ran quickly down the avenue after Mrs Montmorency, telling her not to run like that. When he had caught her up he took the umbrella from her and went still more quickly, shouting, after Mr Montmorency, who pretended not to hear and walked on with a back view of positive hatred.'

'But how do you know all this if you were in the dining-room?'

'When they were under way I went to the library window and looked after them . . . Lois, did Lesworth tell you he has captured Peter Connor? He was in bed, apparently.'

'Laurence!' called Lady Naylor from the end of the gallery. 'Where are you? What about Marda's letters? . . . They can't go now,' she went on, approaching. 'Timothy waited ten minutes, and now he has got to run all the way, but he will certainly miss the post . . . Oh, you are all here?'

She looked at her nephew and niece disparagingly and sat down on the bed. 'It is an extraordinary thing,' she said generally, 'the way nobody in this house can be trusted to remember messages . . . It has been a tiring day,' she added. 'Nobody could be nicer than that young Mr Lesworth, but certainly he is not intelligent. And since then they have all been running down the avenue with umbrellas. And oh, what do you think? They have been raided for arms at Castle Trent. They think the whole thing must have been organized by their gardener's cousin. They took some boots away.'

13

When they had all gone to bed, lamps downstairs extinguished, doors upstairs shut with a rattle upon the last voices, Francie talked of Marda's engagement and said she was glad. She was glad as a wife that the net should be flung wider. She talked, but Hugo did not answer; he was still too angry about the umbrella to speak when they were alone. So till well on into the night they lay beside each other under the darkness in an intent and angry silence. Then she wept and said they should never have come back to Danielstown.

'It's as though I couldn't remember where anything was.'

'Look here, if you can't sleep, you'd better take something.'

'Hugo!'

'Oh, I suppose this place disagrees with you, too.'

He had resigned an insult, he could not bear her to intrude upon his wakefulness. Whichever way he turned in that mournful freedom – and the perspectives of his regret opened fanwise, profound avenues each white at the end with a faceless statue – she would come stumbling after him, hand to heart. 'Try and sleep,' he said, and sent her away angrily.

She feigned sleep rigidly, hardly bearing to lie there. Her mind clenched tight, like a fist, at the isolation of this proximity. She longed to resume the life of day downstairs in the empty rooms. She had lain awake in the South of France hearing palm trees creak in the gritty and dry wind, hooked-back shutters rattle against the wall; she had lain awake in town with her room a battle of lights through the thin blinds, lights like her thoughts, flashing and crossing – But across this battle-piece, under the long lances, had swarmed like Uccello's roses, small comforts, a kind of content at suffering, the tenderness of imagined contact. She had wept because he was not with her. Now a nostalgia for that solitude, for a wall so patient and smooth to the reaching hand where there was now a sleeper, came on her, quenching tears. He thought she slept.

But, 'I remember,' she said, about two o'clock, 'a Miss Lawe. I met her last in a tram in Dublin. I remember then she was talking of a nephew – I wonder would that be Leslie?'

'Did she say his name?'

'I can't remember; I got out of the tram . . . Hugo, I'm so thirsty.'

Sighing, he got out of bed.

Laurence could not sleep either. There must have been something at dinner . . . He longed for the raiders and strained his ears in the silence – which had, like the darkness, a sticky and stifling texture, like cobwebs, muffling the senses. The rain had paused, the trees had shed the weight of it, never a drop came through them or tapped on his window-sill. Once he heard, he thought, a fleet of bicycles in the avenue; he sat up propped on his palms, assembled his attitude, and was prepared to go down and admit the party courteously. He meant to offer them bread and apples and leisurely conversation – and jam and whisky, but in relating the incident he would only mention the bread and apples, he liked that smack of austerity, an Oriental graveness. But there were no bicycles; no one knocked; all he had to say went sour in him. It was only some cattle come up close to the house, rubbing against the wires. They moved away.

He lit a candle, blinked at the startled flame and blew it out again. Darkness resumed, with a discomfortable suggestion of normality. There seemed proof that the accident of day, of action, need not recur. And from this blank full stop, this confrontation of a positive futurelessness, his mind ran spider-like back on the thread spun out of itself for advance, stumbling and swerving a little over its own intricacy. He caught trains he had missed, rushing out to the boundless possible from the shining mouths of termini, re-ordered meals in a cosmopolitan blue, re-ate them, thought of thought but sheered away from that windy gulf full of a fateful clapping of empty book-covers. Far enough back, in a kind of unborn freedom, he even re-made marriages. Laura Naylor gave Hugo, scoffingly, bridal tenderness; they had four sons and all hurried out to coarsen in Canada. Here, in this that had been her room, Laura had lain on her wedding morning, watching a spider run up the canopy of the bed, while Hugo made ready, five miles off, to be driven over to take her hand at the altar by poor John Trent, and the four young sons in excitement jiggled among the cherubim. And it was Richard who married Francie, who came to him all in a bloom at his first request and made a kind of a basinette of a life for him, dim with lace. Aunt Myra enjoyed a vigorous celibacy, while Laurence, to be acclaimed a second Weiniger, blew out his brains at – say – Avila, in a fit of temporary discouragement without having heard of Danielstown. Lois, naturally, was not born at all.

But this involved a certain rearrangement of Laurence's character, for not for anything would he have put a pistol into his mouth, though he would have liked to fire a gun out of a window. This neglect of the raiders pricked his egotism. And alarmed by the dragging tick of the watch under his pillow, slowing down as at the mortal sickness of Time, he turned over and thought in a fury that he could not think why Laura should have married Mr Farquar. The rudest man in Ulster he was, with a disagreeably fresh complexion and an eye like a horse. Her confusion had clotted up in the air of the room and seemed, in that closest darkness under the ceiling, to be still impending. Here, choked in the sweep of the bed-curtains, she had writhed in those epic rages; against Hugo, against Richard, against any prospect in life at all; biting the fat resistant pillows, until once she had risen, fluttered at her reflection, dabbed her eyes, buttoned a tight sleek dress of that day's elegance over her heaving bosom, packed her dresses in arched trunks (that had come back since to rot in the attics) and driven off, averting from the stare of the house an angry profile. Hotly, she went up North to attract and marry Mr Farquar. It was in her to have done otherwise, but there is a narrow and fixed compulsion, Laurence recognized, inside the widest ranges of our instability.

Below, through the floor, a light drawling scrape climbed into stuttering melody, syncopated dance music, ghostly with the wagging of hips and horrid in darkness. Lois, child of that unwise marriage, was playing the gramophone. Laurence listened, paralysed with indignation, then reached out and banged a chair on the floor. She attended; the music broke off with a shock, there was a tingling calm, as after an amputation. He above, she below, they thought of each other with outrage.

Certainly, thought Laurence, there must have been something at dinner.

But Sir Richard and Lady Naylor were soundly asleep. She was dreaming about the Aberdeens, while he rode round the country on a motor-bicycle from which he could not detach himself. His friends cut him; he discovered he was a Black and Tan. But night rolled on over them thickly and uneventfully. The others exhausted themselves to sleep. The darkness clamped round their waking brains did not any one moment seem to abate its insane pressure; only, within an hour of breakfast they found themselves restored without reason to the illusion of daylight. With a kind of fatedness, a passivity, they resumed the operation of living.

The morning gave birth to a disappointment. Livvy arrived just as Lois was starting out for the village with Marda to send the telegram. Her horse was lame so she came over on a bicycle, and certainly, thought Lois, watching her lean the bicycle into the privet hedge, there were many things about Livvy that were a pity. For Marda stood at the top of the steps in a green jumper, fanning the telegraph form on the air to dry the ink. The green, queer and metallic, cut surprisingly into the steamy tones of the house and the morning. She would be gone in three days. And now while Livvy settled her hat and her front and prepared her speech, Marda, smiling, came down the steps and walked away down the avenue, not caring. She missed nobody. The dogs went with her: gloomily Lois's eyes went after their wagging sterns.

'Listen,' said Livvy, clutching Lois's elbow. 'Ah, listen, Lois: what is the matter? – That is a natty jumper she's got. I wonder, has she the pattern? Of course, it's partly her figure. I wonder now that she didn't marry . . . Lois, will we go up to your room?'

Lois did not believe the bed was made. Livvy blushed in her little defined way and said she wished to be confidential. So they went into the drawing-room – where Gerald's kiss was hanging: all the doubts of the night could not disperse it – and leaned on the grand piano. Lois was surprised to notice Livvy breathing on to her breast-bone and drawing something up on a long blue ribbon from intimate depths. A ring dangled. 'No one could be more surprised than myself,' said Livvy modestly, averting her eyes from a finger on which the ring had flowered.

'Oh, well *done*!' Lois could have exclaimed with spontaneity. Checking this, she said doubtfully: 'Oh, my dear . . .'

'Who do you guess?'

'Mr . . . Mr Armstrong.'

'Aren't you quick! Listen – swear that you won't tell. For my father doesn't know and I think he'd kill me.'

'How did you . . . how did he . . .'

'Well, it was like this. You see, he asked me at Mrs Fogarty's when would he see me again, and I said I might be going to Cork to the dentist Thursday, and he said he might be going to Cork too. So I thought no more of it. Think what I felt when, I getting out at the station, I saw him there standing as large as life and watching the train like a dog. So he asked me where was I going for tea, so I said if I wasn't alone I might have dropped in at the Imperial because of the band, but that my father didn't like me to go there alone because of the officers. He said would I go with him, and it was raining and my appointment wasn't till half-past five, so I said that we ought not to be seen together, but I turned my hat right down and we went in and heard the band. He seemed very much confused, so I asked him was there anything on his mind and he said there wasn't and I said there must be. So he went very scarlet and pulled his belt and looked up at the ceiling and said he did love me. Then the waiter came with the tea, and I only hope he will not recognize me again. When the waiter had gone I said he might speak lower, and he said he couldn't because of the band. Then I said that of course a thing like this came as a shock to a girl, and he said did it, and I said indeed it did. I said I was not sure if I could get accustomed to the idea of marriage at all, and he looked very much surprised. I said when would he wish it to be? And he said the worst of it was he had no prospects. I said we Irish were not mercenary, and that anyway I knew he had an uncle – It was a great disadvantage to me, Lois, having to keep down so low under my hat all the time – for I could see the Hartigans' aunt, Mrs Foxe-O'Connor, the other side of a palm-tree, and a man my father buys cattle from kept rising up and staring round the room. And what with this and my being naturally very much confused, and David creaking about in his chair, and the band, I don't know how much he heard of what I said at all.

'However, we thought it might be well to buy a ring, though I can't wear it. David looked quite wandering and I had to get him across the traffic. And I felt pretty curious myself. You see, we have neither of us been engaged before, though I have had two offers. Then he said he must go to the barracks, so he put me into a tram to go to the dentist's. Presently I noticed it was the wrong tram, but I hadn't the heart to get out till it was round the corner after the trouble he'd taken, the poor boy. But the tram kind of bolted and I got out near the Cathedral and had to take a very expensive car. I was late at the dentist's – he had out two of my teeth.'

All in a dream, it appeared, Livvy had wandered through wet

residential Cork. All in a dream she had sat and bled from the gums in a train. She opened her mouth to show the two holes the dentist had made as though they were wounds of love, and Lois looked into them solemnly. Had they kissed at all? No, they had not had the opportunity. They could have taken a cab, but Livvy did not think it moral to drive in a cab with a man, for it roused his passions. Lois said she thought the smell inside of a cab would put anyone off, and Livvy said that in that case a cab would be waste of money.

'But can he marry? *Can* a second lieutenant?'

'Oh, I can wait some years. But I shall go and stay with his relations and wear a ring and all, so that there need not be any uncertainty.'

'Why not tell your father now and have it announced?' said Lois hopefully. She watched her own face looking up from the mottled piano-top and felt very singular, distant and destined, like Melisande. 'I don't think,' she said, 'that *I* should be afraid of your father.'

For Livvy's father seemed really a very despondent, mild man with a yellow drooping moustache that he had always to lift up over the edge of his teacup. It was hard to picture his chasing round after Livvy with a blackthorn, or smiting his fist on the dinner-table so that (as Livvy declared) the plates leaped, or going down with the half of a tart in his hand to destroy the cook. The worst she had seen him do, when Livvy was late, was to take his watch out and stand with his thumb on the lid – not looking at it, as though he could not abide the thought of Time – while two or three bubbles ran up his throat. He was a widower: Livvy declared her mother had died of him. He was a teetotaller: half a decanter of whisky was in his tantalus, but he had lost the key. Lois now assured Livvy her father would be the ideal father-in-law; she was sure that David would like him. He would come and stay and be so absolutely unobtrusive.

'He has a prejudice against Army officers,' said Livvy despondently. 'He wouldn't mind if it was the Navy – but what chance have I, living so far inland? If David was a general with gold all down his front and spoke of marriage, I think he'd still kill him. He says I'll get the house burnt over his head with my goings-on.'

'But if he heard you'd been compromised at the Imperial?'

'A girl can't be compromised in the afternoon,' said Livvy gloomily.

Mr Thompson did not entertain very much, but Lois remembered once staying to supper there, early that summer, with David and Gerald. That was before times got so bad and the officers had to be back early to barracks. Mr Thompson's dining-room looked on to trees, that fanned little gusts of light over the table then closed again in green darkness; it smelt of meat and there was an enormous pilastered mahogany sideboard like the front of a temple, inside which they could hear mice running about. Mr Thompson was silent – from fear, they thought, rather than disapproval – he kept drawing long black horsehairs from the seat of his chair and laying them out on the cloth. At each hair, David and Gerald leaned forward and opened their mouths to speak. But Mr Thompson went down in his collar so that they could not: they spoke to each other. And Lois, looking under her lids, had marvelled at this fortress of many opinions. His sister Miss Thompson was present, but she was deaf. The dining-room was dark red, with a smoky ceiling, and Gerald said afterwards he had felt like a disease in a liver. When the blancmange came in it lay down with a sob and Miss Thompson frowned at it. 'Death of the cow,' thought Lois, and saved this up. Livvy kept looking warningly at her friends, but they were all polite. Some ducks filed in at the French window; the guests flapped with their napkins, but Mr Thompson said: 'Oh, let them be,' and sure enough the ducks went round the table with their usual urgent look and out by the window again. Mr Thompson got up and shut out the May air. 'Times change for the worse,' he said to Gerald, who agreed with him so emphatically that David had to repeat the interchange to the anxious Miss Thompson. No wonder Livvy found home dull.

But the happiness of the evening, the closeness-up of the four to each other, the tremors they all transmitted, the cramp of inside laughter, remained with Lois, as though they had held hands tightly under the large oppression. And – under that pressure of laughter compact to bursting-point – a particular stored excitement of pride and pleasure, a jump of intimacy at each other's voices and movements. And the awareness stayed when, afterwards, they had laughed themselves out and were empty and solemn, tinging their interchanges with unusual shyness. That supper marked a degree in her appreciation of Gerald – his crystalline niceness.

For Mr Thompson, still with a little blancmange hanging off his moustache, got up and left them. And later Miss Thompson stood pulling down her skirt across her hips, when Gerald opened the door so beautifully that she had to go out through it, to perfect an experience. Then Livvy, to show what she thought of her family, got up and waltzed round the table, tugged open the window, ran on to the lawn and with unabated gentility jumped on all the croquet hoops, David following. And Gerald turned for the first time to look at Lois, who looked away. They poured out more barley-water and, in an ecstasy of bad manners, bubbled into their glasses. They went out and sat on the seat by the croquet lawn, under a bush of syringa. Waxy petals touched Lois's arm stretched out along the back of the seat, the air smelt of almonds, moths came slanting out of the bush and glittered off on the dusk.

Miss Thompson declared it had been a pleasure, and had asked them to come again. Lois now said: 'I should tell your aunt, she has so little to interest her; I am sure she would be wonderfully sympathetic.'

'I always find it difficult,' Livvy said, 'to open the subject of marriage.' And as she looked down, looked significant, the word did flower over with implications, so that it was, to Lois, at once in a pit and upon a pinnacle that she leaned and frowned and dangled her garnet ring.

'If only David were more determined!'

'But aren't you certain he wants to marry you?'

'Yes, but he needs to have it all arranged for him. Just because I'm such a capable girl . . . Listen, Lois: if you were to be engaged to Gerald Lesworth it would in a kind of way set the ball rolling. Then I should say to my father –'

'Oh, but then I –'

'Of course he may not ask you. But that being so, I should say to my father –'

'Ssh!'

Laurence was well into the drawing-room before he recognized Livvy's shoulder-blades and saw her pink reflection nodding at him in a glass. He flushed with annoyance and bowed. There was ink on his forehead, between the eyebrows, where he had rubbed with the tip of his pen. 'How d'you do,' he said, and to Lois: 'Has Miss Norton started? Started – set out – gone to village? Eh?'

'Oh . . . yes.'

'Pity. Did she seem to be . . . waiting about at all?'

Livvy giggled. Lois said, oh no, she had not seemed to be waiting about. Why?

'Curiosity. I could have gone for her; I have nothing to do.'

'She hadn't got anything to do either.'

'Naturally.' The two girls leaning shoulder to shoulder on the piano filled Laurence with an unutterable depression. He could not leave them. He went to a table of books, took up a book on Nigeria, looked intently into it and blew some dust from between the pages. He felt the only living thing had gone out of the house. He felt hungry, though it was not yet half-past eleven. He could not go upstairs and work, or in fact settle down to anything. He felt as though he were the weather: 'Le temps, c'est moi!' He wished he were the sort of man who would go out to the yard and take the car to pieces. Marda was the only person who found him amusing – but perhaps he was not amusing, perhaps they were right. 'Mrs Montmorency did not sleep either,' he said. 'Notice her eyes this morning?'

'Eh?' said Livvy.

'This is a dreadful house, Miss Thompson. I should not stay to lunch if I were you. Besides, it's only mutton, I asked the cook. Lois, have you any foolscap? I thought I might write a novel.'

'Oh, *do*! Oh, how lovely! But I have no foolscap; ask Uncle Richard. He has some paper over from when he was going to write his memoirs . . . Laurence, *are* you going to stay in here?'

'Well, I'd rather not.' It occurred to him that he might do worse than walk over to lunch with the Careys. There would be a freshness in their dullness and dampness after the dullness and dampness here, while his own would have a charm for them, a fertilizing strangeness. The households had not seen anything of each other for three days. Both families had driven over to Castle Trent to hear about the raid, but had missed each other by half an hour. There would be the raid to discuss, and how the Trents were taking it; also, the Careys lived well – at the worst there could be nothing worse than mutton. 'I am going to lunch at Mount Isabel – any message to Nona?'

'*Oh!*' said Lois. Her eyes went dark with vivid and deep disappointment at the thought of anybody doing anything without her. She missed everything, no one would ever care, she would never marry. She blinked as Laurence went out and shut the door.

'Funny thing,' said Livvy, 'the way your cousin blushes whenever he sees me.' She looked at herself in the tall glass and settled her side hair. 'Now, Lois, what I always feel: a girl is only young once –'

'I expect,' said Lois, 'that that is all for the best.'

14

'Though to tell you the truth,' said Lady Naylor, circulating among the begonia beds at Mount Isabel, 'though I am in a way sorry, I am not altogether sorry that she is going.'

She glanced closely at Mrs Carey's profile, to see that her exact shade of meaning had been taken. Mrs Carey nodded and wrinkled up her forehead, very profoundly. She was thinking about something else. She stopped, pulled off three dead begonias and crumpled them into her pocket.

'Because if that should be what she is going to do, I should rather she did not do it with us. For one thing, the Lawes are relations, they are cousins to a cousin of mine by marriage. One does not know what they might not say about influence. Though no one could interfere less than I do, one never knows, does one, what might go round through the family? And really I am superstitious about her visits, already this time she has lost a suitcase. One cannot help feeling responsible.'

'But are you certain,' asked Mrs Carey, looking critically round this part of her garden as though she were wishing to have it all up and replant it again, 'that she is going to break it off?'

'I shouldn't like to say. She has got into a kind of a nervous habit of sending telegrams. Up and down, up and down all day to the village. Surely that is abnormal in an engaged girl? It is not even as if they were buying a house or anything. It's bound to be so unintimate – unless she does not consider the postmistress, and I do think really she ought to because it is our postmistress. And another thing – I don't really know that I ought to speak of this, but I really cannot discuss it with poor little Francie – I don't think she has at all a good effect on Hugo. You know what he's like usually? Well, he's quite different. Quite *empressé* ... But I don't expect there is anything in that really. One so easily says too much.'

She paused, sighed and waited. Mrs Carey looked at her mildly. 'Oh?' she said. 'Oh yes. But how do you mean?'

'I know Francie notices; I know she is unhappy. Of course she always is unhappy, but she's unhappy now in a different way. Of course one hates to say it, but one does know what Hugo *is* . . .'

'Oh – is he really?' said Mrs Carey, startled.

'What Hugo needs is real trouble. Now if poor little Francie died –'

'Is she seriously – ?'

'No, I feel that he will die first, he has just that way of avoiding things. Look how he didn't marry Laura . . . However, I expect I am being quite ridiculous; I hate to exaggerate – it is from having Laurence so much in the house. Have you noticed how clever young men –? I believe he's worse in England; they think him amusing. Of course there is no harm in Marda; one has known her since she was little. She's only wild – two of her uncles were like that. Shall you ever forget how her knee bled that afternoon? You know, I didn't give another children's party for three years!'

Coming to the edge of the lawn, they looked down on a court where Marda, Lois, Laurence and Nona Carey were playing tennis. The two ladies, at peace and with the faint self-congratulation with which one generation watches another, gazed with a statuesque remoteness over the foreground. 'She is, somehow, I don't know . . . charming,' said Mrs Carey, as Marda and Lois crossed and recrossed. 'Shall we go round before tea and look at the dahlias? I wanted to ask you . . .'

They turned, having cast an imposing shadow over the consciousness of the players, and went softly, heavily over the grass to the iron door of the garden. It seemed natural to Mrs Carey, half dissolved in the brightness and depth of the afternoon, that Hugo should be attracted towards a fellow visitor; such things came on and passed, transitory as a summer. She did not see that there was anything one need do; she said so to Lady Naylor.

The fine weather was back again. Over the roof of Mount Isabel a mountain sheathed in pink air looked gentle and distant. Light slid over the heavy burnished trees; the cream façade of the house was like cardboard, high and confident in the sun – a house without weight, an appearance less actual than the begonias' scarlet and wax-pink flesh. Begonias, burning in an impatience of colour, crowded over the edge of heart-shaped beds. As the four came up from the court there was silence over the sheen of grass. Then a maid leaned out from the dark through the drawing-room window sounding the brass tea-gong: a minor note.

Marda perhaps was wild, like her uncles, but not inconsiderate. She had realized, almost upon arrival, that the worst thing she could do would be to attract Mr Montmorency. To be loved by him would be the culminating disaster of her unfortunate visits. The idea seemed to her silly – she could not think of herself as fatal – but rooted itself during a fit of extreme apprehension induced by the loss of her suitcase. She dreaded the suitcase might not be the close of her record; having made the acquaintance of Hugo she saw it would not be. She might not be fatal, but *here* she was certainly fated. She thought: 'Damn him!' with conscious injustice and drew on every resource, all that might once have been called the arts of her sex to repel, to annoy and to bore him. That day of the beech walk, in old Dannie's cottage, she had had in a flash the measure of her unsuccess. Persistently charmless, untiring in her attempts not to please, she had still to retreat, resentful, upon a female wariness, guardedness, circumspection she had always despised. Her reward: at the foot of the stairs at bedtime, a contact of finger-tips – all of himself in the touch – as he gave her her candlestick: a startled look over the flame. And as the four candles went up with the ladies, drawing a tide of shadow, she and Lois had turned at a turn of the stairs to see him still there, looking up from the staggering mounting dark. She took Lois's arm.

That was the night he did not sleep, and Lois did not sleep either.

Today, Smith had ridden over to Mount Isabel for tea and Nona. He stood smiling over the glittering tray, in the high dark-yellow shadows, pleased but anonymous. He was a man whose name one could not remember. But his appearance agitated Mrs Carey, who recalled that he did not eat any tea. She hoped it would all be all right.

She said to Marda distractedly: 'I am glad you are going to be happy: I hope you will be really, really married.'

'Thank you so much,' said Marda. 'I am sure I shall be.'

'Of course,' continued Mrs Carey, still watching Smith, 'I ought not to congratulate him, I ought to congratulate you.'

'I am very fortunate.'

'Oh *no*, I don't mean that at all. Show me your lovely ring – oh, you haven't got it on. But I expect you have got a lovely ring. Mr Smith, I hope you will play tennis?'

But Smith, who did not feel like tennis, had not brought shoes. Tennis was not his idea at all. He had thought perhaps a little walk in the garden, a few plums . . . And Nona got up very pink and conscious and circulated with plates of cake. She knew that she must throw off people like Mr Smith because next summer she was to be presented and have a season in London. Lady Naylor could not help raising her eyebrows at Mrs Carey.

'Such a pity,' remarked Mrs Carey, as they slid up arm-chairs to the tea-table, 'you didn't bring over the Montmorencys. Wouldn't they come?'

'*He* might have come,' said Laurence, 'but as I am not allowed to drive there was not room in the car. There were too many of us.'

'Never mind,' said Marda. 'I am going on Saturday.'

'Oh no, you aren't!' cried Lois, and added respectfully: 'Don't be so silly.'

Lady Naylor sighed. 'Unfortunately, Marda must go back to England. I don't know what we shall do without her . . .'

'Do you like England?' said Nona Carey, moving away from Smith. 'Are you really going to live there? I always think it's so new-looking. But of course there's a great deal going on . . . Where do *you* live, Mr Smith?'

'Eastbourne.'

Though Lady Naylor said at once that that must be very bracing, Smith wilted under a general commiseration. He re-crossed his legs, frowned at the toe of his shoe and said he thought sometimes of going to East Africa. A forlorn and slighted feeling the announcement of Marda's departure cast over them was heightened by this proposed defection of Smith's. Lady Naylor remarked disparagingly that that would be rather lonely, while Mrs Carey, seeing Smith at once against hot African skies in a silhouette of nobility, felt they had been unkind and asked him to come over here on the sofa and tell her about himself. He told her. Nona sat and twirled on the music stool.

'Smith,' said Laurence, 'you ought to stay and defend us.' And Smith had to promise he would not leave the Army and go to East Africa till they were all settled.

But to Laurence and Lois this all had already a ring of the past. They both had a sense of detention, of a prologue being played out too lengthily, with unnecessary stress, a wasteful attention to detail. Apart, but not quite unaware of each other, queerly linked by antagonism, they both sat eating tea with dissatisfaction, resentful at giving so much of themselves to what was to be forgotten. The day was featureless, a stock pattern day of late summer, blandly insensitive to their imprints. The yellow sun – slanting in under the blinds on full-bosomed silver, hands balancing Worcester, dogs poking up wistfully from under the cloth – seemed old, used, filtering from the surplus of some happy fulfilment; while, unapproachably elsewhere, something went by without them.

Marda wanted more tea – but they were all distracted, an argument raged round Smith. 'You must, of course, go on Saturday?' said Laurence, taking her cup. 'Oh yes – why?' She leaned back from the bar of sun, into the shade of the curtains. Shadow gave transparency to her colours; its brown clarity hardened her face revealingly so that she was exposed a moment, in her anxiety, without the defence of manner. Her green linen dress went ghostly against the cretonne's rather jarring florescence.

'Just when it's fine,' said Laurence, banal with sincerity.

'That is because I'm going.'

He listened a moment and, as the uproar of argument was sustained, said quickly: 'Lois and I aren't a good addition – the Montmorencys think so. Is that what bored you? Nobody's ever gone so soon. There was a walk I wanted to take you.' He rattled the cup and saucer at her in desperation. 'I think you make a mistake, going.'

'Oh, I expect so, but –'

'Look at Lois, her eyes are starting out of her head. When you've gone, she'll go up and cry on your bed. It will fill her mornings.'

'Oh, shut up, she can hear you.'

'No,' said Laurence, 'she can't, though she's trying to. I'm not so sorry, but I do think it's unimaginative of you going. Why have you got to see Mr Lawe? I mean, quite dispassionately, isn't there heaps of time for him? . . . You see,' concluded Laurence, 'I am enraged – by all this – past snubbing-point.'

'I want some more tea,' said Marda, 'more than anything in the world.'

Unable to attract the attention of their hostess, Laurence leaned over the tray and took the teapot. On his way back to Marda he guessed from the unmoving intentness with which she was staring out at the begonias – they gave back little vermilion flecks to her eyes – that there was someone at the bottom of this and that it was Mr Montmorency. He had learnt – from leaning out of his window while his aunt talked to Mrs Montmorency down on the steps – that they all thought she contemplated breaking off her engagement. Personally he thought this improbable. Mr Montmorency himself was the supreme objection; but also she would be getting herself a good home and what went with it – money, assurance and scope. He himself only wished he could do so as easily. He now stood above her holding the cup of tea and could have counted three before she turned round. But then – oh, the waste of his comprehension – he saw she was laughing.

She had laughed at a thought of the subdued surprise with which they would come to her wedding; barely dressed as befitted because of that unshaken disbelief in her; buttoning, till well up the aisle, their white gloves. But the origin of their disbelief did not seem to her funny; had acquired for her, in fact, a tragic vulgarity. So that she did not explain the joke to Laurence; she thanked him and drank the tea, which was all wrong.

Out, at last, through the window, dazzled, threading and separating between the flower-beds, the party dispersed with their cigarettes. Large to themselves, to each other graduating from a little below life-size to an eye from the mountain ant-like – but smaller and less directed – or like beads tipped out. A sense of exposure, of being offered without resistance to some ironic uncuriosity, made Laurence look up at the mountain over the roof of the house. In some gaze – of a man's up there hiding, watching among the clefts and ridges – they seemed held, included and to have their only being. The sense of a watcher, reserve of energy and intention, abashed Laurence, who turned from the mountain. But the unavoidable and containing stare impinged to the point of a transformation upon the social figures with their orderly, knitted shadows, the well-groomed grass and the beds, worked out in this pattern.

Driving home, tightly packed hip to hip in the back of the car between Marda and Lois, and bumping conjointly over the inequalities of the road, Lady Naylor told them of a discovery she had made. Mrs Carey, also, did not understand modern young people. They seemed, Mrs Carey had said, to have no idealism, no sense of adventure, they thought so much of their comfort – Possibly Mrs Carey was wrong? But almost she thought she agreed with her. In their youth, Mrs Carey and she would have been deeply excited by all that was happening round them. Lady Naylor thought all young people ought to be rebels; she herself had certainly been a rebel. But since the War, they had never ceased mouching. She herself had had a deep sense of poetry; she remembered going to sleep with Shelley under her pillow. She used to walk alone in the mountains and hated coming in to meals. Mrs Carey had noticed that Nona would not miss a meal for anything – she was unpunctual always, but never absent. But perhaps Mrs Carey misjudged the girl? Mrs Carey and she had passed through periods of profound unhappiness. And yet their youth was a golden period; they would not have missed it. It did seem a pity, they both had agreed, to be born middle-aged.

These last remarks were directed with a degree of resentment at Laurence's back view, in the front of the car by the chauffeur. His ears, of unfortunate conformation, curled out semi-transparent against the evening light. Laurence said nothing, but thought; he must write that novel, for here lay a gold-mine (then Spain and those first editions, a Picasso and curtains for his rooms). He would vindicate modern young people for his aunt and her generation. Only he did not know if he should write about cocktail parties or whimsical undergraduates.

15

Hugo was dumb, his companion inattentive to him in silence. They walked on the turf of the Darra valley, along the edge of the water: he beat with his stick at the gold, strident ragwort. At every flash of the stick she glanced in surprise, but did not say: 'Spare them.' Lois, straggling behind, threw in twig after twig to the swollen, hurrying Darra; ran a short way with each in intense excitement, lost it and threw in another. She seemed absorbed but remotely dependent, like one of the dogs. If she had fallen in with a loud enough splash and a cry she might have distracted the couple ahead, but she was surefooted and not quite certain enough of herself to fall in on purpose.

Recollections of Laura were now wiped for him from the startlingly green valley, leaving the scene dull. Not a turn of the rocks with the river, not a break-down of turf along the brink, not the Norman keep with perishing corners (where they leaned and quarrelled till Laura had wished aloud it would fall on them) gave back to him what they had taken of that eroding companionship. He and she might never have come here; they were disowned. The sharp rocks breaking out from the turf, the impassive speed of the water, were naked and had to be seen as themselves, in some relation excluding him; like country seen from the train, without past or future. And, having given proof of her impotence to be even here, Laura shrank and drew in her nimbus, leaving only – as in some rediscovered diary of a forgotten year – a few cryptic records, walks, some appointments kept, letters received and posted.

He now guessed, in fact, he had never loved her. Shocked but with an enlivening sense of detachment, he turned to Marda – but still had nothing to say. She walked rather too quickly beside him, with long steps. She was leaving tomorrow; she was to be in England indefinitely: she seemed content. And for this, his anger, released from Laura, settled upon her. He loved her: a sense of himself rushed up, filling the valley. The rocks again were transmuted: broken all over in planes of light, a defeated sharpness, they were no more limestone.

'Mrs Montmorency knows Leslie's aunt,' said Marda suddenly. 'Do you? It seems so extraordinary!'

'If I ever did I've forgotten her.'

'She's so nice.'

'I have no doubt.'

'Let's ask Lois to come and talk to us.'

'She seems quite happy. Where do you go – after tomorrow?'

'Oh, Kent. Doesn't it seem extraordinary?'

Having given the matter rather too marked attention, he pronounced that her sense of the extraordinary seemed to him extravagant. She agreed there did seem to be some disparity in their outlook. 'Disparity!' he cried out. 'Everything! What a good thing we shall never need to understand each other.'

'I never try to understand anybody,' she said mildly.

'No, indeed,' he replied with sarcasm. 'Who is worth it?'

At this she looked back again for Lois. She remembered Francie, seeing them off from the steps in a pink blouse, and the look that fluttered after them down the avenue. No wonder Francie looked like a windflower – her husband had this unfortunate ability to be young at any time. His unordered moods gave him the churlishness of a schoolboy; his silliness embarrassed her. Yet anger did illuminate him becomingly: brighter and harder, for the first time he could be conceived as lovable. Though in this personal atmosphere generated by his temper she was feeling least herself, most nearly negative.

'I should like to go over there,' she said, looking across the water to where trees began on a skyline and went down steeply, powdered yellow with light on their tops.

'We can't,' he said, triumphant, 'the stepping-stones are covered.' He showed her a line of faint scars, a hesitation across the current.

'I never thought of there being stepping-stones. I only wanted to cross because we couldn't. Why does one always seem to be on the wrong side?'

'I should have thought you never were – don't you even make rather a point of that?'

She was exasperated past caution. 'Mr Montmorency, what *is* the matter?'

Seeing that he had overreached himself, been absurd, he raised his eyebrows in courteous mystification – 'Matter?' – did not reply but began talking about his travels – the greenest river he knew was the Ain, he said; had she ever looked down on the Ain? – an appointment he had held in the North (a deterrent from travel), his five years in London (release from the North), a business enterprise with which he had once been connected. It had never been sound, he now saw, he said, but had once had a chance of success. She took him as he had intended, as the practical man *manqué*. They discussed the question of Canada, whether he would have succeeded. She thought, emphatically, it was a pity he had not tried. 'But my wife's health –' 'Oh, yes, Mrs Montmorency . . .'

'The fact is, I have not made her happy.'

'She would always be happy a little; she is wonderfully unselfish.'

'Do you mean –'

'Oh, what *is* that? The ghost of a Palace Hotel?'

The mill startled them all, staring, light-eyed, ghoulishly, round a bend of the valley. Lois had to come hurrying up to explain how it frightened her. In fact, she wouldn't for worlds go into it but liked going as near as she dared. It was a fear she didn't want to get over, a kind of deliciousness. Those dead mills – the country was full of them, never quite stripped and whitened to skeletons' decency: like corpses at their most horrible. 'Another,' Hugo declared, 'of our national grievances. English law strangled the –' But Lois insisted on hurrying: she and Marda were now well ahead.

The river darkened and thundered towards the mill-race, light came full on the high façade of decay. Incredible in its loneliness, roofless, floorless, beams criss-crossing dank interior daylight, the whole place tottered, fit to crash at a breath. Hinges rustily bled where a door had been wrenched away; up six stories panes still tattered the daylight. Mounting the tree-crowded, steep slope some roofless cottages nestled under the flank of the mill with sinister pathos. A track going up the hill from the gateless gateway perished among the trees from disuse. Banal enough in life to have closed this valley to the imagination, the dead mill now entered the democracy of ghostliness, equalled broken palaces in futility and sadness; was transfigured by some response of the spirit, showing not the decline of its meanness, simply decline; took on all of the past to which it had given nothing.

Rooks disturbed the trees, disturbed the echoes. '*Don't* go in!' cried Lois and clutched Marda's arm convulsively.

'Come on,' said Marda, 'I feel demoralized, girlish. Let's hide from Mr Montmorency.' Lois shied through the gateway with more than affected nervousness. This was her nightmare: brittle, staring ruins. Mr Montmorency, disgruntled, still dawdled by the river; the idea of escape appeared irresistible. But the scene was strangely set for a Watteau interlude. Inside the mill door, a high surge of nettles; one beam had rotted and come down, there was some debris of the roof.

'If he starts shouting,' Lois said, apprehensive, 'he'll certainly bring the mill down. Oh, I can't come in, oh, I can't possibly. Oh, it's beastly here; I feel sick. I think you are quite mad!'

'I think you're a shocking little coward.'

'I'm not afraid of anything *reasonable*. But I'm simply nervous, one can't help that.'

'Come in through that door.'

'But it's so *high*.'

Marda put an arm round her waist, and in an ecstasy at this

compulsion Lois entered the mill. Fear heightened her gratification; she welcomed its inrush, letting her look climb the scabby
and livid walls to the frightful stare of the sky. Cracks ran down;
she expected, now with detachment, to see them widen, to see the
walls peel back from a cleft – like the House of Usher's.

'Hate it?' said Marda.

'You'd make me do anything.'

The sun cast in through the window sockets some wild gold
squares twisted by the beams; grasses along the windows trembled
in light. Marda turned and went picking her way through the
nettles; there was a further door, into darkness – somewhere, a
roof still held. 'Marda, help; here's a dead crow!' 'Tchch!'

'But it's very dead!' Shuddering exaggeratedly, leaping in a
scared way over the nettles, Lois also made for the dark doorway,
eager for comment, contempt, consolation. She was a little idiot –
appealing, she felt quite certain, to a particular tenderness.

In the dark of a lean-to, Marda was moving dimly. 'Stairs!'
she exclaimed with interest. Then she was back in a flash and
stood in the door, barring it. She stood intently; menace contracted about her attitude.

'What?' whispered Lois.

'Ssh – someone's asleep here.'

'Perhaps they're dead?' She stared past Marda's shoulder into
the darkness, and, desirous, laughed, then clapped the back of a
hand to her mouth – unnatural gesture, adequate to the drama.
Gradually, she was able to see a man lying face down, arms
spread out; a coat rolled into a pillow under his face which twisted
sideways a little to let him breathe. One fist, clenched loosely,
strayed to a clump of nettles; the knuckles must have been stung
quite white. He could not feel the nettles – one had to imagine
sleep like that! Behind him, stairs went up into visibility, to a gash
of daylight.

Ashamed, the two young women stood elbow to elbow. Marda
stepped back, some plaster crackled under her heel.

'What's that?' said the man softly.

'Come away quickly – come –'

But the man rolled over and sat up, still in the calm of sleep.
'Stay there,' he said, almost persuasively: a pistol bore the
persuasion out. They were embarrassed by this curious confrontation. Neither of them had seen a pistol at this angle; it was
short-looking, scarcely more than a button. The man sat looking

at them with calculating intentness, like a monkey, then got up slowly: the pistol maintained its direction.

'Don't be silly,' said Marda. 'Go to sleep again. We're not –'

'Are there any more of yez?'

'One – not interested either. Better let us go now, there will be less talk.'

'We're just out for a walk,' said Lois, surprised at her own voice.

'Indeed,' said the man. 'It is a grand evening for a walk, no doubt. Is it from Castle Trent y'are?'

'Danielstown.'

The man's eyes went from one to the other, and remained ironically between them. His face was metal-blue in the dusk and seemed numbed into immobility. 'It is time,' he said, 'that yourselves gave up walking. If you have nothing better to do, you had better keep in the house while y'have it.'

Marda, a hand on the frame of the doorway, remained unmoved, but Lois could not but agree with him. She felt quite ruled out, there was nothing at all for her here. She had better be going – but where? She thought: 'I must marry Gerald.' But meanwhile Marda, holding her arm all the time, had softly, satirically pressed it. They could not but feel framed, rather conscious, as though confronting a camera. The man, who did not cease to regard them with uneasy dislike, asked which way they had come, whom they had met, if they had observed any movement of soldiers about the country. He remained dissatisfied; evidently they had the appearance of liars.

Meanwhile Mr Montmorency, suspicious of merriment somewhere and determined to humour no one, had sat down to smoke on a parapet. At its base the bank descended; the river rushed loudly, dark with its own urgency, under his dangling feet. The mill behind affected him like a sense of the future; an unpleasant sensation of being tottered over. Split light, like hands, was dragged past to the mill-race, clawed at the brink and went down in destruction. He looked at the opposite hill, its distinct and peaceful trees. Marda belonged there and might be imagined composedly walking. Knocking some ash off, he leaned forward and groaned at the intervening water – 'On the wrong side' – He missed Francie; there welled up in him one great complaint to Francie. She – selfless woman – would noncommittally rustle; some tender fidgeting always relieved her intentness of listening. Distressed for her husband, she would let out little sighs. He would tell her everything . . . Yet he could not, for Marda was everywhere present, a clear ruddy-white mask of surprise. She impinged on the whole of him, on his most intimate sense of himself, with her cool sombre amusement. Had she a ghost everywhere? – there was something of her in Francie.

'It is like this,' he began to rehearse, 'what I need is –'

A shot, making rings in the silence. Eardrums throbbing, he gathered up the reverberations with incredulity. A battle – a death in the mill? *Whose* death? He leapt to one thought, a flash of relief in the panic. The front of the mill – he ran round it – grinned with vacancy: corpse of an idiot. He steadied himself in the door, watched his cigarette drop into the nettles, then stumbled in over the debris. A crow's flight, stooping wildly among the rafters, dislodged a trickle of plaster. He paused in the well of ruin, terrified for them all. But the crow swerved out through the roof.

'Marda!'

'All right,' said Lois. They appeared in a doorway and looked at him gravely, rather suspiciously. Marda put up a hand to her mouth – in an incredible half-glimpse, he thought he saw blood round the lips.

Something released in his voice; he said: 'Marda – for God's sake –'

Lois, as though the mill were falling, went white, then crimson. He had, distantly, some apprehension of an emotional shock. Marda, perplexedly, continued sucking her hand. Then she took Lois's handkerchief, dabbed at her knuckles, wiped the blood from her lips – where no more came – returned to her knuckles. 'I have lost some skin,' she said at last resentfully. 'Just, a pistol went off – you heard? – by accident. I seem to have lost some pieces of skin.'

'Let me go past,' he said violently.

'We swore –' began Lois.

'Someone went upstairs backward, not very sensibly, not having eaten much for four days. There was some plaster – the pistol went off, naturally. It was silly, really. Look at my beastly hand – I was holding on to the door.'

'Let me get past –'

'But we *swore*, Mr Montmorency –'

'*You* deserve to be shot!' He turned in a manner terrifying to all of them – most of all to himself – on this interruption. 'You don't seem to see, you seem to have no conception –'

'Then why sit there and smoke?' said Lois, trembling. 'I saw you – you and your old conceptions.'

'Shut up,' said Marda, 'oh, do shut up!'

'Don't stand there, let me go past; I'll –'

'Oh, do let's talk about something else –'

'We swore,' went on Lois priggishly. 'There never was anybody, we never saw anybody, *you* never heard –'

But nobody listened. Vaguely, he waved her silent.

'The fact is,' said Marda, 'we are neither of us good at explosions. Perhaps if we sat down and thought it over? Perhaps if you went for a walk – *not* up in the trees?'

'No more hide-and-go-seek,' he said, playful with fury. 'Still bleeding –?'

'Not like I can – I have rather a high standard. Do you remember the scraper? No, I might have done – *this* – on the broken edge of a slate: it will be the edge of a slate if you don't mind. And, being me, it was bound to happen.'

He was set on transgressing the decencies. 'Don't you *realize* you might have been –'

Marda laughed, coming out through the door of the mill beside him. He looked at her lips – no higher – angrily – burningly. Lois looked quickly away. She thought how the very suggestion of death brought this awful unprivacy.

They took his place on the parapet. Warily, they watched him walk back the way they had come, with effort, as though breasting a current. Lois took up his forgotten matchbox, shook it and put it away in her pocket. Their sex was a stronghold, they had to acknowledge silently; traditionally, one could always retreat on collapse. Mr Montmorency having taken away with him any element of agitation, they were left with a particular sort of shyness.

'How one talks!' said Marda.

Lois tied up the hand, she said it seemed like Providence that her handkerchief should be clean today. Marda's was coloured, that would never have done. One had always heard that dye ran into the blood.

'I don't think it would,' said Marda. 'It boils, it is really a good handkerchief. . . This is the worst of big hands.'

'I suppose they are rather big.'

'Sorry we went in?'

'No.'

'You are being nice to me . . . One won't be girlish again – I think, as a matter of fact, we were being goatish.'

'But I've had a . . . a revelation,' said Lois. She bent forward over the river, felt streaks of light fly over her face and felt that speech did not matter when so much was being carried past. 'About Mr Montmorency . . . he's being awful about you, isn't he?'

The statement, almost a query, fluttered up at the end. But Marda's face was inscrutable with reflections.

'About you. I had no idea – I was too damned innocent,' she explained with precision – 'till we all stood in there and shouted. – Hear him tell me I ought to be shot?'

'He was all – dishevelled. He had to be adequate.'

'Oh, I didn't mind. But, I mean, aren't you rather – embarrassed?'

'One can't help things.'

'*I* was awful, I said, "You and your old conceptions." They are rather old, aren't they? . . . I mean, really: he was in love with my mother.'

'Well, I'm going away, aren't I?'

'But, I mean, what is the good of this? It doesn't make anything.'

Marda said, inconsequent: 'I hope I shall have some children; I should hate to be barren.'

'Once I really meant to love him, but it would never have done.'

Marda leant against Lois's shoulder. 'You are wonderful!'

'Not so protected as you imagine.'

'Nothing gets past your imagination.'

'I wish,' said Lois thoughtfully, 'I had really been shot. But I couldn't be.' Later she added: 'I'm sorry I said that about Mr Montmorency. What will become of him?'

'Nothing.'

'I'm glad he wasn't my father.'

'He couldn't be anything's father.'

'Where shall you be this time tomorrow?'

'In the train.'

'Funny,' said Lois. 'Queer.' Her heart thumped, she looked at her watch. 'Half-past six,' she said. 'It's harder, for some reason, to imagine what I'll be doing or where I shall be.'

'A nice walk with Laurence, a nice cheerful squabble. If you want something to talk about, talk about me.'

'No, no, I mean . . . No.' She looked up from the water. 'You know,' she said, 'all this has quite stopped any excitement for me about the mill. It's a loss, really. I don't think I'll come down this part of the river again . . . Will you have to tell Leslie? I don't think you ought to: a swear *is* a swear, isn't it, even in England?'

Nothing would have induced Marda to confirm Leslie's opinion that her country was dangerous as well as demoralizing. He hated to think of even his aunts at that side of the Channel. She expected, some forty-eight hours ahead, to be walking with him in a clipped and traditional garden, in Kentish light. Under these influences, she would be giving account of herself. Leslie's attention, his straight grey gaze, were to modify these wandering weeks of her own incalculably, not a value could fail to be affected by him. So much of herself that was fluid must, too, be moulded by his idea of her. Essentials were fixed and localized by their being together – to become as the bricks and wallpaper of a home.

At present, the mill was behind her, tattered and irrelevantly startling, like a dream of two nights ago. And Lois kept turning upon her a tragic and obstinate gaze: she could sense a persistence of Leslie upon the mental scene. Lois said, but defeatedly: 'He is certain to be suspicious.'

'I certainly won't tell.'

'So it will be a secret?'

'A perfect secret.'

'Thank you so much,' said Lois. As though breaking a spell, she shifted away down the parapet, put her feet to the ground, and was surprised to feel her legs trembling under her. 'Here,' she said generously, 'comes Mr Montmorency.'

He came: 'with demurest of footfalls.' They smiled and shouted along the bank. Yes, they could come now; yes, they were feeling splendid. 'Shan't we be late for dinner?'

'That is impossible,' shouted Mr Montmorency, who was coming back to them looking formal and pleasant.

16

Marda was not due to leave until after lunch, but throughout that morning they were all distressed and sympathetic, could not settle down to anything, walked about the house. Every time Lady Naylor saw Marda she asked her if she ought not to be packing, and while Marda packed, with her door open, Lady Naylor kept looking in to remark how sad it was to see her thus engaged. Francie sat and sewed in the ante-room, looking anxiously up whenever anyone passed. The rain fell, the windows were open, the rooms smelt of window-sills. Francie rolled up her work with a sigh and went up to tell Marda how sorry she was about the rain.

'You'll have a wet drive,' she said.

'But the hood works,' said Marda, folding together the sleeves of a scarlet dress.

'But rain is so sad when one's going away. Nothing, I mean, but a train to arrive at.'

'But I really like trains: I am always talked to.'

'Hugo will be so sorry, he has so much enjoyed talking to you.'

'It's been very nice of him.'

Sir Richard looked up Marda's train in a May time-table and was worried because he could not find it. Had she really any proof, he came up to inquire, that it had been put on since? Would she not be wiser to catch the 12.30 and have plenty of time for dinner in Dublin? Also, what was he to do about her suitcase if it ever turned up? But he almost feared now it would never turn up. He sighed and went back to the library.

Laurence sat in his room with a book with the door open; he could see across the landing into Marda's room. Evidently she could not make up her mind which hat to travel in: she tried on three and looked at herself in each. He did not care for her looks or her clothes, really; both were over-assured. But then he could not recall whose looks or whose clothes he did care for. Finally, he went across to say he did not want *South Wind* back, she could keep it to leave in the train, or simply pack it.

'Oh, thank you,' she said; 'do write my name in it.'

He recoiled at this awful suggestion.

Her room had all come to pieces – dresses swirled on the bed, hats perched everywhere; she had lost the wedge from the mirror so that it wagged right forward, showing its blank side. She was taking more from the house than herself and her luggage.

'You will have a wet drive.'

'The hood works,' said Marda mechanically, throwing some rolled-up stockings out to make room for some shoes.

'Hasn't Lois been up?'

'I don't think so.'

'What can she be doing?'

'Last time I saw her she was bouncing a tennis ball on the dining-room wall between the portraits. She says she has not much to do at present.'

'Anything I can –'

'Oh, if you'd write my labels –'

'I will indeed, but I hate block printing – need they –?'

'Well, I'm afraid I would rather –'

'Remarkable orange labels,' said Laurence, taking the packet from her politely.

'Here is Livvy Thompson,' he added, looking out of the window. 'She must have ridden over to say good-bye.'

'But I don't know her.'

'She doesn't know that: you have met.'

Marda leaned out and called her good-byes to Livvy, who waved and shouted up to her that she would have a very wet drive. Marda withdrew, shutting the window abruptly.

'I am sorry,' said Laurence, 'that our young men will not have a chance to say good-bye to you.'

'I've only met one of them – Gerald.'

'Oh yes, you weren't here for our last party. What a very short time you *have* been here . . . I hope you'll come back again soon – with your husband?'

'Thank you, it's very kind of you.'

Laurence bowed and went away with the labels.

When Lois heard Livvy's voice on the steps she fled to the back of the house and hid in a box-room. Sir Richard had to tell Livvy he did not know where she was; last time he had seen her she had been sorting out some packs of old playing-cards in the drawing-room and seemed very busy. Livvy was much disappointed; however, she took her horse round, then sat in the hall to wait.

Lady Naylor – who had spared her attention to Marda with

difficulty: this was a busy morning – was agitated by this development. She stood at the foot of the stairs, calling Lois.

'She doesn't seem to be anywhere,' Francie at last called helpfully, from the ante-room.

'But Livvy Thompson is sitting in the hall.'

'Ask Hugo to find her.'

'I can't find him either.'

'Perhaps they have both gone out to the garden?'

'Not in all this rain.'

Lady Naylor sighed, gathered up two of the kitchen kittens that were trespassing on the stairs and plunged away through a swing door. It was twenty to twelve: extraordinary how one's mornings went! Lunch was to be unnaturally early because of Marda's departure: evidently, Livvy would remain for it. She looked reproachfully into the library. But there Sir Richard was engaged with the herd, discussing the Darramore pig fair.

Meanwhile Lois was very melancholy in the box-room. The window was dark with ivy, she could not see out. The room was too damp for the storage of trunks that were not finished with anyhow; mustiness came from her mother's old vaulted trunks and from a stack of crushed cardboard boxes. On the whitewash, her mother, to whom also the box-room had been familiar, had written L.N.; L.N., and left an insulting drawing of somebody, probably Hugo. She had scrawled with passion; she had never been able to draw. Lois looked, and strained after feeling, but felt nothing. Her problem was, not only *how* to get out unseen, but *why*, to what purpose?

She did not really know Marda well; to go up and offer to help her pack would surely appear unnatural? Or worse, one might seem to be taking advantage of yesterday? One had been passingly intimate under the pistol's little acute, pig eye – but one had not spoken again of it. If she were free, she could search the rooms for something that looked plausibly Marda's – a magazine, a handkerchief – and bring it up. But then Livvy was unavoidable, varnished up to the height of a shine with love and bursting open with confidences like a cotton-pod. She was appalled by these thoughts of Livvy.

But Livvy was privileged. If she chose to announce her engagement even Sir Richard must stop and listen. It was a passport at any frontier, that kind of announcement. Spurred by an impulse she did not examine, Lois picked up two cardboard lids and with infinite breathlessness crept from the box-room. Through the back-stairs banisters she peered and listened. Lady Naylor had given up calling, but could still be heard complaining to someone in the basement that she did not know where Lois was.

Marda had finished packing, but felt it would not be decent to reappear so soon. Especially when weather did not permit of the 'last walk', a formal parade of the grounds with her host and hostess before lunch-time. She was pleased to see Lois appear in the doorway.

'I brought up some cardboard in case you were packing photographs.'

'But I haven't got any photographs.'

'And you're packed ... Would you like me to sit on anything?'

'No, I think they will all shut.'

'What about Leslie?'

'Oh, he is in talc – unbreakable.'

'I say, I have never seen your engagement ring.'

'Oh yes, we must see the ring,' called Laurence, from over the landing. Surprised by a sudden stillness inside the whirlwind, he had been settling down to a half-morning's work. But he came across and breathed on the ring with Lois, in an imitation of reverence, then returned to his work, shutting the door loudly. Lady Naylor was heard on the stairs again, talking to someone below as she came up. Lois uttered an exclamation of despair and dashed behind a window curtain. Lady Naylor came in with some cake in a cardboard box. She said she did not believe the train had a tea-car, but that Marda should be able to get a tea-basket at Ballybrophy. 'But I am sure you won't care for tea-basket cakes, we none of us do.'

'Thank you *so* much –'

'My dear,' said her hostess, 'it is really a terrible pity about your hand. Especially as it's the left hand, as I'm afraid you will have to be conventional and start wearing your ring again, now you are going to England. It is extraordinary, Marda, the way things happen to you.'

'We must be thankful,' said Marda, 'that nothing worse has happened this time.' Both thinking of Hugo, they looked at each other benevolently, brightly and blankly. 'At least she has not thought of *that*,' they both thought.

Lady Naylor looked with surprise at Lois's feet. 'If you are hiding there,' she said, 'it is simply silly. I have been calling you everywhere. Livvy is waiting for you down in the hall.'

'But I don't want to see her.'

'But she is waiting for you in the hall.'

'I've got nothing to say and I'm sick of always having to keep on saying it.'

'I can't help that, she is your friend. And I thought her feelings seemed very much hurt.'

'She will stay to lunch, you know,' Lois retorted.

'How fickle girls are!' said Lady Naylor, sitting down on the window-sill. Her manner of sitting and waiting most strongly encouraged an exit.

Lady Naylor was more than busy, but could not resist this last opportunity to discover, before the veil of an international marriage descended, what Marda really thought of the English. For nothing of Leslie was Irish except his aunts.

'Of course really,' she said, 'you are very adaptable. I dare say we all are, but with some of us it does not have to come into play. I dare say you'll be very happy indeed. Where did you think of living?'

Leslie had thought of London, Marda confessed an omission on her part.

'Of course that is hardly England,' said Lady Naylor, encouraging. 'And of course it will be lovely for you being able to go abroad so easily; you will be so much nearer everything. And you will have no neighbours, one never has, I believe.'

'Demoralizing . . .'

'You could certainly never be happy living like Anna Partridge. She has an unnaturally sweet disposition: I often pity her . . . I always find the great thing in England is to have plenty to say, and mercifully they are determined to find one amusing. But if one stops talking, they tell one the most extraordinary things, about their husbands, their money affairs, their insides. They don't seem discouraged by not being asked. And they seem so intimate with each other; I suppose it comes from living so close together. Of course they are very definite and practical, but it is a pity they talk so much about what they are doing. I can't think why they think it should matter: supposing I came up here and insisted on telling you what I had been doing the whole morning!'

Marda, feeling how true this must be, pulled open an empty drawer and looked into it, much depressed.

'Though I don't think it is fair,' pursued Lady Naylor, 'to say they have no sense of humour, and of course they are anxious not to appear conventional, and they are kindness itself once they have "placed" one . . . Marda, surely you are not going to travel in that thin coat? Well, for heaven's sake do not develop a cold till it can be obvious that you haven't caught it here. How very unfortunate you have been in your weather! Just that one fine day at Castle Isabel and yesterday evening when you went for your walk. Before you came it was brilliant – such a pity you missed our last party – and as I was saying – Why, Hugo . . .'

He did not seem pleased to be with them. He was nonplussed at finding the door open, having prepared to tap on it inexpressively. Francie had insisted on sending him up with some eau-de-Cologne. She expected that Marda, being so modern, would not care for eau-de-Cologne, but wanted to give her some little token for the journey: this was all she could think of. To the idea of this present he offered surprising resistance. Or could she not take up her present herself? Her large eyes of protest reminded him – their plan of life must eliminate stairs for her; already, she had been up to the top once. So here he was, prepared to recede three steps when Marda should come to her door: he was of that school.

He stood back from the door, looking past with surprise at the room's non-committal features – the chairs, the window – as though he were specially struck by there being a room at all in this part of the house, and especially this room. Some tree-tops fidgeted under his scrutiny. Where had he been all the morning, his hostess wanted to know; no one could find him. Indeed? They could not have looked far: for he had been in the dining-room, down at the dark end, taking out those old *Illustrated London News*, old bound volumes he remembered since he was a boy. There was that Tsar being bombed by Nihilists: very interesting.

'I can't think how any of those Tsars had any confidence,' said Lady Naylor gloomily.

He looked doubtfully at the bottle of eau-de-Cologne; Lady Naylor asked at once what he had there, was told, and exclaimed at Francie's imagination.

'There is nothing like eau-de-Cologne at the end of a crossing, when one is trying to look like something again. Of course, it may not be so bad tonight: at present I don't like the look of those trees. Our inland weather does sometimes go by contraries; it may be surprisingly calm when one gets to Kingstown. I often wonder if living on an island does not make one more deeply religious – the French, for instance, could never have our sense of dependence – though of course they have railway accidents. But I shouldn't think of it, Marda, that's much the best way. I am sure one is often sea-sick from nervousness.'

'I don't know what Miss Norton's friends will think of her hand,' said Hugo. 'Their worst suspicions will be confirmed; they will think we have been shooting at her. Her stumble was most . unfortunate.'

'I ought to have brought back that piece of slate from the mill.'

'I hold you responsible, Hugo; you should not have let her go climbing about. Never mind, it will give them something to talk about.'

'You must draw on your imagination,' said Hugo to Marda. 'Don't let them suspect how tame we all are. They will expect you to be a bit of a heroine; you must tell them everything that might have happened.'

Marda, finding a place for the bottle of eau-de-Cologne at the top of her dressing-case, declared: 'That would be inexhaustible.'

'They may think it odd that you should have cut the *back* of your hand . . .'

The three closed suitcases had a look of finality. Marda wished to go down and find Francie and thank her, they all three crossed the landing at a high pitch of affability. Laurence gripped the hair over his temples in larger handfuls and crouched lower down over his book. His thoughts, tight with concentration, were darkened by a wave of malignance. Marda's door, which no one had shut, remained flapping and clicking.

In the yard, under the dripping chestnuts, Lois and Livvy walked about in their mackintoshes. This afternoon, Lois intended to wash the dogs; they might anticipate the occasion by disappearance, so she thought it better to go down now – they had had their dinners – and shut them up in the stables. They had gone up and looked for no reason into the loft, at the chaff and the dead swallows. They went back slowly, listening in vain for the gong.

'It seems odd,' said Livvy, 'she should be going away; she seems to have only just come. I generally get so accustomed to your visitors. I have said good-bye to her once – I had no idea I should be staying to luncheon. However, I don't suppose she will remember, she seemed rather flurried. Laurence was up there with her; it seems odd to me to have a man in one's bedroom even in the morning, but I dare say she is rather cosmopolitan . . . It does seem a pity, Lois, you forgot to ask her about that jumper pattern.'

'Do you remember those Black and Tans on the Clonmore road? They always remind me of her.'

'Why?' said Livvy. Then with her holy look, which Lois had up to now managed to keep in abeyance, she added: 'That was a memorable day for me, naturally.'

'Why?' said Lois crossly.

'David and I decided to go to Cork.'

'I thought you said that was just chance.'

'It was predestination. Now I must tell you, Lois –'

'Things that have come just before people seem like part of them.'

'How you do talk . . .'

'No, I don't.'

'Lois,' said Livvy sagaciously, 'I hope things are not going wrong between you and Gerald?' Since her engagement, she spoke of all young men by their Christian names and made motherly little impulsive advances in all directions, like Mrs Vermont.

Hugo wished to return to the *Illustrated London News*, but the parlourmaid was laying the table and looked at him in surprise. In the hall the two young girls, hair damp from their excursion, were playing left-hand catch with a tennis ball. So he had to go into the library where his wife and Marda were still talking about eau-de-Cologne – Marda against the mantelpiece, bright and hard-looking in her coat and skirt. Eau-de-Cologne wasn't scent, Francie summed up; she hated scent for it seemed a kind of advertisement. Sir Richard joined them; they all four talked in an eager, unnatural way, as though they had just met for the first time.

Indeed, the unfamiliarity of the moment made them strange to themselves, though it now seemed to have been waiting ahead of them like a trap into which they had stepped with a degree of naturalness. Sir Richard, the least affected, thought the Montmorencys unduly animated and deplored departures. Visitors took form gradually in his household, coming out of a haze of rumour, and seemed but lightly, pleasantly superimposed on the vital pattern till a departure tore great shreds from the season's texture. Francie rubbed the palms of her hands lightly on the tapestry of the chair-arms. She knew that life was unkind and that Marda must have begun at least to suspect this; she wondered how much Marda had understood from the eau-de-Cologne. Marda, turned half-away from them, tapped a tune on the edge of the mantelpiece, laughed at every shade of a silence and felt how resolutely Hugo did not look at her now. There was to be no opportunity for what he must not say to be rather painfully not said. Hugo wished there had been a fire: the room was cold with rain and branches went restlessly up and down beyond the windows. Her face and figure, at which he dared not look, compelled his imagination with ghostly sharpness.

'You will have a very wet drive, I'm afraid,' said Sir Richard finally. To Francie, the remark had a faint echo. Had it been what she was going to say, or had she once said it?

Outside in the hall, Livvy skidded over the edge of a rug and came down heavily, knocking over a wicker chair. The tennis ball bounced away, Lois shrieked her condolences. They all made a movement of consternation and were delighted.

Livvy came into luncheon fragrant with Pond's Extract, a shiny patch on her chin. She kept putting up a finger and feeling the bump: David must 'kiss it better' for her tomorrow. David should have witnessed her courage: he seemed increasingly struck by her moral qualities; he had never observed these things in a girl before. Yesterday he had taken her over to tea at the Vermonts; at her suggestion, they had 'told' the Vermonts, in confidence. It had been a success: she had been made to feel at once she belonged to the regiment. She had had no idea Mrs Vermont was so jolly; she had taken Livvy off for a real little chat in her bedroom; they agreed what a rag it would be if the regiment went to China. Livvy looked voluptuously from Sir Richard to Lady Naylor, thinking what a surprise she had here for them both. She ate two helpings of fricasséed chicken, in absolute silence, designing her trousseau dressing-gown; and old Mr Montmorency, who sat beside her, did not speak either.

'I like lunch at one,' said Lady Naylor, surprised. 'It shortens the morning, but gives one so much more time in the afternoon. I can't think why we don't have it always.'

'I see no reason why we should not, my dear,' said Sir Richard, who, unlike an English husband, was not conservative in these matters.

The car came round twenty minutes too early, but Sir Richard said the chauffeur was quite right. He could hardly bear to let Marda drink her coffee and was but slightly mollified when she burnt herself. Mr Montmorency sugared his coffee twice over, to Livvy's delight. They drank coffee out in the hall, standing up; it was like the Passover. Marda went upstairs and came down in her travelling coat. Hugo stood at the foot of the stairs, in the back hall, tightening the screws of his racquet press.

'Good-bye,' she said. 'Thank you for being nice to me.'

'Oh,' said he, looking blindly at her with his pale eyes, 'have I been nice to you? Good!'

'Good-bye.'

'Good-bye – Marda.'

'Don't come on to the steps –'

'No, I'll finish this press –'

They both half-turned, heard the pendulum of the clock swing once: she went on into the hall. Everybody was there but Lois.

Lois stood behind the door in the drawing-room, waiting. 'Marda,' she said through the crack. 'Hullo?' said Marda. She came round the door, pushing it a little way to behind her. They kissed.

'Marda, I can't –'

'Never mind.'

'*Darling!*'

'Be good!'

'Happy journey!'

'Oh yes.' They parted.

Marda came back to the hall, not looking at anybody in particular, putting her gloves on. Lady Naylor asked her if she had packed the cake. Sir Richard patted her arm and said she was a good girl and must be sure and be happy – then looked very much abashed and startled at what he had done. Laurence looked bored, so bored; she was sorry for Laurence. She said: 'I am really going.' 'I'm sorry you're going, I don't think it's –' They shook hands, he immediately turned – rather rudely, his uncle thought, and walked into the library.

After all, there were only Sir Richard and Lady Naylor and Francie to wave Marda off from the steps and watch the car up the avenue into a veil of rain. Rather few, they felt, considering what a dear she had been and how they had come to love her. Wondering why and where the others had gone, they tried to present the broadest possible expanse of smile and flutter. And of this effort the flick of Marda's gloved finger-tips round the hood conveyed the friendliest, the most satirical recognition.

'Well, that's that,' said Livvy, at last discovering Lois in the drawing-room. 'Partings make me ever so sad. Now listen, Lois –'

'I'm afraid I'm not well, I've eaten something,' said Lois. 'I'm sorry –' She clapped her handkerchief to her mouth and fled from the drawing-room by the other door, stumbling over the *portière*. Livvy went a little way after her, talking, then came back: 'It is a disadvantage to a girl,' she reflected, 'that kind of stomach.'

Lois found in the empty spare room a piece of paper that crept on the floor like a living handkerchief. Through the defenceless windows came in the vacancy of the sky; the grey ceiling had gone up in remoteness. More wind came through, flowers moved in the vases, the pages of a book left open beside the bed turned over hurriedly. The pillow was dinted, as though half-way through packing Marda had lain down lazily. Or as though since last night the pillow had not forgotten the feel of her head.

The Departure of Gerald

17

Captain and Mrs Rolfe of the Gunners were giving a dance in their hut. Denise Rolfe and her dearest friend Betty Vermont of the Rutlands had been more than busy the whole morning. Flustered and happy, they darted about the hut, cutting sandwiches, scattering floor powder, pinning draperies round the walls. They masked the electric lights with pink crinkly paper to produce the desired enchantment. Every now and then, one would collapse on to what remained of the furniture and, catching the other's eyes, burst into delighted laughter. It was all such a rag. They smoked cigarettes and ground the ash into the floor to enrich the polish; they tried the new records over again and again till Mrs Rolfe declared that the needles would give out and snapped down the lid of the gramophone resolutely.

Mrs Rolfe's Colonel disapproved tacitly; Colonel Boatley did not think the dance was a good idea either. Entertainments in barracks had been given up long ago. But it was not easy to veto what ladies described as 'a little fun in the huts'. Married quarters in barracks were limited; as the army of occupation was reinforced, lines of hutments began to extend up the hill at the back of the Gunner barracks. There was nothing to beat these hut dances; for one thing, the floors were so springy. And the fewer the couples, the more intimate the occasion. Denise and Betty both thought with contempt of the Rutlands' official dance in the barrack gymnasium, full of majors waltzing, where you were nearly blown off the floor by the regimental bassoon.

'All the same,' said Betty, rubbing a board with her toe, a shade despondent, 'I wish this would polish *more*. You're certain it won't be sticky?'

'Nothing could be stickier than the C.O.,' said Denise wittily. 'If it wasn't for him, we should be keeping it up till breakfast.'

'It's these wretched patrols and things,' said Mrs Vermont.

'It seems odd being short of girls. I do feel I should be getting my sister over.'

'There will be heaps for tonight,' said Mrs Vermont, who thought people's young sisters rather a bother. The ladies of the neighbourhood had praised Mrs Rolfe's kind intentions, but said that they feared the roads were not fit for their girls these nights. But their girls, meeting Mrs Vermont at the tennis club, had told her they would be certain to come. 'In fact, if they all come,' said Mrs Vermont, apprehensive, 'I may have to telephone down to the mess for some more of our boys.'

Captain Rolfe came off duty at lunch-time, and during the afternoon friends kept dropping in, by twos and singly, with offers to help.

'But don't *look*!' shrieked Denise every time, flinging herself against the wall to conceal the draperies. 'It's all a surprise for tonight.' The subalterns, after a hasty look round, prepared to be perfectly blind. They began to slide industriously, buffeted on the head by the Chinese lanterns which Betty had hung too low. Tubby, Mr Simcox, sat down on a mat and was whisked round the room by his friends to perform the functions of polisher.

'Really,' volunteered someone, 'we ought to be rolling the floor with champagne bottles . . .'

Girls who succeeded in coming over for the dance had arranged to be 'put up' in Clonmore, or in married quarters. The two Miss Raltes from Castle Ralte in the Tipperary direction looked in about four o'clock, pink from a twelve-mile drive and parental opposition. Father, in fact, had been more than difficult. 'He says,' said Moira Ralte, looking beatifically round at the decorations, 'that the whole proceeding is not only criminal but lunatic. He says he can't understand the C.O. allowing it, with the country the way it is. We really did think, till we got past the gates, he was going to stop us.'

'But we came,' said Cicely. Every one laughed. The Miss Raltes had been cast as wild young Irish and rather liked themselves. But they exchanged glances, uneasy. It had not been quite the thing, perhaps, to have laughed at Father.

'It takes two to make a war,' said Mrs Rolfe wisely. '*We*'re not fighting.'

'More's the pity,' said a Mr Daventry of the Rutlands with violence. '*God*, if they'd –' The Miss Raltes, unaccustomed to swearing, looked down their noses. There was a moment of slight discomfort, of national consciousness.

'Wouldn't it be a rag,' said Moira, relieving the tension tactfully, 'if they tried to fire in at the window while we were dancing?'

'*I* shall draw the curtains!' cried Mrs Vermont.

Cicely glanced at the gramophone, hummed a fox-trot and tapped her heel on the floor, looking most unconscious. But the subalterns continued to slide violently, rebounding against each other, and dancing was not begun till the D.I.'s niece came in. The D.I.'s niece came in with a flourish and was greeted with uproar. She was priceless. She had light-red hair fluffed over her forehead, a wide smile punctuated by gaps in her teeth and tireless repartee in a Cork accent. Denise and Betty adored her. She was a Catholic; it seemed so queer to think that she worshipped the Pope. The Miss Raltes hardly knew her. As she came in, Daventry opened his arms, she ran into them with a gurgle and they began to dance. The gramophone spurted hoarse music; other couples followed the gramophone.

Mr Daventry, the senior subaltern, elegant, tall and a shade satanic, was 'taken', obviously, with the queer little person. She could talk and dance at once with an equal skimmingness and she did. Daventry shook her, murmuring: 'Do shut up!' He whispered into her hair that she danced like thistledown and that he hated to have it spoilt.

'Like how much?' shrieked the D.I.'s niece above the music, bobbing her face up at him.

Mrs Rolfe, as distracted hostess, allowed herself to drift into the arms of the adjutant, who had looked in for a moment or two. He spoke of himself as a busy man, but she knew this to be a pose. She danced remotely and kept repeating: 'Glasses for claret cup ... Glasses for cider cup ... Cigarettes ... Cover the washstand ...'

'Washstand?' said the adjutant, solicitous.

'They will have to sit out in Percy's and my bedroom. Do you think it will matter?'

The adjutant took a firmer grip of Mrs Rolfe, an ethereal girl with a habit of drifting just out of one's reach like a kite. He gulped, and said rather too genially: 'It will be no end of a rag tonight. We – we must make the most of it; it may be the last for a bit. As it is, we're doubling the guards. The C.O. –'

'Pig!' said Denise, looking deep into the adjutant's eyes.

'Mum,' said the adjutant, blinking. 'And another thing: I'm afraid you won't have Dobson of the Rutlands. I've just met him – he's to be out on patrol.'

'Oh, but he *said* he'd get out of that! Oh, but he promised me –'

'He'd no business to; he's been due for patrol for ages. Their C.O. –'

'He spoils everything. Captain Dobson is one of my best dancers.' She stopped short and turned off the gramophone. 'Listen, Percy! They're sending Captain Dobson out on patrol at a moment's notice. *Now* I'd like to know what I'm supposed to do? I'd calculated the numbers exactly.'

'But, Dens,' said her husband conscientiously, 'we had four men spare. And you're certain of Lesworth and Armstrong.'

'*He* won't count!' They all laughed: Betty had told a few friends in confidence . . .

'And for a matter of that,' Denise, still clouded, complained to the adjutant, 'Mr Lesworth won't count much either. He's awfully keen on the Farquar girl.'

The adjutant thought: 'These attachments!' His C.O. did not like these attachements, either. The gramophone in a perceptibly minor key began again, they went on dancing.

'Suppose,' said the D.I.'s niece, during an interval, 'all we girls are left sitting tonight and nobody comes to dance with us?'

'Dance with each other,' said Cicely Ralte firmly.

'But I wouldn't care to dance without men,' said the D.I.'s niece, frankly languishing. She had hoisted herself on to the cabinet that held the records and sat swinging her legs in their shiny stockings and pulling her dazzlingly checked skirt over her knees. Her green eyes roamed round, returning attention confidently.

Daventry, a hand on the edge of the cabinet, stood leaning with his back to the wall's art-muslin draperies. He kept shutting his eyes; whenever he stopped dancing he noticed that he had a headache. He had been out in the mountains all night and most of the morning, searching some houses for guns that were known to be there. He had received special orders to ransack the beds, and to search with particular strictness the houses where men were absent and women wept loudest and prayed. Nearly all beds had contained very old women or women with very new babies, but the N.C.O., who was used to the work, insisted that they must go through with it. Daventry still felt sickish, still stifled with thick air and womanhood, dazed from the din. Daventry had been shell-shocked, he was now beginning to hate Ireland, lyrically, explicitly; down to the very feel of the air and smell of the water.

If it were not for dancing a good deal, whisky, bridge, ragging about in the huts, whisky again, he did not know what would become of him, he would go over the edge, quite mad, he supposed. He opened his eyes: afternoon light lay in bars on the smoky air. The flash of his partner's legs in their glassy stockings exasperated him, he gripped one of her ankles – harshly, as though it had been a man's. She kicked, and a high-heeled slipper went rocketing through the air. A forest of hands went up. The D.I.'s niece looked down complacently on the compact and plaited backs of the subalterns. The other girls tittered and hung on the outskirts.

'Oh, take care,' wailed Denise, 'mind my draperies!' She freed an end of the muslin and, as no one listened, began with angry laughter to pepper them all with floor-powder. The D.I.'s niece looked at Daventry queerly and suddenly: their eyes were now on a level. His eyes, dark with fatigue and nervousness, were set in too close together, like a good-looking shark's.

Cicely Ralte yawned slightly; the struggle did not abate. 'We shall all be tired when it comes to tonight,' she said to the adjutant.

But he said: 'Here comes Miss Farquar, looking as fresh as paint.'

Lois came to the door with David Armstrong. Livvy would not come up to the hut till this evening, she would be confused, she feared; she didn't know how much they knew. She was down in Clonmore now, buying sophisticated-looking black pansies to wear in her dress. She and Lois were spending the night in Clonmore, with the Fogartys. Lois was dazed still from her long drive under the strained white sunless sky. Sir Richard and Lady Naylor had viewed her departure with the gloomiest apprehensions, but Francie had insisted she would enjoy herself. It must be flat for her these few days, Francie said, after Marda had gone. And she had slipped a sachet of Californian Poppy into the top of the suitcase, with Lois's green tulle dress.

Lois and David looked through the door at the young men all in a tangle with a sensation of helplessness, as though it devolved on themselves to unwind them. Then they stepped in and shook hands with Mrs Rolfe and her girl friends. Lois, pleasing the adjutant by her freshness, wore a light-blue felt hat and a blue cardigan. She suspected she should not be walking about the camp without a chaperon, but could not see how to avoid this: she had come up here to look for Mrs Vermont. She went pink from the heat of the room and felt Mr Daventry look at her – then shut his eyes again. There was a desperation about Mr Daventry she could have loved. But he apparently craved relaxation: she had found out she did not relax Mr Daventry.

Gerald was not here – she guessed from the eyes of commiseration. He was a serious dancer and did not care to tire himself by sliding. Possibly he was on duty, possibly would be waiting at Mr Fogarty's. Now, she could remember nothing of him but the leg he had drawn so tenderly into the armoured car. She had heard nothing of him from that moment; he might have been sealed up permanently in tin, like a lobster. Did he regret the kiss? – he had not added a word to it.

Mr Simcox, the fattest and sweetest of all the Gunners, started the gramophone with an eye on herself and came to ask for a dance. He looked so hot, she said she would rather wait till the evening. 'Remember,' said Mr Simcox, spreading a hand on his heart. And by some mysterious evocation, the hut, lit up, vibrated; the air was warm like smoke on her cool arm, and she went throbbing along with Gerald, feeling his hand on her back through her thin dress – too near to see each other – his lashes reverent by her hair. She thought she need not worry about her youth; it wasted itself spontaneously, like sunshine elsewhere or firelight in an empty room.

She thanked Mr Simcox and said she would keep number six and would not lose count. Mrs Vermont, looking peevish suddenly, said it was tea-time now and shooed the young men out of the hut like chickens. They dispersed through the mud in the tired, wise light of the afternoon.

That evening a wind came up. Lois and Livvy dressed in Mrs Fogarty's spare room, stumbling round the edge of the large bed. They took turns at the looking-glass; in the intervals of their toilet they ran to the window to look out. It was strange and pleasant to Lois to be in a town again. The square, where some crisp leaves whirled autumnly, was pervaded by an excitement. Though only twelve couples had been invited to Mrs Rolfe's dance, all Clonmore seemed to know of it. People kept coming out quickly through the swing doors of the Imperial. Someone played half a waltz and broke off, discouraged; two commercial travellers clapped one another on the shoulder. Livvy pinned the black pansies under her bosom and turned to invite admiration. Lois thought the pansies looked common, but, knowing they must have cost four-and-six, said they were most original. Lois's green tulle dress slipped over her head like a cataract. She shone, coming out through the top of it. If only Marda could see her . . . It was half-past six: she had promised herself to think of Marda.

They were dressing early, they were to dine with a Mrs Perkins up in the huts. Mrs Perkins could not promise there would be much for dinner, but after all this was Ireland and it would be rather jolly.

Captain Vermont was to call for them: they buttoned their over-coats over their ball-dresses. Mrs Fogarty kissed them half-way downstairs, and warned them not to break hearts. She would see them later, she was coming to watch the dance.

Since the acquisition of Betty, Captain Vermont's stock of conversation to pretty young things had given out naturally; biologically the time was past for it. They walked rather silently up past the barracks and picked their way over the mud between the huts. A chill of darkness was coming down on the air. The wind came, knife-like, down through the lines of huts from the mountain, over a gulf of land where the farms were dark – apprehensive, the young girls patted the whorls of their hair. The hut exposed a flank to the wind; it was chilly, one slipped one's bare arms out of one's coat reluctantly, going to table.

The dinner was not so jolly as Lois had feared. Mrs Perkins looked distraite and had a whispered argument with her husband about a tin-opener. Mrs Vermont could talk of nothing but poor Denise ('as though,' said Livvy, 'she were having at least a baby instead of only a dance'). Captain Perkins and Captain Vermont apologized repeatedly to the girls for being old and married; their wives told them not to be so silly. Their wives said the girls could perfectly well see there was no room for young men here: already their six chairs grated against the match-boarding. The girls would have young men in the course of the evening. Lois agreed politely, but Livvy wished they had stayed to dinner down in Clonmore where one could have at least watched Mr Fogarty drink. She sat squinting, watching the wasted powder flake off her nose.

A bottle of white wine was divided among the ladies with depressing impartiality; the men drank whisky. Mrs Perkins' pince-nez glittered with more animation. But the wind like a lunatic fidgeted with the hut, frames creaked, doors rattled, a shudder went down the walls; a gust through a crack set the lights dementedly swinging. During a strained little silence, between two gusts of the wind, Mrs Vermont observed that an angel must be passing over the house; she wanted them to listen for its wings. They listened; they thought of empty country blotted out by the darkness. 'Quiet here, isn't it?' said Mrs Perkins.

'Better not circulate too far between the dances,' said Captain Perkins, 'and don't go down to the wires. It's dark, for one thing; we don't want any of these girls lost.'

'Grandpa!' said Mrs Vermont. Livvy noted there seemed some communal feeling between the married: any wife could be faintly rude to anyone else's husband. 'I don't go for walks between dances,' said Livvy, bridling.

'You don't know what you'll do *now*!' said Mrs Vermont, and they all laughed.

Lois was anxious, there was a tight little ball in her throat; she could hardly swallow. She was always 'strung-up' before a dance. But tonight it was worse; she had not the expectation of being claimed: she was really doubtful. She had not had a word from Gerald; he hadn't been round to the Fogartys'. Was she not nice to kiss; was he disappointed? Her green frock glinted under the light; she kept looking down at her breast, and into her lap, where the folds ran off in shadow under the table. If he were not there when she came, if she did not see him before he saw her (as she came uphill in the dark) standing full in pink light by the door, staring eagerly on to the slab of darkness that was to give her up – she should die, she thought. For this morning she had written to Viola that she intended to marry Gerald.

18

The Rolfes' door swung open and shut; bursts from the gramophone came downhill like somebody coughing. As the Perkins' party stepped up from the duckboards Gerald spun past the door with the D.I.'s niece, in a nimbus of gauze draperies. The room was sticky with strawberry light, unlit lanterns wobbled between the electric light cords; the dancers seemed to be moving slowly in jam. A group of young men stood by the door, coughing. But one hadn't yet made one's official appearance: Lois blinked and began to tug out her silver shoes from her pockets; somebody pulled her on down a passage to change.

In what Denise called the kitchenette at the end of the passage the five spare men were smoking, looking into their glasses of whisky and wishing to play bridge. Lois looked in and they all waved to her, but Livvy pulled her away quickly: she said that must be a gentlemen's cloak-room. Lois met, with surprise, her own eyes of interrogation in six inches of mirror between the coats.

David came to claim Livvy, Betty went swooning off over the chalky lake of the floor with Mr Simcox, Mr Daventry stared at the passage door with severity, balanced his cigarette on the rim of the gramophone and came up to Lois and frowned, without speaking. He opened his arms slowly. They danced; she had no idea she could dance so beautifully. At the end of the record Mr Daventry impassively moved back the needle again. 'Tiring day,' he said.

'Oh, I don't think so.' They went on dancing.

The D.I.'s niece picked off ends of her tangerine draperies from various parts of Gerald and walked away with an aquiline-looking gunner. Over Lois's temple Mr Daventry's jaw moved slightly; his neck muscles strained. Again he revived the gramophone. Lois, breathless, said: 'Isn't there going to be an interval?' 'Not necessarily,' replied Mr Daventry. Meanwhile, one wall of the hut seemed propped against Gerald's rigid, resentful back.

'What a crowd . . .'

'I beg your pardon?'

She did not speak again. Anxiously dancing, she merely constituted Mr Daventry's revenge. Mrs Vermont, going past Gerald, said: 'Oh, diddums?' She asked Mr Simcox if he had noticed, nice-looking boys looked their nicest sulky? Mr Simcox, looking round so carefully that he missed a step, said he would not call that *sulky* . . . More worried.

'Nonsense, Tubby, what's he got to worry about?'

'You never know.'

Mr Simcox was a bit of a philosopher, because he was so fat. He gave up Mrs Vermont with a sigh to another young man and went across for somebody's young, shy sister. 'No luck?' he said on the way, to Gerald. And Gerald looked at him candidly, with despair.

The evening 'went' with a rush, with a kind of high impetuousness out of everybody's control. Everyone looked and spoke and danced close up with a kind of exalted helplessness; intimacy tightened the very air. Sandwiches were ambrosia, brightening the eyes; rims of plates went electric where fingers touched. Mrs Rolfe laughed all the time, you would have said with despair. She climbed past couples very close up at the darkest part of the passage, she entered the kitchenette with a shriek and swept some cards from the table. The spare men danced with each other. She ran in and out of her bedroom, shaking a plate of chocolates at the couples sitting out on the chest-o'-drawers and on the washstand covered with Turkish cushions. If the hut had risen and soared up into the air, so that someone stepping out at the door had to step back dizzily, she would hardly have been surprised. Indeed, two subalterns running down to the mess for more siphons did leap to the mud as from a great height.

The room was hot; they drew the curtains back and opened the windows, then were stared in at oddly by hard little squares of night. Couples went out for walks, to cool their faces. Livvy was kissed twice and went off to powder her chin. 'Of course, this is post-war madness,' said Mr Simcox, standing beside a window.

'Oh yes,' agreed Lois.

'Awful, really . . . I expect *you* understand what I mean?'

'Oh yes.' Wishing Mr Simcox were not intrigued, she put her two hands out of the window, as into a well, to feel wind cold on her wrists. Gerald came up behind her.

'Mine next,' he said, as though they had just parted. 'What a row!' he yelled.

'This jazz,' said Simcox. 'They ought to have let me bring my band,' complained Gerald, 'it wouldn't have taken up much more room than Mrs Fogarty.'

Mrs Fogarty had indeed come in and sat at the end of the room in a purple tea-gown. Her circumference was enormous, her feet stuck out beyond it – but she was such a darling. Every time a couple stumbled over her feet she beamed and nodded in the friendliest way. She had just whispered to Gerald, who brought her a glass of lemonade: 'Here, where's *your* girl?' And her eyes had rolled at him, dark with worry. Gerald could not have borne to disappoint Mrs Fogarty.

Gerald did not dance silently. His hand supported her wrist, cool and familiar. Lois felt she was home again; safe from deserted rooms, the penetration of silences, rain, homelessness. Nothing mattered: she could have gone to sleep. But he woke her.

'Look here: what have I done?'

'How –?' said she, quite inadequate.

'You *know*. But why are you – why must we –?'

'Gerald – oh, do be – ssh!'

A couple sheered off from them.

'I didn't think you'd be cruel,' he said to her hair, almost confidentially.

'But it's you who've been cutting me.'

'But how? When? You've never once looked – Lois, you're lovely, but you're so –'

'Look here, we can't talk and dance.'

'Which does that mean you *don't* want to do?'

She looked at a button of his mess coat. 'Talk,' she said after a little contented interval. He slid his hand up her wrist, they danced on. The D.I.'s niece trailed past them, laughing at Daventry: they had a pool of space to themselves on the crowded floor. The pink room melted round, beatific and syrupy. He was closer than ever under the lovely compulsion of movement.

'You do dance divinely.'

'What?' he said, like the ghost of Daventry. Someone stopped the gramophone, they looked at each other, shocked. Something had made him absurdly unhappy: she would have liked to have comforted him.

'Let's go out.'

'Won't it be cold for you?'

'Gerald,' said she, discouraged, 'don't be an aunt.'

The wind whipped round the edge of the hut, ran through her hair at the roots and stung her ears – a sinister energy in this fixed and angular world, for one could not see anything moving. Gerald walked, unknown, beside her, up in the dark. 'At one time,' said Lois, wrapping her wild skirts round her, 'a girl would have died of this.'

'Cigarette?'

'Oh – will it light here?'

'I can light one most places.' So she bent over his hands, a cup of fire. There were two bright specks in his eyes. – Then the match whirled off and died on the dark. 'I can't think what you think has gone wrong,' she said.

'You were so queer that Thursday. You'd been like part of me the night before; then everything seemed – wrong. I dare say I was a brute; I oughtn't to have – though as a matter of fact I'll never be sorry . . . If you'd been just angry or anything . . . But you seemed to go right away: I didn't know where I was. All lunch you were like a girl at a tennis club. Then you left me down there with them all to talk rot and went off with that beastly gramophone.'

'*That* was not my fault – did you want me to listen to you talking rot? – Gerald, I didn't realize you were resentful; I didn't think you could be . . . I was waiting for you to write.'

'I began so many letters, I used half a box of note-paper. I couldn't think what to say.'

'Still, you might have written.'

'But how?' he said candidly.

She could not remember, though she had read so many books, *who* spoke first after a kiss had been, not exchanged but – administered. The two reactions, outrage, capitulation, had not been her own. 'You were hoping I would write?' she said, seeing light suddenly.

'You see, you had always been so understanding.'

'But, Gerald, I should have thought you'd have been shocked if I'd –'

'Oh? . . . Perhaps I would. But I wanted something to make things natural. I shall never forget what I felt in that armoured car. You will always be connected up in my mind with the smell of oil – Lois, do you think I am terribly introspective?'

'You know, you were tired.'

'Perhaps it was that,' he said, puzzled. 'But bumping along back to barracks, and you going in again with that girl to that topping house . . .'

'Do you think it's a topping house?'

'It seems so to me.'

This new version of the changeable afternoon was a shock to her. It had gone on for him, too; doors that she had not thought of shutting and windows opening, the drone in the drawing-room, rain with a different importance. Might she perhaps have thought more about Gerald and wondered less? Splashing along the brown road to Clonmore she could now see the armoured car diminish – with Gerald its only nerve. But she thought of the empty spare room and how it avenged him.

'Marda's gone, you know.'

'But she had just come to lunch, surely?'

'*Gerald!* . . . Can't you feel any difference between someone to lunch and somebody staying?'

'She hadn't a hat,' said Gerald after consideration.

'She went two days ago: she's in Kent now.'

'I'm sorry,' said Gerald civilly. Feeling a strained, fierce pause, he added: 'She seemed awfully nice, I thought.'

'Don't you wonder at all if I miss her?'

'I expect you must. I always miss visitors, though they're a bother beforehand.'

'She hadn't any beforehand – that seems so odd now.'

'Lois . . . you aren't angry, then?'

'Oh?' Recollecting herself, she looked round the darkness vaguely. A couple were coming towards them; she put a hand on his sleeve to make him be quiet, his other hand came over it. They heard Daventry's angry laugh, his partner's feet ran stickily on the duckboards. Gerald and Daventry passed in the dark with, it seemed, a queer silent interchange.

'Mr Daventry seems old to be a subaltern.'

'It's absurd that he should be – all this peace-time bother. He had a company in France in 1916, later on he was acting major. He's a splendid fellow, I'm sorry you haven't seen more of him. He won't go about much, outside barracks. The fact is,' he added apologetic, 'he's sick at being over here. It doesn't seem to agree with him.'

'Do *you* really like it?'

'Oh, well, it's a job. Though I rather see Daventry's point – it doesn't seem natural.'

They had come to the end of the huts – at the foot of the steep slope a wall, the top heavily wired. Under the wall a sentry inhumanly paced like a pendulum. The country bore in it strong menace. Gerald looked out at it, his face blinking in and out of the dark, faintly red with the pulse of his cigarette. She nursed her bare elbows, unconsciously shivering. He seemed at once close and remote, known and un-personal; she understood why, up to now, she had searched for him vainly in what he said. He had nothing to do with expression. She put out a hand to where he was, shadowy and palpable. He threw his cigarette away, turned – and said nothing. The sentry passed.

They went back the way they had come, between the huts.

'Gerald, I *wasn't* angry . . . at what you did . . .'

'No, you were wonderful all the time.'

'Don't you understand?' she said sharply – '*Gerald?*'

'Understand? . . . *Lois!*'

While they kissed, she heard, in the silence of their footsteps, someone moving about in a hut up the lines. The sound was a long way off, at the other side of a stillness.

'Your arms are so cold.'

'I've been so lonely.'

'They're so *cold*.' He kissed them, inside the elbows. Later: 'I like the back of your head,' she said with exploring finger-tips.

'I never thought you looked at me.'

'Gerald, I've been so . . . vacant.'

'I never thought you wanted me.'

'I –' she began. The soft sound of her dress in the wind became, by some connection of mood, painfully inexplicable to her – the pain was its own, from not being understood. 'Gerald, your buttons hurt rather.'

'My darling –' He let her go, but still, above consciousness, held one of her hands, solemnly. 'Shall you really be able to marry me?'

'I don't know till you've asked me.'

'Don't laugh –' he cried.

'Can't you *hear* I'm not laughing?'

'Lois –' Something more was coming; she waited, hearing him draw a breath. 'Let's go back and dance,' he said almost religiously – 'shall we?'

The hut was compact with movement: she stood back in alarm, as before a revolving door in destructive motion. Now it was gone, she remembered sharply the smell of earth . . . David Armstrong leaned from his partner wildly and struck Gerald over the head with a red balloon.

Mrs Rolfe had had an idea that the dance might well finish up with a cotillion. She was vague about cotillions, but towards this end she had distributed balloons, whistles that ran out long tongues when you blew them, and streamers from striped cardboard batons with which dancers might hit one another over the head. Mrs Vermont thought these things went better with fancy dress, but Denise said a rag was a rag at any time. Girls ducked and shrieked and waved their streamers over their partners' shoulders. Denise, radiant in black with a trail of nasturtiums, was waltzing – affair of prolonged 'hesitations' – with Betty's husband. She bit off a streamer, spat out a mouthful of paper and said, with a shiver of happiness: 'Isn't it marvellous, Timmy? I can hardly believe I'm awake!'

'Ra-*ther*!' replied Captain Vermont, with blurred enthusiasm. He was being buffeted by Mr Simcox and somebody's sister.

'Betty's been just too marvellous,' went on Denise – 'Oh, Timmy, do have a shot at Reggie Daventry – there, with the girl in scarlet. He looks just too refined!'

But Timmy failed to find Daventry. 'Betty's *tons* the prettiest here,' cried Denise, ecstatic.

'Oh, come!' expostulated Captain Vermont, squeezing her waist. It gave him a warm, tender feeling to think how fond she and Betty were of each other.

'Tell me,' said Denise, as nearly as possible snuggling, 'are we terribly reckless? Would this annoy the Irish?'

'They won't know.'

'They have heaps of spies.'

'I say, *sssh*, Denise, there are heaps of them here tonight.'

'Spies?'

'Irish – the Raltes and Co.'

'They're different.'

'Still, they've got feelings.'

Denise sighed. 'I could go on like this for ever.' But Captain Vermont rather thought he would like a drink. A balloon exploded. 'Glory!' cried Mrs Fogarty. So they burst four more to keep her amused.

'Is this like a bombardment?' asked Moira Ralte.

'No,' said Mr Simcox.

If they were not careful, they would knock over the gramophone. Mr Daventry thought it was time they did. It was time something happened. He danced the D.I.'s niece down the passage and kissed her with her head pressed back in the coats. She struggled, futile, slippery as a weasel. As he kissed again her face went stiff and she shut her eyes. When these opened, they were as shrewd as ever: still he did not know what she thought. The drums in his temples were now insistent; he could not forget them even while he was dancing. She had dabbed herself over with White Rose. Her frizzy hair tickled his mouth as he bent close to her.

'Do you get kissed a lot?'

'Englishmen never could keep their mouths to themselves.'

'You won't know yourself when we're gone!'

'You should get back home while you can, the lot of you.'

'What would become of Uncle?'

'Did you like your whisky?' She put a hand up rudely to shield herself from his breath. This reminded Daventry, who let go of the common little hell-cat abruptly and walked away to the kitchenette, where he heard a siphon. Lois stood in the door, waiting while David got her some soda-water. But wouldn't she try a little something? Just a little something to dance on – no? Daventry, standing back and tilting his drink about in his glass, stared at her feet with owlish ferocity.

'Sorry about your silver shoes, Miss Farquar.'

'There are some beautiful walks round here,' said David, grinning.

'Miss Farquar should float, not walk; she looks like a water-lily,' said Daventry, looking over her green frock with his discomforting eyes. 'Come on and dance,' said David, taking her empty glass. Lois began to say she was keeping the next for Gerald. But: 'Miss Farquar and I are hungry, we are going to find a sandwich,' said Daventry.

In the box of a dining-room plates of dishevelled sandwiches sat in unmasked electric light. There was no one there. Mr Daventry, looking hard at her, put the palm of his hand to his left temple with a curious, listening air, as though to see if a watch had stopped.

'Chicken and ham,' he said, 'tongue and turkey; they're all cat, they say.' ('What shall I say?' thought Lois.) He looked at a chair with contempt, then sat down on it. 'I don't think I've met you before,' he continued.

'Perhaps you didn't notice.'

'Dear me,' said Mr Daventry, looking into a sandwich. 'No, I don't think it could have been that.'

'Then it can't be explained,' said Lois, and (she felt) glittered excitedly. He suggested the army of Wellington; buckskins. Looking up thoughtfully, he directed upon the wall just over her head his strained dark look that was almost a squint. 'You live round here?'

'More or less –' She was startled to meet the dark look on a level. Hers was, he said, a remarkably beautiful country.

'I am afraid *you* –'

He affably shrugged. Did that matter? He stared at her arms, at the inside of her elbows, with such intensity, she felt Gerald's kisses were printed there. Was this a bounder? – She knew she had no criterion.

'Have a nice walk?' he inquired.

'Did you?' she countered.

'I expect so,' said Mr Daventry, after consideration. 'As a matter of fact, I am not quite at my best.' They looked hard at each other. 'Nothing,' he said, 'appeals to me.' She moved her arms nervously on the silk of her dress. For she saw there was not a man here, hardly even a person.

'How do you mean "more or less"?' he said suddenly.

'Well, I don't live anywhere, really.'

'I do: I live near Birmingham.' He put the half-eaten sandwich down, with distaste, on the edge of the cloth and pulled up a plate to cover it. She felt she was quite finished with. Suppose, she thought, they were all like this! Should she go? She made a movement, he did not see; she was disappointed. He put the hand to his temple, again listening.

'Tired?'

'Oh, no,' he said, with irony.

'I'm going back now.'

'Such a pity. Anyone so charming . . .'

'Well, I'm bored,' she said.

'It's a pity you don't know about my head, it's a most curious head, it would interest you . . . How shall I keep you? Look here, seriously, about Lesworth –'

'Oh?' she inquired, suddenly cold inside.

'About our young friend –' He pulled up his chair close; she had a feeling like gates shutting. 'Tell me this –'

But the roar of merriment, solid and swerving evenly as a waterfall past the door, splintered off in a crash. Silence came, with hard impact. 'Thank God, *they've upset the gramophone*!' Daventry smacked his knee, remotely, as though rehearsing the gesture. His look decomposed in laughter. 'Done in,' he said, drawing life from the thought. Simultaneously, a universal shriek went up: it was smashed, finished. 'Really,' she thought, 'you laugh like Satan!'

'Well, well,' said Daventry, tilting his drink about, 'it's been a pleasant evening.' Here they all came – a stampede in the passage. She was glad of them, for under the storm of his mirth that swept their island, disarranging the interlude, she had sat cold and desolate. A gramophone passing, a gramophone less in the world, it was not funny. But between bursts of laughter she had felt him look at her lips, at her arms, at her dress, like a ghost, with nostalgia and cold curiosity. About their young friend? – she wasn't to know.

Mrs Vermont seemed broken also, she leaned on the adjutant. 'Stay her with sandwiches,' called out somebody, 'comfort her with – with – more sandwiches!' Moira mopped her eyes with a trail of her dress, but nobody noticed. They jostled about the table. Plates rang, shunted in all directions. 'Sitting in here?' cried Gerald, exalted, 'splendid!' Somebody waved a mouth-organ: could one dance to that? More and more squeezed in at the door: the room would burst. The cracks of the walls that had been straight a minute ago like bars now seemed to bulge out visibly: light glared down on the resolution of backs and pink, reaching arms. '*Our* young friend, our *young* friend, our young *friend*,' thought Lois, and watched Gerald. Though she watched wherever he went, she could not see him. There was nothing, in fact, to which to attach her look except his smoothness and roundness of head, which seemed for the first time remarkable. She looked for his mouth – which had kissed her – but found it no different from mouths of other young men who had also been strolling and pausing between the huts in the dark. The page of the evening was asterisked over with fervent imaginary kisses. And one single kiss in the wind, in the dark, was no longer particularized: she could not remember herself, or remember him.

As he came up, she looked quickly away. She looked at an empty plate down on the floor, at a thin disk of cucumber flaccid against its rim. 'What have I done?' she thought: she looked at the plate with dread. And: 'Oh, sandwich?' said Gerald, turning to bring up some more. '. . . Or perhaps it will seem natural tomorrow?' Nothing could keep her from having to eat a sandwich. 'Darling . . .' he whispered, brushing against her shoulder.

'Tired?' asked Mr Simcox, seeing her face.

'Oh no,' she said, with Mr Daventry's best irony.

19

Mr and Mrs Montmorency were sitting on the steps as Lois drove up the avenue. Francie waved, Hugo looked warily round the *Spectator*. 'Well . . .?' cried Francie, as Lois came into ear-shot. Above, twenty dark windows stared over the fields aloofly out of the light grey face of the house. The trees had rims of light round them; everything seemed a long way away. With a sigh, Hugo put down the *Spectator* and came to lift Lois's suitcase out of the trap.

'Well . . .?'

'Oh, marvellous . . . But what *do* you think: we broke the gramophone!'

'Oh, the poor gramophone!'

'It was the Gunners' gramophone . . . Where are the others?'

'We have no idea.'

The Montmorencys now felt certain it must be a tiring day: even Lois looked pale. They had been having an intimate conversation about the future, both with a sense of courage as from sweeping aside some decency. Why not, Hugo had said, build a bungalow somewhere? 'With no stairs?' Francie kindled at the idea, slipping a hand under Hugo's. 'And live there always?' Certainly – why not? – they would un-store the furniture. And at the thought of their tables and sofas coming again out of limbo, Hugo's face was illumined by a look of defiance.

'But where would we build?' said Francie, wrinkled up with delightful anxiety. Hugo said they would motor round for a bit and no doubt some idea would suggest itself. 'We could choose the view,' said Francie. But at this point, for some reason, he had taken up the *Spectator*.

The man came round for the pony: Lois sat down on the steps and began to chatter. It was surprising, really, how much had occurred. And fancy, the Colonel had been furious . . . Even Hugo listened with some attention. 'Dear me,' he said when they heard about Mr Daventry. Francie expected it must be a great relief for a man in that state of mind to meet a girl to whom he could really talk. 'But he didn't talk; he really was most extraordinary. Of course, he was once a major.' Francie wished she had seen her go off in that green frock – all, how should she say? like a poppy, only a different colour. Would Lois put it on for them all tonight?

'It's not really a frock one sits in,' said Lois discouragingly. Francie said it was almost a pity in some ways that Laurence was so intellectual. 'I know, we'll make Hugo waltz with you, he waltzes beautifully.' But the thought of Hugo waltzing – as Hugo suspected – made Lois melancholy.

Laurence, disturbed by her voice, shut an upstairs window. His industry nowadays was remarkable. He dragged at his chair and stared at the trees through a flawed pane, across which Laura Naylor had scratched her name with a diamond. At his elbows, books were in toppling stacks; movement produced an avalanche. A wasp hung round him, tentative, scrawling Z's on the air. 'Go away,' he muttered, 'you are superfluous.' Finally, he was obliged to open the door and shoo the wasp out of it; it undulated across the landing and in at the half-open door of Marda's room, as though it had an appointment. Though he did not care for the wasp, Laurence went in after it, to see if she had not left *South Wind* behind. She had indeed – which was like her. The wasp dithered above the looking-glass in triumph; he took aim with the book and almost hit it. An eight-day clock still ticked; it was five to four, it would soon be tea-time.

As he came out, Lois appeared at the top of the stairs, carrying a suitcase.

'Hullo! what have you brought *that* up for?'

'Oh yes,' she said, putting it down in surprise. 'I meant to have left it half-way.'

'Well –?'

'Really,' she cried, unreasonably, 'this house is nothing but Montmorencys; they are an absolute state of mind ... I only wanted to see if you were here.'

'Well, I'm not, practically: I'm working.'

'Oh – why do you work in the spare room?'

'I was dealing with a wasp.'

'Laurence, I had a marvellous dance.'

'Splendid!' He turned to his door, but she, in tremendous need of his un-sympathy, brought out, imploringly: 'They were all there, every one. And my dear, the wind; I thought the hut would be blown away. And we broke the gramophone. There was a most sinister man called Daventry, with shell-shock . . .'

'Good,' said Laurence, 'and *you* look sleepy!'

Lois, lamblike under the force of suggestion, leaned back against the banisters, yawning. 'Livvy kicked all night, she will be a horrible wife . . . Laurence, I wish you would tell me something to read.'

'I should go to sleep.'

The idea seemed grateful: she thought of her room with the high ceiling, the foreign touch to the cheeks of afternoon pillows, the delicious crime of crossing one's stockinged ankles over the rucked-back quilt and the slow recession of fact down a long tunnel till the windows stretched and faded. But, pulling at her fingers, she said impatiently: 'But I want to begin on something; I do think, Laurence, you might understand. There must be some way for me to begin. You keep on looking into rooms where I am with silent contempt – what do you think I am for?'

He leaned against the frame of his doorway, looking at her with surprise and a degree of humanity. Today four weeks, Term would have begun again; he did for a moment stretch to an effort of comprehension: there was nothing for *her* to go on with. The vacancy, more than negative to him, which had succeeded Marda made the natural claims of a life on his young cousin. With that concession to fancy one makes for the doomed or the very weak, he suggested she should go on with her German. He gave her two grammars, a dictionary and a novel of Mann's, which she took from him doubtfully. When he was back at his table, his door ajar, she went across stealthily to the door opposite.

'There's a wasp in there,' called out Lawrence.

'Oh, I just thought I'd see if . . .'

But she went downstairs, defeated, forgetting her suitcase.

She had not seen Gerald again this morning, though all contracted with apprehension she had waited in Mrs Fogarty's drawing-room – the multiplicity of the photographed young men's faces, candid and vigorous, further appalling her. An orderly had come down with a note from barracks. The crested envelope, handed in with its air of a claim on her, had austerity, like some limb of an institution. She lost her last sense of Gerald, she felt committed. Fumbling open the envelope, asking: 'What have I done?' she wondered what had become of that last lonely disk of cucumber on the plate. After 'My darling darling' – she was reprieved, provisionally; Mrs Fogarty, coming in in a wrapper – greatly worn, she said, after last night's gaiety – had insisted that if she would not drink port she must drink milk – it was a long morning – and eat some of this nice sponge cake.

And: '*I* know who has been breaking hearts!' said Mrs Fogarty, knifing the sponge cake which was moist and eggy and 'gave' to the knife deliciously, like an eiderdown.

The ante-room chairs, now looking at Lois askance, knew also. What she had done stretched everywhere, like a net. If she had taken a life, the simplest objects could not more have been tinged with consequence. The graded elephants on the bookcases were all fatality. She went into her room hurriedly. 'All the same,' she thought, looking round with patronage at the virginal wallpaper, 'it *is* something definite.' And with curiosity, with complicity almost, she looked at herself in the glass.

Gerald's straight, round writing had – to her imagination – a queer totter, like someone running for life in tight shoes.

'– I have so much to say to you; though there is all time now there seems to be no time. Lois, when I am with you you make me awfully dumb with your darling wide-awake eyes, and when we are apart you seem so close I feel you must understand, so why try to explain when I am so stupid? So I won't try to say what I feel; all that matters is that you are beautifully beautiful. Sometimes, till now, I have felt you must think me awfully stupid and introspective and dull; I have wondered so much what you did think about all the time: it seems unbelievable now that I am really to know. You seemed so complicated, it was cheek to associate you with the sort of person that I am, and now you are lovely and simple and all mine. Last night doesn't seem like part of my life at all – I can't believe it was me who danced and drank whiskies and tinkered about with the gramophone – and yet it's the reallest thing ever. And what I am doing this morning seems so important – although it keeps me away from you – because I am doing it *for* you. It is awful to think of you here in Clonmore and not to be able to get to you, and yet it is wonderful to think of you waiting, and of who you are waiting for being me. Lois, your dear cold arms were so lovely, I mustn't think of them now. All your life I am going to keep you and wrap you up and protect you and never let you be cold again. It is awful to think you have ever been lonely and sad – you are so brave, you know, and I never guessed – and yet I am almost glad of that, because it makes some reason for me. Darling, I kiss the thought of you and feel so terribly humble. I must not write more now. If you can, leave a letter for me at the Fogartys'. Does she guess? I thought perhaps you might like to confide in her. But of course I will tell nobody, as you wish. Good-bye, my most beautiful woman; I cannot write how I love you. – GERALD.'

Folding the sheets again in their order, she thought: 'It is you who are beautiful,' and later: 'If this thing is so perfect to anyone, can one be wrong?' An escape of sunshine, penetrating the pale sky in the south-west, altered the room like a revelation. Noiselessly, a sweet-pea moulted its petals on to the writing-table, leaving a bare pistil. The pink butterfly flowers, transparently balancing, were shadowed faintly with blue as by an intuition of death. Lois bowed forward, her forehead against the edge of the table.

Steps in the ante-room; she slipped the letter under the blotter and turned round consciously. 'I hear you are back,' said Lady Naylor, entering. 'I hear it was such a success that they broke the gramophone. Now I want to hear all about it.' She sat down.

'Well, to begin with –'

'One moment – have you unpacked your frock?'

'Oh! I left my suitcase . . . I went up to Laurence to borrow a German grammar.'

'Oh, I shouldn't go on with German,' said Lady Naylor, 'it still offends so many people; Italian is prettier and more practical. I could lend you *Il Piccolo Mondo Antico*, or Dante – However, tell me about the dance.'

'Well, first of all –'

'– By the way, I've just heard from Marda. She has arrived quite safely, I'm glad to say. She says Kent is dull, which I dare say it would be, but of course she is glad to be with Leslie.'

'Did she say so?'

'She naturally would be. You can read it; I've got the letter downstairs . . . Who broke the gramophone? I hope you weren't anywhere round when it happened: these things are always remembered. Were the Raltes there? Did they look pretty? I wonder, really, at their mother allowing them; she professes to have them in such control. However, I dare say this will be the last of these dances.'

'Oh, why?'

'If you had heard what we heard at the Trents' . . . There was a man there from Kerry. He really made us feel quite uncomfortable. Though, as your uncle said afterwards, one knows what the

Trents' friends are: everything happens to them. However – Were the Vermonts there? *She* would be quite in her element. And Mr Armstrong? I have heard he and Livvy were seen in Cork together at the Imperial, by Mrs Foxe-O'Connor. And the young man who was here to lunch, who talked so much ... in the armoured car ... oh – Lesworth?'

'Yes, he was there.'

'I am surprised at them all having time,' said Lady Naylor. 'However, if they danced more and interfered less, I dare say there would be less trouble in the country. It appears that in Kerry ...' Her voice became colder with inattention and dwindled away. Lois was certain she eyed the pink blotter. This zigzag approach to Gerald, this ultimate vagueness, were sinister. Lady Naylor, after some moments of odd and oppressive silence, observed that the sweet-peas were dying. 'The water must be unhealthy, it's going green. In fact, all the flowers need doing. Perhaps after tea – How would you like to go to a school of art?'

'Marvellous,' said Lois after reflection.

'Francie was very much struck by your drawings. And Marda said you certainly needed an interest.'

'Oh. Was she discussing me?'

'We were all saying that girls needed interests, and I thought she seemed to agree particularly. *She* has not made much of her life, so far – though of course if she marries Leslie – and I've always thought that music or drawing, or writing a little, or organization of some kind –'

'Did Marda say what she thought of my drawings?'

'She seemed to think they were nice ... A quarter to five!' exclaimed Lady Naylor reproachfully. 'The tea will be cold ... You look sleepy, Lois. Did you hear the Montmorencys are going to build a bungalow?'

'Here?'

'Don't be silly – Besides, according to that friend of the Trents, it would be blown up or burnt in a month or two. Certainly,' added Lady Naylor, looking out at the sky, 'I call this a tiring day.' She got up with a sigh.

Later that evening Lois, half-way up to the garden with scissors and basket, overtook Mr Montmorency walking all by himself up the shrubbery path. Pulling leaves from the laurels he shredded them carefully.

'I hear,' he said, as she came up alongside, 'you are taking up German?'

'Unless Italian might be more practical . . . I hear you are going to build a bungalow?'

'Oh, I don't know; that is chiefly Francie's idea.' They walked in silence, she dragging her basket against the laurels. They had not been alone since the drive from Mount Isabel. She remembered how once she had hoped so much, and how he had been infinitely disobliging. Now she had a tenderness for him, devoid of attraction, as though they had been a couple of widows.

'No stairs would be nice.'

'But it would be certain to have other disadvantages.'

'Apparently,' she said with effrontery, 'Marda arrived quite safely.'

'It should be a surprise to us all,' said Hugo, sarcastic, 'that she has not fallen out of the train. Even she cannot think of anything better to say to a hostess. And the information, I always feel certain, leaves hostesses cold. Once one is clear of their gates, interest ends with responsibility.'

'And she says Kent is dull.'

'I cannot believe *she* finds it so.'

'She is frightfully philosophic. Perhaps she was dull here.' (She thought: 'Even now, shall we never be natural?')

'Have you seen her letter?'

'No . . . have you?'

'No, your aunt has lost it.'

He pushed open the door, then followed her into the garden which, deep in its walls, seemed impossibly large, for one could not see to the end of it: it was crossed by espaliers and crowded with apple-trees. Down the borders, the September yellow and scarlets were metallic in unsunny light. Dahlias, orange and wine-coloured, blazed and gloomed. He turned down one path, she kept to the other; they silently parted. Here she had come with Marda – never with Gerald – they had sat on the green seat, pressed blisters out of the paint and spat out their plum-stones into the box border opposite. Entered today, the usual breath of the garden was cold to her face. The branches were quiet as though in anxiety, the flowers appeared to be clamouring vainly, forgotten. Coming to the hedge of sweet-peas she began at the purple end, diligently. 'Though myself,' she could not help saying, 'I do not care for purple sweet-peas.'

When she reached up to the top of the hedge her sleeves fell back from her arms and she thought of Gerald. She felt him looking at her through the thinning stems. The sweet-peas were practically over, and indeed she was glad, she thought, snipping and tugging with blunt garden scissors. In yesterday's dusk the Square with its flitter of leaves had been all autumnal; smoke was blue in the air and, later, the dark where they kissed had a sharp intimation of autumn. She loved in autumn a stronger, more shadowy keen spring, sweet shocks of good-bye, transition. Summer meanwhile stayed on inside these walls, forgotten.

The fact was, that though one determined tonight to sit under the lamp and learn verbs, her Italian or German would not dispose of last night, which remained, like the tear in her green tulle dress, to be dealt with practically. After an anxious glance at the possible, a pain so sharp that it seemed her own forbade recantation. It was inevitable that she should marry Gerald. Mrs Montmorency at least – she thought with relief as she came to the red sweet-peas – would be infinitely sympathetic and pleased. The unbelievable future became fixed as the past under the flutter and settling down of a flock of comments, which, as she turned in imagination back to the house and steps and saw lips forming themselves in unconscious readiness, seemed already uttered. And as Mr Montmorency came up a path at an angle, with the two garden kittens toppling after him, she was surprised he did not repeat: 'Well, I hope of course that you may be happy. And decision of any kind is an excellent thing in your mother's daughter.'

Instead, he came to the other side of the hedge and, picking off some bleaching tendrils, observed that the sweet-peas would soon be over. The house flowers must keep her busy, he added. And taking out his pocket-knife he cut three sweet-peas, with precision. Having made this gesture of sympathy, he continued to move with her down his side of the hedge.

'It is extraordinary,' said Lois. 'I feel as if I had been away for a week.'

'Yet you find us going on much the same?' He looked at her through the stems ironically but without intelligence. And she could not try to explain the magnetism they all exercised by their being static. Or how, after every return – or awakening, even, from sleep or preoccupation – she and those home surroundings still further penetrated each other mutually in the discovery of a lack.

20

Lady Naylor, who wished for a clear steady light these lengthening evenings, saw to the lamps personally. In big yellow gloves she accurately trimmed the wicks, between the morning's headlines and a thorough talk with the cook. But the smell of oil was repugnant to her and now she said with some sharpness:

'You have no conception of love – You are in my light.'

Lois moved from the lamp-room window. 'I really have,' she said, 'really.'

'Nonsense,' her aunt said, looking round for a rag. Lois began to slide a match-box about, and her aunt, taking the matches away mechanically, thought how hard it was that a woman like this, who could bring the matter on to an intellectual plane at once, should have to do lamps at all. Anna Partridge, whose brain was all shreddy with rabbit-combing and raffia, had had electric light for years, just from living in England; even the Trents talked of harnessing their waterfall.

'When I was your age I never thought of marriage at all. I didn't intend to marry. I remember, when I was nineteen I was reading Schiller.'

'I don't think about marriage, I . . .'

'Then you can have no conception . . .'

'I read,' said Lois, with dignity.

'Girls nowadays do nothing but lend each other these biological books. I was intensely interested in art.'

'But, Aunt Myra, young men are quite usual.'

'It all comes of dancing and all this excitement.'

'But Gerald is not excitable; he was in love with me the other day before lunch.'

'He was half asleep,' said Lady Naylor. 'At the best of times he has not much conversation. Of course, I rate brains so highly; perhaps I am wrong. But remember, you cannot hope to be always in love, and then . . .'

'But you said I had no conception . . .'

'There you are, in my light again.'

Lois moved further away from the window. She wished she had not started this explanation. She had felt, somehow, that it should be less embarrassing in the lamp-room. She thought of Gerald's unquestioning shoulder, where she would lean her head. 'But I can't explain,' she said; 'I never heard of a girl being asked to explain. I always thought . . .'

'Real feeling explains itself,' said Lady Naylor and polished some oil off the base of a lamp triumphantly.

'But if he comes to tea . . .'

'Oh, we cannot help that, of course.'

'But if he spoke to Uncle Richard . . .'

'Your uncle would be very much worried. Really, Lois, I do think you might be more sensible and considerate.'

Lois saw this point of view only too perfectly. She wrinkled her forehead. She did not want to be hard on her Uncle Richard and she could not help sympathizing with Aunt Myra, who had so much to organize as it was. Feeling did seem to her out of proportion with life, and that this disproportion should be so evident generally, that her aunt should think she was making an irrelevant fuss, strongly discouraged her. But she reassembled herself; she had been led to understand that love . . .

'But surely love . . .'

'You have no conception of love,' repeated Lady Naylor, and thought again of electric light in Bedfordshire.

'But shall I never do anything?'

'Go to a school of art.'

'Where?'

'It could be arranged.'

'But I don't think I really draw well.'

'There is no reason why you should marry.'

It was, of course, no reason; acknowledging this, and seeing light from the barred window fall so coldly on the oilcloth top of the lamp-table, Lois felt quite at a standstill.

'However . . .' said Lady Naylor. She looked with her brilliant eyes dubiously, almost shyly, at the door behind Lois's head. She swept the rags and the lamp scissors into a drawer, shut the drawer on their malodour, and pulled off her gloves, sighing. She saw life, perhaps, as a shuffle of setting to partners, then a drawn-out, coupled but somehow solitary curtsying, to him, the other, the rest of the eight. 'However . . .' she said. And the qualification committed herself and her niece, a shade alarmingly. Lois knew that Gerald might come to tea.

'You do see,' said Lois, and stared at her aunt's ringed hands which reappeared from the gloves, 'that I didn't want to be clandestine?'

'Oh, of course you were quite right,' said Lady Naylor without enthusiasm. She went down to talk to the cook.

Kathleen, the cook, who resembled her mistress in personality so closely that their relation was an affair of balance, who had more penetration than Lady Naylor and was equally dominant, inferred much of the situation from her mistress's manner. Herself, she had felt this was bound to occur. For an hour or so, they had countered each other amiably in the lime-washed gloom of the kitchen, over a basin of green-pea soup. Lady Naylor announced with unusual deprecation, there would be an officer coming over to tea. Kathleen, refolding her hands royally, asked, would she slap up a sally-lunn? On the whole, Lady Naylor thought drop-cakes. Kathleen immediately placed the officer. Strolling down the yard in the course of the afternoon to execute a couple of chickens, she watched dispassionately from under the chestnuts Gerald crouch on his motor-bicycle up the avenue. Lois, standing about with the dogs, went down to meet him. For tea, Kathleen sent up an unaccountable iced cake, ironically festive.

Francie was glad Mr Lesworth was coming to tea. For the day strained with ominousness, as though it were going to burst. Hugo, pacing about on the avenues with *The Conquest of Mexico* under his arm, disparaged repose. 'By the way,' he said once, coming up, 'if you should be happening to write to Marda Norton . . .'

'Oh, but I shan't be; not till I send her our little present. Besides, I have nothing to say.'

'She might write to you about the eau-de-Cologne.'

'Oh no, she thanked me.'

'There was a point I wanted to clear, about Metternich – you remember that argument? I've just come on a book – I suppose I had better write myself.'

'But no one knows her address; Myra lost the letter.'

'Ah yes, of course . . . That settles it.' He smiled – one would have said with relief. Francie, looking down in despair at her blouse as he walked away, saw that the jabot was crumpled. She could not understand how a woman who travelled with suitcases could look as *smooth* as Marda. But then, she was all outlines: detail seemed to collect and obtrude in the middle of Francie. She went up to change, glad that Gerald was coming, sounding with some attention the silence under the avenue trees. For the fact was, life attenuated to the snapping-point; in Gerald's continuity, in Lois's, she must invest her own.

Gerald propped up his motor-bicycle, looked up carefully at the closed windows – in one, from behind a blot of light, Francie was nodding – and said that he should not really have come. Troops had been fired on coming back into Clonmore, near that level-crossing. The situation was tightening; there was a lot to do.

'Oh. Then it is a pity you came,' said Lois.

Gerald said nothing; his ears faintly coloured.

'*Clonmore!*' said Lois with indignation, and thought of the little friendly town with its tennis club.

'So it happened,' said Gerald, looking at her. 'It might have been anywhere else.' He whistled and greeted the dogs, her dogs.

'Then . . . it was dangerous coming?'

'Oh no, not to speak of.'

The house so loomed, and stared so darkly and oddly that he showed a disposition – respectful rather than timorous – to move away from the front of it. They walked to the tennis courts and round one court in a circle. '*Lois* . . .' She veered off quickly, Laurence was working up there in his window. Gerald waved, but had no response. 'Doesn't he concentrate!' he said wistfully.

'I suppose so . . . Does Laurence matter?'

'You know *you* . . .'

'Gerald, you are the frightfully concentrated person, really.'

'But I can't read . . . Where can I . . . where could we –?'

'– Here comes Mr Montmorency.'

Hugo, coming up to shake hands with Gerald, said it seemed a long time since they had met. The young man, by his way of standing and looking clearly and being positive, strongly connected himself with Marda. With an unexpected and crooked stab of nostalgia, Hugo thought of the trees, the morning mountains, the tinkling and knocking stream. Of all of her he had kept and had never had and must try to regain appeared most sharply the moment of that encounter: irrelevant moment, when, outside something, he had watched light run down her hair as she stooped for Gerald to light her cigarette. The quality of their silence, their separation after Gerald had left them – pressing on up to the house to look for Lois – now seemed the very ground of his closest approach. But he knew how the scene was perishable, how having drawn up into itself for life, like a plant, any reality that there was in him, it would die of his barrenness. Until finally, by even the same conjunction of mountains and light and trees, it would not be evoked again.

'No shaving under a hedge this morning?' he said genially.

'Oh no,' said Gerald, surprised. Why should there be?

Lois, encouraged to find that by some growth of womanhood in herself her attitude was already a wife's, at once proud and deprecating, stood there watching Gerald, most grateful for the repose of this interposition and willing that Mr Montmorency should be detained. She knew, from a glance they both gave her, that she must have been startled by some sort of consciousness into beauty, and a particular placidness, a sense of being located, warmed her surroundings, the smooth lawn and heavy trees. Balancing, foot behind foot, on a line of the court faint from rain, she constructed a life in China – most regimental, alert and pleasantly surfaced – from Japanese prints she had ignored in shops, an idea of odd, angular archways and some strips of vertical writing. He must no doubt some day be a captain, and 'captain's lady' had a ballad-like cadence. She almost took Gerald's arm.

'You find us diminished,' said Hugo, 'and a good deal quieter. Miss Norton has gone.'

'Oh?'

'*Marda*,' she hastily prompted.

'She was awfully nice and amusing,' said Gerald, beaming out like the sun from behind a moment's perplexity. 'I'd have loved to have met her again.'

She explained to him afterwards, taking him off through the shrubberies, how things were at present with Mr Montmorency: he was a ruined man. Gerald went rigid, something shut like a door on his sensibilities – the thing reeked of adultery. He produced an appalled silence. But about Lois's mother, he brought out finally, hadn't one heard he had once been . . .?

'But a thing *can't* be final,' said Lois. 'Not while one's alive.'

Was this what she read? 'But there's *Mrs* Montmorency . . .' It seemed fixed here, the Montmorencys' conjointness, among the stately furniture and long mild meals – earth to Lois's roots.

'But one can't arrange oneself; one doesn't altogether live from inside: Marda just happened.'

'And did *she* . . .?' cried Gerald, appalled. Above this extraordinary undercurrent, it seemed to him his Lois was poised too perfectly.

Lois, in pink linen, perfectly sophisticated and cool, said: 'No. She was just regretful. Also, she is engaged, you see.'

'*Is* she? I should never have thought . . .'

'. . . Her engaged? Well, how ought she to look? Like a kind of hen bird, all dim?'

'She was all herself. Doesn't love kind of finish people off . . . with something that isn't them, in a way you can feel?'

She understood him, but did not know how to agree. What must one then be for him? She was shy of his uncomprehension of a particular notion of living she seemed only now to have formed. Did she give out an untrue ring to his touch? Where was the flaw? Or was Gerald, sublimely, the instrument of some large imposture?

'Complete – you mean finished? . . . Perhaps she is not really in love.'

'But surely she isn't that sort . . . she wouldn't just marry?'

'I don't think what Marda does matters; she simply *is*.'

He looked desperate suddenly, as though she were behind bars. 'Look here, no one matters. Don't let's talk . . . I mean . . . don't let's talk. Lois, there's so little time now, I'm desperate. I don't see when I am going to see you, ever. Lois, this miserable waiting; even happiness never lets one alone. When shall we be quiet?'

'But, Gerald, we're quite young.'

'I want nothing to happen but you. You are everything. I want so much of you.'

She stood, perplexed, at the edge of the path; he kissed her with frightened violence. The laurels creaked as, in his arms, she bent back into them. His singleness bore, confusing, upon her panic of thoughts, her physical apprehension of him was confused by the slipping, cold leaves. Her little sighs elated then alarmed him.

'What's the matter?' he said, his lips close to her face.

'I don't like the smell of the laurels. Let's come out of here.' They went back, she put up anxious hands and asked him about her hair. 'Is it twiggy and awful?' 'Lovely.' She wished that he were a woman. As they approached the steps where her aunt and uncle and Francie composed an abstracted group, she told him: 'Aunt Myra wants me to go to a school of art.'

'Oh . . . Can you draw?'

'*Gerald . . .!*'

'Darling, I've never seen them. How could I know?'

Lady Naylor exclaimed how delightful it was that Gerald had come over. Now they would hear some real, *real* news, she said: they always relied on Gerald. Sir Richard, taking his pince-nez off in amazement, could hardly believe it was Gerald again; he still thought subalterns came in rotation. Surely, he said candidly, it was yesterday they had had that interesting talk about the Militia? Gerald was given a chair of such voluptuous depth that his chin came barely above the edge of the tea-table. They congratulated him on the Rolfes' dance. In fact, they united to carry off the situation with such brilliance that Gerald might well have been a dun or a tax-collector. Then, at a moment when talk seemed precarious and Marda obtrusively absent and Lady Naylor sat eyeing Lois's hair, the Trents arrived unexpectedly. They brought over another friend, this time from County Clare, to whom still more had happened. Gerald went into joyous eclipse; the Danielstown party sat breathless – hardly a chair creaked – the Trents looked at their friend complacently while the Trents' friend curdled the tea in one's mouth with tales of assault and cattle-driving.

'Well, I suppose *we've* a certain amount to be thankful for,' smiled Mrs Archie Trent as their friend, having been put through his hoops, settled down to tea. And she told Lois that she was looking remarkably well, and they hoped they would see her out with the Ballymoyles this winter. And meanwhile, what about cubbing?

'Lois is going to a school of art,' said Lady Naylor.

'That seems a pity,' said Mrs Trent.

The friend, finishing his tea, said all the Irish art schools ought to be searched. He wouldn't say for certain, but he had a pretty shrewd suspicion what you would find there. If it came to that, he said, casts were hollow and you could keep a good deal inside the Venus of Milo. Sir Richard looked vaguely offended.

'I should go to the Slade,' said Lois.

'Oh,' said Mrs Archie Trent, 'not Rome, I suppose? Well, I shouldn't do anything of that sort in a hurry.'

'Art is long,' said Laurence, who liked conversation of this sort. The Trents' friend asked him how he liked Cambridge; he himself had a nephew who hoped soon to be going up. Laurence said he had heard that Cambridge was very nice.

The Trents' friend took Gerald aside after tea, to explain to him where the Army was going wrong. Mrs Trent at once drew closer up to the teapot and said, in a loud voice of confidence, she had heard Livvy Thompson was really engaged to that young Armstrong. 'Nonsense,' said Lady Naylor.

'But they were seen in Cork having tea, and the aunt denies it too vigorously. After all, it would be something for the Thompsons.'

Lois, who was unfortunate, blushed; both ladies looked hard at her. 'To begin with,' declared Lady Naylor, 'these young men are not at all marriageable. Besides, to tell you the truth . . .'

'But I don't see what else the girls are to do. I mean, look at the Hartigans.'

'There's a future for girls nowadays outside marriage,' said Lady Naylor inspiringly. 'Careers – how *I* should have loved one. One reads so much about . . .' She was an advanced woman: Mrs Trent, who did not read, paused in respect but preserved an honest, bright-pink expression of incredulity. She pictured those indoor women with clutched little bags getting hurriedly into the Dublin trams. It was no life. Her friend seemed, moreover, unwisely persistent in encouraging art for Lois: this, for young girls, often resulted in worse than spinsterhood. 'All the same,' she said, returning, 'Livvy seems set on the young man. And she has a great deal of character.'

'Well, if I were her aunt and her father, I'd never hear of it.'

'Dear me,' cried Mrs Trent, kicking the table cheerfully, 'we've made Lois blush at the very idea.'

'Lois knows better,' said Lady Naylor. And she gave Lois one of her rarest, most charming, direct and personal glances.

And indeed what a friend, thought Lois, going out to the steps to escape them all, if one had only just met, might Aunt Myra be.

21

A cloud slid over the sun; the stream went opaque as tortoiseshell. Then, startling Hugo, the water suddenly flushed with light as the cloud moved east. Minnows, disturbed like thoughts, darted shadowy over the clear yellow stare of the stones. He dipped his stick in the water, then, drawing it out, thoughtfully looked at the shining end. At this point: eighteen inches; the stream, divided in two deep channels by the island of turf where he stood, went hurrying to the Darra. In its fold of the Darra valley, the high white mill would remain sardonic. He was swept by an irresistible anger back to that affair of the pistol. For Marda had written: her hand had healed; no one had asked any questions or wondered, she said.

She had written to Lois, sending Hugo this message. It had pleased both the girls to underline his exclusion. She wrote also, Leslie had given her a dog – a correct dog, Lois expected, like all that was best in English country-house life. Marda could not think what to do with the dog till she married; she would have to leave it in Kent . . . And what else did Marda say, Francie had wanted to know. But Lois, who seemed to have swallowed the letter, postmark and all, could not remember. Later, she did seek out Hugo and offer to show him . . . But he had put up surprise. 'Oh? Was there any particular –?' No, he did not think on the whole he would trouble her . . . Would the child see, he wondered, that the little oblique snub was not intended to stop at *her*, but to go past? His look now fell empty, reflective, on the tawny glass sliding water.

The child, having seen, went upstairs to describe his behaviour to Marda. Her unreticence was immoderate, though she was sensitive for him. She wrote scrupulously, with an affect of hardness.

'He is terrible, and, as the end of everything, they are to build a bungalow. *She* has it all her own way now; I don't know if he still even brushes her hair. Since you went, it has been the same time all day: three o'clock, after a long lunch. We all talk about my future (by common consent I am about nine now, very distracting and sunny; they like to have me about). It is to be a school of art, certainly. – Why did you never tell them I couldn't draw? – But we can't decide where. London, in view of my age, is supposed to be too large. In Dublin, a man who came to tea yesterday said there might be high explosives inside all the casts with capacious figures. In Cork I might pick up an accent, and Paris they will not hear of – my wretched virtue. But as a matter of fact, I have no future, in their sense. I have promised to marry Gerald.'

Here she paused, for from now on it was all obscure ahead of her. Reading back, she was surprised at the woman she was. She took this merciless penetration for maturity's. But when she looked for Gerald there seemed too much of him. He was a wood in which she counted from tree to tree – all hers – and knew the boundary wall right round. But how to measure this unaccountable darkness between the trees, this living silence? So she turned back to Mr Montmorency, adding a paragraph. He had, this morning, snubbed her.

She would have been surprised to have seen him, at this same moment, step across to the island and stand there rootedly. And he, his whereabouts even so much as guessed at, would have been quite at her mercy. For to have followed the stream to this loneliest reach, beyond the plantation wall, where the meadow's hedge trailed unknown blackberries over the water, was not to have walked, to have strolled even, but to have betrayed oneself in an emotional kind of straying. Further down, stepping-stones had been displaced by last winter's flood, there was a ruined cottage; nobody came here. Even Lois had given up, since her eighteenth birthday, coming to lie on her stomach along the bank, weep out a bottomless despair at nothing and look at herself in the stream. And this wildness within the demesne boundaries, within sound of the farmyard bell, had a particular desolation.

Hugo was pleased with the place; here he seemed to have stepped through into some kind of non-existence. And here, divorced equally from fact and from probability, he set up a stage for himself: the hall's half-light. Marda's hand is on the wide scrolled curve of the baluster rail: he touches her still and electric hand with the deliberation of certainty, all the senses running into his touch. She stares recognition fixedly, darkly back ... For though in actuality she had had only one mood for him – cool and equivocal – he, now frantic with this power disconnected from life, could command her whole range imaginatively: her very features became his actors. And if this were not love ...

He was pleased with the place. They must all, he expected, be looking for him: it produced the faintest vibration behind the solitude. This morning, Myra was driving into Clonmore to lunch with the Boatleys; she had asked him to come, he had said he would see. He had intended by this 'Good God, no,' and if she were fool enough to interpret it otherwise there was a rightness about her delay in starting. Francie would certainly go; she was painfully fascinated by military society. She would now be standing out on the steps, grey net veil strained elegantly over the tip of her nose, looking at her gloves in despair, persisting: 'He must be *somewhere*!'

'How many of us do they really expect?' said Francie at last, getting into the car disconsolate.

Lady Naylor had not the slightest idea. 'But they are accustomed to Ireland. She was a Vere Scott. And they know that I usually fill the car.'

'You're not taking Lois?'

'Lois goes into Clonmore quite enough,' replied Lady Naylor.

For Lady Naylor had further reasons for going into Clonmore. She had an assignation with Gerald at half-past three, in Mrs Fogarty's drawing-room. Fridays were Club days, Mrs Fogarty would be 'up at the tennis', and her drawing-room, disembarrassed for once of her large personality, remained at the disposition of friends. Lady Naylor, though she deplored Mrs Fogarty's taste in beads, her husband, her stays – which stuck out half-way up her back in a frill – and her too overflowing maternity, had fallen into the general habit of using her house as a kind of Ladies' Club, dropping in there at all times to leave parcels, wash her hands or meet friends. And she had the impression, always, that the maid who admitted her ran upstairs at once to put Mr Fogarty under lock and key. Still, one knew that one's coming gave pleasure and gratification: she would enter the little drawing-room, even when empty, with her queenliness at its full.

Gerald, questioning but elated, turned up a little before time, much braced in and polished about the belt. He had never been given an assignation so directly. For she had said (this now divinely probable aunt of his) : 'I may be at the Fogartys', resting, about half-past three. If you should be passing – though of course you may not be and I do not want to keep you away from the tennis – you might look in and have a chat. For it has been too bad today, I have hardly seen you. I have missed our usual talk. There is still so much . . . But I dare say you won't be passing.' Her look, a special point to its wide-pupilled eagerness, transposed this to the imperative. The vigorous arch of her eyebrows insisted strongly. He, feeling himself ordered like a taxi – better still, like a nephew – had flushed with pleasure, *Rath*-er; he'd make a point – (would she then call him Gerald?). 'Of course, I may not be there; we may not even come in; it is all quite uncertain,' said Lady Naylor.

Riding home, the intoxication of Gerald had mounted. He guessed that she never rested, rarely leaned back in a chair, never pushed up her hat with a sigh or stretched tender feet out, unbuttoned shoes. She would remain imperious, even in Oxford Street. So she was contriving for him; a special tribute.

Lady Naylor, coming into the Fogartys' soon after four, was annoyed to find Gerald before her. She had now, instead of being discovered, to manoeuvre more or less openly for position. Disregarding the chair Gerald trundled up with its load of cushions, she placed herself (unaccountably, it would have to appear) on the narrow window-seat. Thus, she conceded no more to the room than an imposing silhouette of hat and boa, while Gerald, glancing round pessimistically at the chairs, remaining with elbow planted among photo-frames on the mantelpiece, was exposed to her full in the strained green light coming over the bushes.

'Such a day,' she sighed briskly. 'We have lunched with the Boatleys. What a delightful Colonel he must be! *She*, you know, is Irish; a Vere Scott. We must seem ridiculous to you, over here, the way we are all related.'

'Topping, I think,' said Gerald.

'Oh, I don't know! Now you lucky people seem to have no relations at all; that must feel so independent.'

'I have dozens.'

'Indeed? All in Surrey?'

'Scattered about.'

'That sounds to *me*, of course,' remarked Lady Naylor, pulling her gloves off brightly, 'exceedingly restless. But you all *came* from Surrey, didn't you?'

'More or less,' said Gerald, who was not sure. The Boatleys had not been sure where he came from, either; her day so far had been unsatisfactory.

'Now I do hope I'm not keeping you from smoking?'

She was. He smiled and lighted a cigarette. 'You don't . . .?'

'Oh dear me, no, I am quite old-fashioned. Now tell me – you know how I hate all this gossip in a garrison neighbourhood, but there is something I must set right. What is this nonsense I hear about Livvy Thompson? You know she's a friend of my niece's and comes a good deal to our house, and I do feel I ought to refute these stories about her.'

'Oh?' said Gerald, alarmed. 'I had no idea.'

'Hadn't you?' said Lady Naylor. 'Well, you are a friend of the young man Mr Armstrong, so I felt I'd come straight to you.

It appears they were seen in Cork having tea rather intimately, and in consequence there are all sorts of rumours. Now it doesn't seem fair to a young girl, at the beginning of life, having her name coupled.'

'I should have thought,' said Gerald rather stiffly, 'anyone could see Miss Thompson was entirely straight. And as for Armstrong – They are engaged, as a matter of fact.'

'Oh, nonsense,' said Lady Naylor pleasantly.

'Oh yes,' he nodded, then with his rather engaging childishness looked at her under his lashes. 'But they don't want –'

'To begin with, the Thompsons would never hear of it. And they would be quite right. Of course, poor Livvy is motherless –'

'But many people are,' said Gerald, faintly aggressive. 'Lois is.'

'Oh, naturally we should never consider a marriage like that for Lois! The point would not even arise. But even for Livvy – And then think of the young man's career: these early marriages ruin careers, and engagements are nearly as bad. I know Colonel Boatley feels – No, what you should do, I think, is: have a straight sensible talk with your friend Mr Armstrong. I know how much you young men will take from each other. I think as a friend you should say to him –'

'But look here –' began Gerald, and paused. 'Look here, Lady Naylor –' He stopped dead and looked round the room, which was darker since she had come in: the afternoon was clouding over. He was disengaging himself with some anguish of illusions which he had brought here and which during the first minute or so of their talk had been fortified. When they came to Surrey, he had thought she was hoping to meet his mother. Crossing his legs, he rubbed the side of one shoe on the other with a slight creak at which she, betraying her tensity, started. Standing with lowered eyes, with an air of heaviness and confusion, he noted this movement, a tremor of light round the edge of her boa. With unusual calmness and virility he said:

'As a matter of fact, I love Lois.'

'Oh yes. But I'm afraid, you know, that she doesn't love you,' said the aunt equably.

He overruled this without comment, simply by maintaining his attitude. For all his physical lightness and vigour, there was a quality in him she would describe as stodginess. 'Then I gather she's told you we –'

'Oh, she's naturally pleased that you like her. And at her age, with her temperament, of course it is nice to love anyone.'

'But you've just said she doesn't –'

'Not as I understand love.'

'But so long,' said Gerald, with the particular urbanity of an approach to rudeness, 'so long as she and I both mean the same thing.'

'But you don't,' said his friend in her kind, social voice. 'That is what I am trying to make you see. With her temperament –'

'*I* haven't noticed her temperament,' said Gerald loyally, as if a temperament were a hump.

'Now that alone,' exclaimed Lady Naylor, waving her gloves in a rapid gesticulation, 'would make a marriage quite fatal. . . . Mr Lesworth, I don't want to have to imagine you miserable. I have no sons of my own, you know, and Laurence being so intellectual – And there is another thing . . .' She paused, and with unusual nervousness, with a movement almost of Francie's, touched her boa, her jabot, two carnations pinned in the lace. She had now to tilt straight at indecency. There was this question of money – a subject the English made free with, as free with as what was below their diaphragms, but from which her whole modesty shrank. 'You may think me dreadful,' she said, 'but there are things in life one must face. After all, I am Lois's aunt . . .'

Gerald, blushing, stood agonized to attention.

'There is money,' she brought out at last. 'I mean, you haven't any, have you? Of course, I don't see why you should have. But two people must live, though it's all rather sordid. However, this need not arise. But I just want to show you –'

'I know she's got a beautiful home,' he said glumly.

'However . . . You see, it's impossible every way. But first and last, she does not love you.'

He was forced into the position which he would have described to a friend as bloody, of asserting she *did*. 'Though I cannot think why.'

'Oh, but so many girls would!' she cried earnestly. 'But for Lois I do think – we all think – a school of art. She cares for her drawing intensely.'

'She never speaks of it.'

'Ah, that just shows . . . Lack of sympathy!' said the aunt with mournful complacency. 'And it isn't simply your age; it would be the same thing if you were a captain or even a major. Now I do think you ought to be sensible. It can all pass off so quietly. Nobody knows except me. Now what I suggest –'

'– She might have told me she'd told you!' He stared round the changed room bitterly.

'That was just what I didn't encourage, to tell you the truth. Oh, the child was most honest. But I thought you and I should approach this quite fresh and unprejudiced.'

'Did we have to?'

'Oh, Mr Lesworth!' she cried, disconcerted. She resumed, firmly but with inspiration, something between a hospital nurse and a prophetess: 'The less talk, the less indirect discussion round and about things, the better, I always think.'

While she considered her gloves and with gathering satisfaction prepared to put one of them on, he stood half-turned away from her, stubborn but indecisive. An unusual pendulum swung in him, he was ruined – resolute – ruined. He was dark with perplexed anger, from which his invincible 'niceness' stood, in deprecation, aside. She blasphemed, and yet he had to admire her four-square propriety, her sound sense, the price she set on his Lois. And love, meanwhile, did not so much lie bleeding as sit back stunned, bruised, a little craven from shock. Gerald drew his chin, swallowed, put a finger inside his collar as though to loosen it.

'Then I understand you don't like this: you're going to stop it?'

'Now, my dear Mr Lesworth, do think: would I ever "stop" anything?'

'– You're going to stop it because I'm too young and too poor and not "county" enough – or whatever I ought to be.'

'You have entirely misunderstood me,' cried Lady Naylor, hurt.

'You don't have to tell me I'm not good enough: that's what I've battered my head against ever since –'

'We all think you're charming – the Montmorencys, everyone! You know we're delighted to see you –'

'Oh, I'm all right for tennis,' said Gerald without rancour.

'There is no one I'd rather – as far as that goes –' began Lady Naylor warmly.

'You feel it's up to you to stop it,' he summed up. 'And I can see that from your point of view you're quite right. But there are some things you can't stop. God knows, I've got little enough for Lois, and she ought to have everything, straight off, now. But I swear I'll see that she gets it. I'll give up the Army, anything. I *know* I'm going to work things out. If it were only what *I* want – But she loves me – I dare say she's pretty mad – but she does love me; I've looked at her eyes, I know. If she hadn't seemed – if I hadn't felt – if it hadn't been just the only thing for us both, I'd never have said a word – I swear – I'd have died sooner.'

'But she agrees with everyone,' said Lady Naylor, taking off the glove again in despair. 'She is extremely keen to go to this school of art.'

'Where?' he said violently.

'Some good school.'

'Do you expect me not to trust her?'

'I should have a straightforward, sensible talk.'

'You're not going to stop me seeing her?'

'I don't know what sort of girls' mothers and aunts you're accustomed to,' she said, nettled, 'but how could you expect me to do such a preposterous thing? It would be not only unkind but exceedingly foolish. To begin with, she is not my own niece at all. It would be for her uncle to decide. But Sir Richard is very easily worried: I particularly do not wish – You know we are always delighted to see you at any time . . .'

She paused. 'It's most awfully kind of you,' said he, by reflex action.

'In these days of frank unsentimental friendship between young people, I do not see why you two should not have a perfectly friendly, sensible talk. Of course there must be *no* . . . I mean, I know I can trust you . . . I mean, you do quite understand you are not engaged, and not being engaged there can be no question of –?'

'I promise I won't kiss her.'

Lady Naylor was much embarrassed. She laughed impersonally and arranged her boa. She expressed some envy of this generation, its frank friendships.

'I don't think I am very modern,' said Gerald flatly.

'Now Laurence is too modern: he does not seem to care about girls at all . . . For the present, I'd leave love out of the question –'

'But I thought that *was* the question!'

A shadow went past the window. 'Here comes Mrs Montmorency,' said Gerald. And he touched his moustache and blinked and looked round, wondering which chair to offer.

'That is too bad! I sent her up to the Rectory.'

'Perhaps they were out.'

'I told her to wait; there would be plenty to read in the drawing-room – Well, you do understand, don't you?'

'I'm afraid I –'

Francie was shown in. 'Oh!' she cried, 'what a lot of cushions! Kittens! Fancy sitting on them, I should feel like a cannibal. No, I don't mean – Mr Lesworth! Isn't this nice! Are those photographs of your regiment? I had no idea there were so many officers . . . Myra, I remembered a little something I had to get at the chemist's, so I thought I'd call in here and save you that climb up the hill. They were all out.'

'Well, that was very sweet of you, Francie,' said Lady Naylor.

'Oh, how patriotic!' cried Francie, knocking two cushions covered with Union Jacks off the sofa. 'She's a Catholic, isn't she? Oh, Mr Lesworth, don't bother; I'm so clumsy . . . I had no idea we were going to meet you. Isn't it a pity now that we didn't bring Lois? Myra, isn't it too bad Lois didn't come too.'

'Yes, it does seem a pity,' said Lady Naylor. Still faintly regretful, she got up, looked at herself in a mirror, arranged her boa and pulled down the brim of her hat. Then she shook hands with Gerald warmly, saying how much she had enjoyed their talk.

22

'I shall never forget,' continued Francie, through the open dressing-room door, 'the way he picked up those cushions.'

'Which?' said Hugo, searching irritably among his collars. The feudal system was weak at some points, he reflected – this Danielstown laundry. The laundress's father had helped to defend the house in the troubled 'sixties. Nostalgic, he thought of these neat democratic blue vans labelled 'hygienic' that called on Mondays. 'Well really,' said he, 'I may just as well go to bed. I haven't a collar left fit to dine in . . . Which cushions?'

'Oh, horrors. But then they say the Fogartys are so kind. – Never mind, Hugo; Richard's and Laurence's collars are just the same. – You know how alive he is generally: well, that was all gone. It was like seeing a waterfall stand still. You know, Hugo, it may be horrid, but I don't trust Myra sometimes. She says things aren't, and then she turns and makes these curious little dabs at them. She dislikes the Clonmore rectory people, she says they are breath-y, she knows I don't know them and yet she insisted on my going up. And when I came down again she was charming; I knew I must have annoyed her.'

'My dear Francie, life is too short for all this.' (Though that was not the matter with life, really: life was too long.) Hugo frowned, chin up in front of his glass. 'It's a good thing the evenings are drawing in,' he said, with reference to his collar.

'Now what I should have said . . .' resumed Francie, 'though ideally, really, I shouldn't have said anything . . .'

'Talking of evenings,' said Hugo, 'where do we go next? We've got to fit in the Fitzgeralds before October. Oughtn't you to be writing to somebody? And oh, Francie, you might post some of these collars to the Terenure laundry, if you can get the parcel out of the house quietly.'

'I shall miss here,' sighed Francie, looking out at the trees.

'You miss everywhere.' They both thought of the bungalow which, an eternal present for them, would never be able to shine in retrospect. Throughout dinner, Francie was distraite. She was making out in her mind a little letter to Gerald. But, of course, that would never do.

'Hullo!' said Laurence, earlier, looking at the letters put out for next morning's post on the hall table. 'Lois has written to Marda. I thought no one knew her address.'

'She heard from Marda this morning,' explained his uncle, bending to study the envelope with melancholy interest. 'I understand that it was about a dog. I shall be relieved when Marda is married. I wonder will the young man be able to look after luggage?'

'I ran into Mr Lesworth this afternoon,' Lady Naylor told Lois. 'He came into the Fogartys' while I was resting there. Really, she keeps quite a home for those young men – though nothing would ever take the gloss off those cushions. He seemed very cheerful, he was on his way up to the tennis.'

'He never goes to the tennis on Club days.'

'Oh, well, he seemed to be on his way up to the tennis. He told me of that young Armstrong's engagement to Livvy Thompson.

It seems quite a *fait accompli*, though secret, of course, How things do get round in a garrison town! You knew, I suppose?'

'Well, Livvy did tell me.'

'What a bother for you!' said Lady Naylor. 'It is a comfort to have outgrown one's friends' engagements. I suppose *you* couldn't very well tell her it was preposterous?'

'Well, I . . .'

'Mr Lesworth thought it a pity, in view of the young man's future. He expects Mr Armstrong will not stand well over this with their Colonel at all. I think he can't understand his friend's not being keener on his career. I suppose it will end by their just going out to one of those coffee or orange places in Africa. But, of course, Livvy is used to a dull life.'

'But I don't see . . .'

'And there isn't much else for her. I can't see poor Livvy at a school of art, though she might typewrite.'

'She would do for a model,' said Laurence, who had been listening with interest to this conversation from his side of the table. 'They should be either voluminous or very spiky.'

At this point, the candles were brought in – Lady Naylor had been delayed in Clonmore, they were dining late. The sharp flames shivered, every one blinked; the dahlias became theatrical.

'Autumn,' pronounced Sir Richard. 'There should be less of this ambushing and skirmishing and hey-fidaddling now that the days are drawing in.'

'But as an English friend of mine pointed out,' said Hugo, 'this Irish fighting is not cricket.'

Laurence maintained that this way of fighting was consistent, efficient and very natural. Why, he asked, be high-toned about a war?

'Oh dear,' said Francie, 'you sound just like a pacifist!'

'What else did Gerald say?' Lois wanted to know.

'I really cannot remember,' said Lady Naylor; 'he was as pleasant as ever, but, of course, not original. He seemed in a hurry to be getting up to the tennis.'

Lois, dissatisfied, blinked gloomily in the candlelight.

About half-past ten, Francie – having been taken up to her room by Myra, with a suggestion of having been put away for the night – crept out again to the ante-room, listening. Her candlestick, wobbling with indecision, brushed the ceiling with shadows. Wires twanged where some cattle rubbed on a fence in the damp darkness. Francie went across and tapped on Lois's door.

Lois turned in alarm from the dark window where she stood holding her elbows, not quite thinking. Her heart thumped as the crack of the door widened, letting in foreign light. 'Damn,' she thought with annoyance. She had been up here for more than an hour and had not begun to undress. To look more natural she undid her frock and stepped quickly out of it.

Mrs Montmorency, yellow under the chin, appeared deprecatingly. She had just thought, she said, of a little chat. She looked round hopelessly, she could not think where to put down her candle. This decided – a little table presented itself – her difficulties seemed to be over. She said at once: 'The young man, Lois, seems so unhappy.'

'But we're engaged,' said Lois, tying her dressing-gown firmly round her hips.

'Oh . . . Are you certain? Because . . .'

'What did he say? said Lois, at once defensive.

'My dear, I was up at the rectory. I am sure your aunt meant everything for the best.'

Lois went to the glass and took down her hair distractedly. Shaking it over her face she said, muffled: 'You mean she has interfered?'

'Well, I wouldn't say she'd done *that*. But it seems a pity . . .'

'Really,' cried Lois, glad of the hair because her anger did sound to herself faintly academic, 'she is as designing as . . . a cardinal.'

'As I said to Hugo, you have enough sense, you are so modern . . . and after all you will only be young once.'

'Oh. Were you all there?'

'My dear, I tell you, I was up at the rectory. But from the way he picked up the cushions . . . I can't bear lives to go wrong.'

This came out so vehemently, with such an effect of passion that Lois, surprised, said: 'Neither can I, really.' And looking round, she found the shadows exaggerated with solemnity; the thin candle-flames stretched up anxiously: a predicament must have become noticeable, even to the room. Impressed by strangeness, by this pressure of emergency, Lois plaited her hair in two plaits instead of one and felt herself a different woman.

'What they never see,' she said rapidly, 'is, that I must do something.'

'I should write at once,' said Francie. 'I'm not sure that I shouldn't even telegraph, if it were not for the post-mistress. I should say . . . Well, I don't know really: I do wish Marda were here!'

'If I learn German, they say, why not Italian? And when I learn Italian they take no interest.'

Francie picked up the evening dress that Lois had just stepped out of, stared, and remarked to it, almost with incredulity: 'Love is everything!'

'At least Gerald is definite. He, I . . .'

'I *know* love is so important.'

'At least it may get one somewhere.'

Francie, raising her voice to a scared note, as though she must make quite certain what they were really talking about, cried: 'There are such mistakes!'

'I wouldn't mind being properly tragic . . .'

'If one's not quite certain, one never knows where one is.'

'– It's just that I feel so humiliated the whole time.'

'But the young man . . .' persisted Francie. They looked at each other, or at where the other had been. Francie, deserted at once by the conspiratorial courage that brought her in, dolefully put a finger over her lips, as though betrayed irrevocably by what had come out of them. She visibly shrank with misgiving.

'You seem very intellectual, Lois. Do – do you not love him?'

'I *must*,' said Lois. She put her hands up to the back of her neck, fumbling open the clasp of her corals. She could feel the bright girl she had been for Mrs Montmorency disintegrate: much that even she had taken to be herself went with the illusion.

'I just thought I might have helped,' said Francie, in a spent, remote little voice, as though they were both coming back from a funeral to an imposingly vacant house.

'Oh, you have indeed,' said Lois. And she stood there vacantly and, she felt, rather gruesomely smiling, weighing her coral beads up and down in a hand, trying to remember what they had both said, what they had meant, what it had been about.

Francie took up her heavy candlestick and looked about for the door. She sighed and said it had been a tiring day. She could not bear to feel she was not missed out after all, had not been passed by because there was nothing to pass her. It was late at night for so fundamental a disappointment. There seemed some difficulty about getting her back to her room, though they both desired this. Lois opened the door; they heard Sir Richard and Hugo arguing up the stairs. Francie shielded her candle-flame with her hand and wavered out round the door like a shadow.

Lois, hot with retrospective embarrassment, slipped from her clothes and blew out the candles quickly. The dark was gratefully positive. She lay on her side with knees drawn up to her chin, blankness snowing down on her till, quite snowed up in blankness, she was asleep.

Next day, mist lay on the fields like a blanket, muffling sound so that the postman arrived unexpectedly. He brought a letter from Gerald: 'For God's sake see me.'

She meant to go out to meet Gerald, bright and matter of fact, but this miscarried: when he came, in the evening, she was half-way down from the garden, fighting with Laurence over a snail. He had walked on the snail on purpose.

'Ough – you fool . . . you beast, Laurence!'

'Well, I didn't mean to be kind to it.'

'Just because it had no mentality.'

'Not at all.'

'Ough, it's all over the path.'

'It's scrunched . . . I dare say,' said Laurence, pleased. 'I am pathological.'

'Great fat feet!'

As a matter of fact, he was sorry about the snail; he had thought it was just a shell, but he wasn't going to say so. 'Little mother,' he said unpleasantly.

'Laurence, you're insane. Ough, you're wiping it off everywhere. I shall be sick!'

'Do.'

'Well, I won't then.'

'I had no idea you were so fond of animals,' he said as offensively as possible. But he was not feeling up to much this evening and could not think what else to say to her. He turned and walked briskly away towards the avenue, conscious of having no objective. An unusual evening, however, awaited him. In a boreen in the Castle Trent direction he met three armed men coming out of a gate. They made him put up his hands and march smartly down the boreen ahead of them. He discovered that under these conditions the mind works fast but unfruitfully; he noted details sharply and then forgot. When they came to the wall of the grave-yard he was embarrassed, but they only asked for his shoes and the loan of his wrist-watch. Placing him with his face close up to the wall they advised him for life's sake not to look round or stir for twenty minutes. 'How shall I know?' said Laurence, 'you've got my watch.' But they did not care and went away with his shoes. Laurence remained with his forehead against the stone for fifty minutes, horse-flies biting him through the socks. Then he limped home to dinner and an audience, considerably cheered. Three days after, the watch was posted back to his Uncle Richard: it was in excellent order and ticked as it was taken out of the package. 'Which just shows,' said Sir Richard, holding the watch to his ear with satisfaction. But that was a day of confusion; nobody listened.

As Lois ran down from the garden, swollen about the personality with annoyance, she saw Gerald waiting at a turn of the path by a holly tree. He looked intently at her advancing, without comprehension, as though she had been a picture. Though they were alone, he did not put out a hand or move towards her. He stood there with the vigour, grief and indifference of a tree that cannot help growing.

'Gerald?'

'What's the matter?' he said, impassive.

'Oh, Laurence walked on a *snail*!'

'Bad luck!'

'My dear, he liked it.'

'Queer,' said Gerald, finding the word with difficulty.

'Where shall we go?' she asked, while something in her stopped like a clock with foreboding. The encounter, uncoloured by surprise or passion, left her quite at a loss. Unkissed, her mouth and cheeks felt a touch of ice.

'It seems now,' said Gerald, impersonally, as though delivering a message, 'that we can't ever be married.'

'Why? When?' she cried angrily.

Gerald looked at her under level eyelids. She remembered saying: 'I wish you wouldn't keep looking so pleased the whole time.' Now his look and silence were cold with a doomed expectancy: she nearly hated him. Dumbly, in happy-seeming physical agreement like a pair of animals, they wheeled off down the path together, crossed the yard rapidly and came into the plantation ribbed with shadow and lanced across with light about the eye-level. He told her her aunt agreed he was not good enough: it would never do at all, her aunt had said. Looking angrily up the tree-trunks, she exclaimed that her aunt was mad. She repeated this with vehemence and confusion, pulling at her fingers. He listened to her in silence, wounded, wounded. She wished they had not come down – overruling possibly in each other some desire for space – to the plantation where, constricted by firs, thought and movement were difficult and upright shadows emphasized his severity. 'She advised me,' Gerald concluded, 'to have a frank talk with you.'

'Is this the frank talk now?'

'She was certain you didn't love me.'

'*Gerald* – why weren't you furious?'

'I . . . I don't know,' he said, surprised by the question. She saw him standing confused, like a foreigner with whom by some failure in her vocabulary all communication was interrupted. Her mind halted and she wanted to run away. 'Gerald, come back. I'm wretched. Why do we have to talk?'

'I thought you liked that . . .' Outside himself with passion he cried: 'I'd rather be dead than not understand!'

'But don't you *know* I . . .? Gerald?'

If he did not know, it would be quite over. She watched with agony what seemed to be his indifference. They were each waiting for the other. *He* watched her hand, on a tree-trunk, pick like a bird at the scaly bark. Her hand, which immediately centred her consciousness of him, paused and became quite rigid, fingers spread out. When he saw her hand so quiet, he would have to be certain. And he immediately said with his usual little resigned inflection: 'You see, you are everything.'

'I know,' she said, impersonal.

'I suppose you are what I mean by life . . . Do you understand at all?'

'You sometimes make me.' She wanted to add: 'Touch me now': it was the only way across. In her impotence, her desolation – among the severe trees – at not being compelled, she made a beseeching movement which he, remote in a rather sublime perplexity that transcended pain, either ignored or rejected. From the stables, the six o'clock bell sent out relief in a jerky, metallic passage of sound through the plantation. She wanted something to look at, to follow: a train curving past in a rush. With an exaggerated movement, she put up her hands to her ears. Gerald's face, in a band of light, remained impassible.

'Gerald, you're making us lose each other!' she shouted above the bell.

'But I mean to say: what would *you* lose?'

'Everything.'

'Do you *mean* that?' A light ran almost visibly up inside him. She saw now where they were and why he had come.

She thought of going, hesitating with delight, to the edge of an unknown high-up terrace, of Marda, of getting into a train. 'No,' she cried, terrified, 'why should I?'

'Then we don't mean the same thing.'

'Why don't you make me . . . like you?'

'I thought I could. I know I can – when I'm not with you.'

'Damn, damn,' said Lois. 'I do want you!'

Gerald said piteously: 'Then why can't it all be simple?'

'But it's our being so young,' she said, too eagerly, 'and then, money. I mean, we have got to be practical.'

He explained to her, wide-eyed: 'It isn't anything practical that makes all this – like death. What *she* said was, that if you loved me . . .'

'It's like a nightmare that even you should begin to talk. I thought you were a rock: I was safe with you. Gerald, really, this is all like a net; little twists of conversation knotted together. One can't move, one doesn't know where one is. I really can't live at all if it has all got to be arranged. I tell you, even what I think isn't my own, and Mrs Montmorency comes bursting into my room at nights. Even Marda – nothing we said to each other mattered, it hasn't stayed, she goes off to get married in a mechanical sort of way. She thinks herself so damned funny – it's cheap, really. All that matters is what *you* believe – Gerald, you'll kill me, just standing there. You don't know what it's like for a snail, being walked on . . .'

'I don't understand you,' he cried in agony. 'Who is a snail?'

'I didn't ask you to understand me: I was so happy, I was so safe.'

Gerald noticed a change somewhere; the light was gone from his face, moving down the trees it had disappeared. He looked at his wrist-watch. They had been a short time together, almost twenty minutes. 'When were you happy?' he said accurately. He would have liked to be sure of this, and of several other matters: she was not collected enough to explain. He eyed the incredible

wood, the path, her unchanged figure in the cheerful blue woollen
dress. Something struggled free in his brain and said, quite apart
from his numbed self: 'My darling, don't, don't rack yourself.
You know this will be always the same for me. Whatever's impossible, you will always be perfect. I know we're different about
things: if that didn't hurt you it would never matter to me. I
mean, don't let's be disappointed. You know I'm not giving you
up, I could never have done *that*. But it's just that, you see, you
never . . . I suppose things can't come out as one wants . . . I
suppose it would hardly do . . .'

'But, Gerald, where are we?'

He said, 'Don't worry.' They were both, he knew, entirely lost.

'But what have I *done*? What have I *not* done?' After a minute,
during which she heard him finger his belt – his fingers slipped
on the leather – she shut her eyes and said, 'So you're certain I
don't love you?'

No answer. 'Oh, leave that belt alone, Gerald!'

Still no answer, as though he were alseep. And indeed he felt,
as at the approach of sleep, an immense indifference. She,
tortured by the loneliness of insomnia, had to cry out: 'Won't
you even just try – won't you just kiss me?'

'I don't think . . .'

'All right.'

'Look, I must go now.' Vaguely, he saluted and began to go
up the path, towards the beech walk, towards the house.

'Good bye?' she said.

He only half paused. 'No, don't let's . . .'

'Where did you leave your bicycle?'

He was well up the path; he called back: 'Against the hedge.
You know, under the tennis courts.'

She knew; she remembered him pulling leaves from the privet
hedge, scattering them on the grass and throwing them over her.
She remembered that Mrs Boatley was a Christian Scientist. It
seemed a good thing summer was practically over; there might
not be more tennis parties. But at this the incomprehensible glare
of summer blinded her, bringing tears to her eyes. 'Gerald!' she
called.

But by this time he seemed to be out of ear-shot.

23

Another thing Lady Naylor had noticed about the English was, a disposition they had to be socially visible before midday.

Soon after ten, she had heard, Mrs Vermont and her friends were to be seen about the streets of Clonmore – from behind the still decently somnolent blinds of inhabitants – with gloves buttoned tight at the wrists, swinging coloured baskets. Before eleven, they would be seated behind the confectioner's window, deploring the coffee. Mrs Rolfe had once had Moriarty's shutters taken down for her specially – and she wishful, Moriarty said, to purchase the one pair of stockings only. A Mrs Peake, of the Gunners, demanded attention at the hairdresser's before ten. These unnatural practices were a strain on the town's normality; the streets had a haggard look, ready for anything. Really, as Lady Naylor said, almost English. She thought of the south of England as a kind of extension of Brighton, the north serrated by factory chimneys, the middle a blank space occupied by Anna Partridge. Only Danielstown's being out of dropping- or popping-in distance from Clonmore deprived her, as it transpired, of matutinal visits from Mrs Vermont and her friends.

Mrs Vermont, however, overcame difficulties, hired a Ford and had herself driven over one morning about eleven o'clock. She brought her great friend Mrs Rolfe; they were on their way to lunch at the Thompsons'. This she explained before they were out of the car; *she* knew what Mondays were, she did not want to alarm Lady Naylor – being so much with Mother had made her considerate in these matters. Lady Naylor, as a matter of fact, would have minded them less at lunch-time; one didn't notice people so much at meals, she discovered. When news of the dropping in came down to the kitchen, she groaned: 'My morning!' Nothing could have been worse.

Francie was lying down with 'a head'; Hugo was talking over old times with the coachman, who had been pensioned off and brooded all day in the harness-room, much at a loss. Lois, indirectly responsible for the outrage, was not to be found. She had not been herself at all, these last few days. Her aunt, after Gerald's departure, had made a point of saying: 'Well, I hope,

of course, you have not made a mistake. But we all have to settle
these things for ourselves, you know.' Francie never failed to
inquire if she were getting on nicely with the Italian; her uncle
agreed it was high time she went to that school of art. This
morning she seemed to be nowhere; shouting did not produce
her.

Laurence, always unfortunate, was surprised on the steps with
Locke. 'Oh God,' he said as the Ford came round the bend of
the lower avenue. He turned, too late, to escape; the girl wives
were already shouting and waving.

Betty said: 'Denise, this is Mr – (Oh dear, how awful!) This
is Mrs Rolfe of the Gunners; my great friend, you know.'

'Good,' said Laurence. Denise glanced up, apprehensive, at all
the windows. Laurence stood looking at them with resignation;
he forgot to open the door of the car though they brimmed out
over it.

'*May* we get out?' asked Betty, tittering up at him in the
friendliest way from a perfect swirl of furs and red crêpe de Chine.
On their knees, two little pairs of hands curled like loose chrysanthemums over their kid pochettes. He let them out and they
ran up the steps shaking out their dresses. '*Oh*, what a brainy
book!' cried Betty, pouncing. '– My dear, just look what he's
reading – oh, you have got a brain! I mean, fancy reading . . .'

'You're at college, aren't you?' said Denise, fluttered.

'Sometimes,' said Laurence accurately. Opening his mouth
very wide he shouted for Lois. They shrieked and covered their
ears. 'I expect,' he said finally, 'I had better go in and look for –'

'Don't go! I'm sure they will all come out . . . I did want
Denise to see a lovely old Irish home.'

'Yes, we are quaint, really,' said Laurence, considering. 'And
you oughtn't to miss the Trents; has she seen the Trents?'

'Well, I hardly know the Trents. Here, we always feel that
Gerald is such a link.'

'Missing or otherwise,' Denise added.

'Exactly.' Betty smiled at him sidelong, but all the same, it did
seem a pity it should be Laurence that they had dropped in on
with unintended accuracy. *This* was not at all what she had led
Denise to expect. Laurence's not quite rudeness was, in fact,
rather international – she supposed, Oxford. She said: 'I have a
boy cousin at Reading University. That's quite near Oxford,
isn't it?' Denise, plaintive, said that a wasp was bothering; she

wanted to go indoors and see the reputed ancestors. Betty flapped with her pochette and the end of her fur. 'She's *terrified* of wasps!'

'So am I,' said Laurence, backing, 'absolutely *terrified*. I think I'd better go and – better get a –' He disappeared through the glass door, shutting it.

Denise said: 'Well, I do think people are extraordinary.' They both sat down and yawned. All these trees; it was quite extraordinary. 'Is that Lois's cousin?'

'More or less.'

'Well, I always did think she was an odd girl.'

'Ssh, there's Sir Richard writing in the library – Denise, *just* look through, sideways. He's such a type.'

'O-oh . . . yes. Is he a knight or a baronet?'

'Well, I don't see how he could have been knighted.'

'My dear, ssssh!'

'He's deaf. Oh, darling, look at those little teeny black cows. Those are Kerry cows. They farm, you know; they have heaps of cattle.'

'I always meant to ask you: *are* there Kilkenny cats?'

'Really,' said Mrs Vermont, annoyed, as her friend yawned again and she felt her own jaw quiver, 'when one thinks these are the people we are defending! I wonder if they'll offer us any coffee. What I think about Irish hospitality: either they almost knock you down or they don't look at you. Or I tell you what, we might go out to the garden and get some plums. Only I would like you to see the drawing-room. I wish these were Livvy's people; the boys say her house smells – I hope you aren't bored, darling? – I mean, what I mean about Livvy; she does grow on you. I can't think what Gerald sees in this family, I must say. It isn't even as if Lois –'

'Of course, I always did think she was an odd girl.'

At this point Sir Richard, who was not deaf, came out in despair. He said this was too bad; he couldn't think what could have become of Lois. 'We might shout,' he said helplessly.

'Your nephew has been shouting.'

'Still,' said Sir Richard, and shouted again. 'How are you all getting on?' he said kindly, when he had recovered his breath.

Betty said with dignity: 'There may be going to be an offensive.'

'*Sssh*,' whispered Denise, pinching her elbow.

'Though I ought not really to tell you.'

'Never mind,' said Sir Richard, 'I don't suppose it will come to anything. Besides, now the days are drawing in – But this is too bad really, most unfortunate that my wife should not be here to receive you. She will be most distressed.'

'Oh, but we just dropped in. As I said to Denise, what is the good of being in Ireland if one isn't a bit unconventional?'

'She will be most distressed.'

'Don't bother! We've been admiring your darling cows.'

'I'll just go in and inquire,' said Sir Richard firmly and disappeared, shutting the glass door.

Denise said she would get the giggles: a seizure did seem to be imminent. 'Well, I must say, Gerald is well out of this family.'

'But, my dear, *is* he?'

'Something's happened. He's *black* – even Timmy noticed. I said to Timmy: "You *must* find out" – 'Cause I think, don't you, that when men get together . . . You see, *I* can't – though I can't bear to see the boy suffer.'

'But I thought you said you –'

'Well, I've seen him in the distance and he didn't look like himself at all. But he hasn't been near us, or to the Club, or into the Fogartys'. And as I was saying to Mrs Fogarty –'

'It seems to me he's been treated rottenly. If it were one of our boys, my dear, I should be fur-rious.'

'All the same, I do want to *see* Lois . . .'

'What he sees in her, I cannot imagine. She's what I should call rather affected –'

'Sssh – Oh, hullo, Lois!' they cried in unison.

Lois, unbecomingly bright, came up from the beech walk.

'Oh, hullo,' she said, 'splendid!'

'We've just been talking about you.'

'O-oh! *Can't* you stay to lunch?'

'No can do; we're off to the Thompsons'. My dear, aren't you thrilled about Livvy and David! Isn't it marvellous?'

'Thrilled, it's absolutely marvellous. *Do* stay to lunch – I mean,' she said agitatedly, 'do come back to tea? Oh no, we shall all be out. Oh, how rotten. Or come to tennis – no, I believe there won't be any more tennis; Laurence is going back to Oxford and the rain's washed all the markings off the court. Perhaps we could have a dance or something –'

The two young wives eyed her lightly and curiously; their looks ran over her form like spiders. They were so womanly, she could have turned and fled back down the beech walk. 'Donne ch'avete intelletto d'amore,' she thought to herself wildly. And the pause, the suspicion of some deformity that these ladies produced in her became so acute that she smiled more widely. She buttoned her cardigan up to the top, then unbuttoned it.

'Oh, but don't go *now*,' she said, but looked at their Ford, longingly.

'Oh, we must, we have been here hours, watching your darling cows.'

'I'm afraid they're very much in the distance. Does Aunt Myra –?'

'Oh, we'd hate to disturb her. Unless we might all run round the garden –?'

'It's locked and I've lost the key. I feel quite an outcast. That's what has been the matter the whole morning. Do have something to eat – have some biscuits?'

'Unless we just come into the drawing-room for one moment?'

'I always think drawing-rooms in the morning are so depressing.'

Denise said she did not see how the same room could be much different, but it was no good; Lois seemed determined to keep them out. From the way she shifted her feet and stared round, you would have said she was expecting bad news momentarily: she talked so much that they hadn't a chance to express themselves. She went in for a tin of *petit beurres* and offered it with an odd air, rather propitiatory. Lady Naylor called from an upstairs window that this was too bad, that she was so much distressed, she would be down immediately. 'She spends whole mornings with the cook,' said Lois. 'I cannot think what they do. I believe they fence verbally. More biscuits?'

'No, we shall spoil our din-dins. Denise, we *must* come. I hear old Mr Thompson is a terrible ogre. Any messages in Clonmore, Lois? Any messages to Gerald?'

Lois thought she must blush, but did not; even her blood stood still.

'*I* should ask him,' said Denise, 'why he didn't send *you* a message. *I* think it was odd of him; I should be fur-rious.' Lois saw, with interest, a ripple of light down their dresses; they nudged each other. There must be something odd about her, really, if they had noticed; she must clearly be outside life.

'How is the gramophone?' she said enthusiastically.

'Don't *ask*! Gerald is going to Cork to bring back a new one. We thought we might all go too, it would be a rag.'

'Marvellous!'

'Look, I'll just run Denise in to have a look at the drawing-room.'

'I shouldn't, really. I haven't done the flowers.'

'Gerald says all your looking-glasses make him feel sleepy. He's a funny boy, in a way,' said Betty innocently. 'You don't think we ought to wait till we've seen your aunt? She won't be offended?'

'I shouldn't really; she's probably been delayed.' Lady Naylor did, in fact, arrive on the steps in time to utter exclamations of despair as they drove away. 'Too bad, *too* bad!' she called, waving after them. 'You must come again soon!... Really, Lois, you might have found them some fruit or something. Fancy puffing them out with biscuits at this hour.'

'I tell you what I think it is about Lois,' said Betty cosily, nestling down in the car as the trees rushed over them. 'I think he's left her.'

Denise agreed. 'A boy needs keeping, if you know what I mean.' Betty also told her what she thought about the Naylor family: they were going down in the world. 'I should not be surprised if they never used that drawing-room,' she said viciously. 'It smells of damp. Myself, I do like a house to be bright and homey.'

The world did not stand still, though the household at Danielstown and the Thompsons' lunch party took no account of it. The shocking news reached Clonmore that night, about eight o'clock. It crashed upon the unknowingness of the town like a wave that for two hours, since the event, had been rising and toppling, imminent. The news crept down streets from door to door like a dull wind, fingering the nerves, pausing. In the hotel bars, heads went this way and that way, quick with suspicion. The Fogartys' Eileen, called by a friend while she was clearing away the supper, cried 'God help him!' and stumbled up to Mr Fogarty's door, blubbered. Mr Fogarty dropped his glass and stood bent some time like an animal, chin on the mantelpiece. Philosophy did not help; in his thickening brain actuality turned like a mill-wheel. His wife, magnificent in her disbelief, ran out, wisps blowing, round the square and through the vindictively silent town.

Barracks were closed, she could not get past the guards; for once she was at a loss, among strangers. She thought mechanically 'His mother,' and pressed her hands up under her vast and useless bosom. Trees in the square, uneasy, shifted dulled leaves that should already have fallen under the darkness. The shocking news, brought in at the barrack gates officially, produced an abashed silence, hard repercussions, darkness of thought and a loud glare of electricity. In Gerald's room some new music for the jazz band, caught in a draught, flopped over and over. An orderly put it away, shocked. All night some windows let out, over the sandbags, a squeamish, defiant yellow.

Mrs Vermont heard when Timmy had just gone out; he was to be out all night with a patrol. She was to sleep alone, she could not bear it. Past fear, she ran to the Rolfes' hut. She spent the night there, sobbing, tearing off with her teeth the lace right round her handkerchief. Captain Rolfe kept bringing her hot whisky. 'I can't, I can't, not whisky; it's so awful.' They all felt naked and were ashamed of each other, as though they had been wrecked. From the hut floor – where they had danced – the wicker furniture seemed to rise and waver.

'Percy, where did he – how was he –?'

'Through the head.'

'Then it didn't –?'

'Oh no. Probably instantaneous.'

'Oh, *don't*! Oh, Percy, how can you!'

Denise repeated: 'I can't believe it.' And while the others sickly, furtively stared, she tried to press from her hair the waves she had had put in that morning. 'You know, I *can't* believe it. Can you, Betty? It's so . . . extraordinary.'

'Why can't we all go home? Why did we stay here? Why don't we all go home? That's what I can't understand.'

'Percy, can *you* believe it? I mean, I remember him coming in and standing against this table –'

'Oh, don't! – Percy, what became of *them*? Where did they go? Those devils!'

'Oh, got right away.'

'Didn't anyone hear anything, any firing? I mean, didn't it make a noise? . . . Couldn't they be tortured – why should they just be hanged or shot? Oh, I do think, I mean, I do think when you think –'

'Well, we've got to get 'em, haven't we? Look, just try –'

'Oh, I *can't*, I tell you – Why can't we all go home!'

'Percy, leave her *alone*! Oh God, my head; I shall cut my hair off. I mean, he came in and stood there against that table. Why did they get just Gerald? – Oh, yes, I know there was the sergeant – but *he* won't die; I know he won't die . . . I can't believe it! Percy, *can* you believe it? Percy, say something.'

Betty sobbed: 'I should like to – oh, I should like to – Those beasts, those beasts!'

'Look, you two girls go to bed.'

'Oh, how can we!'

'Oh, why isn't Timmy here? I mean, when I think of Timmy, and out all night – *I* can't understand the King, I can't understand the Government: *I* think it's awful!'

But they went to bed – Percy spent the night on two chairs – and lay in what seemed to both an unnatural contiguity, reclasping each other's fingers, talking of 'Him', of 'you know who' and 'that boy' in the eager voices, low-pitched and breaking, kept as a rule to discuss the intimacies of their marriages. In the same moment they fell, dimly shocked at each other, asleep. Then Denise saw Lois clearly, standing affectedly on the Danielstown steps with a tin of biscuits, a room full of mirrors behind her. And Betty woke with surprise to hear herself say: 'What I mean is, it seems so odd that he shouldn't really have meant anything.'

They heard an early bugle shivering in the rain.

24

Mr Daventry arrived before the postman. He had not paid an unofficial visit since he had been in Ireland; it seemed to him odd there should be nothing to search for, nobody to interrogate. It was early, wet tarnished branches came cheerfully through the mist. He had come to the gate with a convoy on its way over to Ballyhinch; two lorries had ground into silence and waited for him at the gate, alarming the cottagers. He walked up the avenue lightly and rapidly: nothing, at the stage things had reached for him, mattered. And superciliously he returned the stare of the house.

He rang and made his demand. Lois came out slowly, dumb with all she must begin to say – for who could an anxious waiting officer be but Gerald? 'Really . . .' Lady Naylor had said, with a glance at the clock, advising her to put down her table napkin. And Francie, smiling, had covered up her egg for her.

'You?' she now said while everything, the importance of everything, faintly altered. 'Come and have breakfast.'

He told her that there had been a catastrophe yesterday, west of Clonmore: a patrol with an officer and an N.C.O. had been ambushed, fired on at a cross-roads. The officer – Lesworth – was instantly killed, the N.C.O. shot in the stomach. The enemy made off across country, they did not care for sustained fire, in spite of the hedges. The men did what they could for the sergeant.

'Will he die?'

'Probably.'

'And Gerald was killed?'

'Yes. Would you –?'

'I'm all right, thank you.'

'Right you are.' He turned round and stood with his back to her. She asked what time it had happened; he said about six o'clock. She thought how accurate Gerald was and how anxious, last time, he had been to establish just *when* she had been happy because of him, on what day, for how long. 'They'd been out all the afternoon?' They both saw the amazed white road and dust, displaced by the fall, slowly settling. 'As a matter of fact,' said Daventry, 'we were mostly ready for things. I don't suppose – if he knew at all – it mattered.' 'No, I don't suppose, to oneself, it ever would matter much.' But she thought of Gerald in the surprise of death. He gave himself up to surprise with peculiar candour.

'Thank you for coming.'

'I was passing this way anyhow.'

'But still, there was no reason why you should take the trouble.'

Daventry glanced at her, then at the gravel under his feet, without speculation. Cold and ironical, he was a stay; he was not expecting anything of her. He finally said: 'It seemed practical. Would you like me to – shall I just let the others know?' She nodded, wondering where to go, how long to stay there, how to come back. Her mind flooded with trivialities. She wondered who would go up to the tennis this afternoon, if there would be anyone left who did not know, who would expect him; she wondered what would become of the jazz band. She saw for days ahead she must not deny humanity, she would have no privacy. 'As a matter of fact, they are expecting me back to breakfast.'

But at the thought of Francie's tender and proud smile, covering up her egg, she was enlightened and steadied by grief, as at the touch of finger-tips. She went into the house and up to the top to meet what was waiting. Life, seen whole for a moment, was one act of apprehension, the apprehension of death. Daventry, staring at her in memory – she was, after all, a woman – went into the hall. Here, it pleased him to think of Gerald socially circumspect under the portraits.

He waited. The dining-room door swung open on a continued argument; they came out one by one, each on the threshold, balanced momentarily like a ball on a fountain by the shock of seeing him. 'Lady Naylor?' he said to Francie. 'Oh *no*!' She seemed appalled at the supposition. 'Isn't ... Mr Lesworth here?' 'Not today.' Lady Naylor came last and stared hardest: really, the Army seemed to be inexhaustible. He told her. 'Oh, no!' she said quickly, as though to prevent something. He told her the circumstances. 'Oh – *no*,' she repeated, and turned in appeal to her husband. 'That is ... that is too bad,' said Sir Richard and in despairing confusion touched her shoulder. He looked back into the dining-room at the chairs and plates and table, incredible in their survival.

The fact was, they did not at all care for the look of Mr Daventry. They felt instinctively that he had come here to search the house. Lady Naylor, still statuesque from the shock, made, even, a little disdainful gesture, a kind of: 'Here's everything.' He, unconscious of her impression of being brought to book, remained staring darkly and piercingly past her. Behind her, across the dark dining-room, he saw through a window the lawn striped with mist and sunshine. In Clonmore it had rained that morning: they seemed to have escaped that too. She said sharply: 'Where's Lois?'

'I'm afraid I don't know,' he replied, indifferent.

'She – you have –?'

'Oh, yes.'

Her defensive dropped; she said with heart-broken eyes on his face: 'You know, we knew him so well. He came out here so often to tennis. It seems queer that one can't – that one never – He was so –'

'Yes he was, wasn't he?'

'His mother, he used to tell me about his mother. Who will write? I should like to write to her. Yes, I want very much to write to her. I think she might like – we did know him so well, you see – Richard, don't you think I –?'

But Sir Richard had slipped away quietly; he was an old man, really, outside all this, and did not know what to do. He was wondering, also, about the Connors. Peter Connor's friends – they knew everything, they were persistent: it did not do to imagine . . .

Mr Daventry said that was all, he thought; he must go now. He took leave with unfriendly courtesy and went off abruptly, with an air that obliterated them, as though he had never been into their house at all. Then she exclaimed, recollecting herself: '*He* must be unhappy; I ought to have said something.' There was so much to do now, more than would fit into a morning; she had some idea of postponing lunch. And hearing the postman, she half thought, terrified by a sense of exposure: 'Suppose there should be a – suppose he should have–'

But there was no letter for Lois from Gerald.

No one was on the steps to hear the news from the postman; he went away disappointed. Lady Naylor thought firmly: 'Now I must go and find Lois.' But she did not go; things seemed to delay her. She looked into the drawing-room to see whether something – she wasn't certain what – was there. Francie, red-eyed, looked guiltily over the back of the sofa. They did not say anything. The room became so sharply painful that Lady Naylor almost exclaimed: 'Lois has not done the flowers!'

It was Laurence who, walking about the grounds unguardedly, was exposed to what they all dreaded. He came on Lois, standing beside a holly tree. She could have moved away, but seemed not so much rooted as indifferent.

'It's all right,' she explained, and added: 'I'm just thinking.'

His look became almost personal, as though he had recognized her. He said: 'I think I should. I expect – I don't know – one probably gets past things.'

'But look here, there are things that one can't –' (She meant: 'He loved me, he believed in the British Empire.') 'At least, I don't want to.'

'Perhaps you are right,' he said, studying, with an effort of sight and of comprehension, some unfamiliar landscape.

'Well, don't stop, Laurence. You're going somewhere, aren't you?'

'Nowhere particular. Not if you –'

'No, I don't specially. Though if it has to be anyone, you.'

Taking this for what it was worth, he went on, brushing awkwardly past her against the laurels.

A fortnight later, Mrs Trent drove over, the very evening of her return from the North. She had been inexpressibly bored up there and wished to complain. Lady Naylor, delighted, came out to meet her; it was like old times again.

'The house feels empty. They've gone, you know.'

'Yes, dear me. I was sorry not to have seen the last of Hugo and poor little Francie. What about their bungalow?'

'Oh, that was just an idea; they are quite off it. Bungalows inland seem so pointless, cliffs are so windy and one cannot live on a flat coast. No, they think now of going to Madeira.'

'Then they won't un-store the furniture?'

'I don't think so; they never cared for it much.'

'It's a pity he never did go to Canada.' Mrs Trent looked round at the pleasant fields and lawns, the trees massive and tarnished, the windows that from their now settled emptiness seemed to have gained composure. Her sense of home-coming extended even to Danielstown. She went on: 'How's Richard? And listen: are you getting in your apples? – we haven't begun. They never get anything done when I'm away. And tell me: how's Lois?'

'Oh, gone, you know.'

'*Gone?* Oh, the school of art!'

'Oh no,' said Lady Naylor, surprised. 'Tours. For her French, you know. And to such an interesting, cultivated family; she is really fortunate. I never have been happy about her French. As I said to her, there will be plenty of time for Italian.'

'Oh, that's splendid,' Mrs Trent said vaguely but warmly. 'Then of course you must feel quiet. Did she and Laurence travel over together?'

'She seemed so offended at being thought incompetent and he was worried at the idea of looking after her luggage, so we sent them over separately; he crossed Wednesday, she Friday. Both nights, I hear, it was rough . . . Yes, it's been sad here, lately, we've been so much shocked and distressed about that unfortunate young Lesworth. I think I felt it particularly; he had been out here so much and seemed so glad to talk, and had come, in a way, to depend on one. Though it was a shock, too, for Lois. You see they had played tennis so often and were beginning to be quite friends. She did not take it as hard as I feared, girls of her generation seem less sensitive, really . . . I don't know; perhaps that is all for the best. And of course she has so many interests. But it was terrible, wasn't it? I still think: how terrible. But he did have a happy life. I wrote that to his mother; I said, it must always be some consolation to think how happy his life had been. He quite beamed, really; he was the life and soul of everything. And she wrote back – I did not think tactfully, but of course she would be distracted – that it was *her* first consolation to think he died in so noble a cause.'

Mrs Trent had for a moment an uneasy, exposed look. She said: 'It was heroic,' and glanced down awkwardly at her gloves. She missed a dog, she felt unstayed, there was no dog.

'Heroic,' said Lady Naylor, and scanned the skies with eager big-pupilled eyes that reflected the calm light. 'Although,' she added, half in surprise, 'he could not help it . . . But come in now and tell Richard about the North, he will be amused, though sorry that you were dull. To tell you the truth, we both rather feared you might be. Ah, don't mind the time, I'm sure it's early; come in, come in!'

But Mrs Trent could not, she was a punctilious person and wore a wrist-watch. She had not even sent round her dog-cart to the back; a man was walking the cob up and down the avenue. 'A flying visit,' said Lady Naylor mournfully, having prolonged the conversation by half an hour. Then Mrs Trent climbed briskly into the dog-cart and gathered the reins up; they sighed at each other their resignation to parting.

'Then we see you on Tuesday. Be sure and come early, before the Hartigans.' To the domestic landscape, Mrs Trent nodded an approving farewell. 'Every autumn, it strikes me this place looks really its best.'

'To tell you the truth, I really believe it does. There is something in autumn,' said Lady Naylor. She remained on the steps looking after the trap, her hands restlessly, lightly folded. Some leaves spun down from the gate with a home-coming air.

The two did not, however, again see Danielstown at such a moment, such a particular happy point of decline in the short curve of the day, the long curve of the season. Here, there were no more autumns, except for the trees. By next year light had possessed itself of the vacancy, still with surprise. Next year, the chestnuts and acorns pattered unheard on the avenues, that, filmed over with green already, should have been dull to the footsteps – but there were no footsteps. Leaves, tottering down the slope on the wind's hesitation, banked formless, frightened, against the too clear form of the ruin.

For in February, before those leaves had visibly budded, the death – execution, rather – of the three houses, Danielstown, Castle Trent, Mount Isabel, occurred in the same night. A fearful scarlet ate up the hard spring darkness; indeed, it seemed that an extra day, unreckoned, had come to abortive birth that these things might happen. It seemed, looking from east to west at the sky tall with scarlet, that the country itself was burning; while to the north the neck of mountains before Mount Isabel was frightfully outlined. The roads in unnatural dusk ran dark with movement, secretive or terrified; not a tree, brushed pale by wind from the flames, not a cabin pressed in despair to the bosom of night, not a gate too starkly visible but had its place in the design of order and panic. At Danielstown, half-way up the avenue under the beeches, the thin iron gate twanged (missed its latch, remained swinging aghast) as the last unlit car slid out with the executioners bland from accomplished duty. The sound of the last car widened, gave itself to the open and empty country and was demolished. Then the first wave of a silence that was to be ultimate flowed back, confident, to the steps. Above the steps, the door stood open hospitably upon a furnace.

Sir Richard and Lady Naylor, not saying anything, did not look at each other, for in the light from the sky they saw too distinctly.

READ MORE IN PENGUIN

In every corner of the world, on every subject under the sun, Penguin represents quality and variety – the very best in publishing today.

For complete information about books available from Penguin – including Puffins, Penguin Classics and Arkana – and how to order them, write to us at the appropriate address below. Please note that for copyright reasons the selection of books varies from country to country.

In the United Kingdom: Please write to *Dept. EP, Penguin Books Ltd, Bath Road, Harmondsworth, West Drayton, Middlesex UB7 ODA*

In the United States: Please write to *Consumer Sales, Penguin USA, P.O. Box 999, Dept. 17109, Bergenfield, New Jersey 07621-0120*. VISA and MasterCard holders call 1-800-253-6476 to order Penguin titles

In Canada: Please write to *Penguin Books Canada Ltd, 10 Alcorn Avenue, Suite 300, Toronto, Ontario M4V 3B2*

In Australia: Please write to *Penguin Books Australia Ltd, P.O. Box 257, Ringwood, Victoria 3134*

In New Zealand: Please write to *Penguin Books (NZ) Ltd, Private Bag 102902, North Shore Mail Centre, Auckland 10*

In India: Please write to *Penguin Books India Pvt Ltd, 706 Er)s Apartments, 56 Nehru Place, New Delhi 110 019*

In the Netherlands: Please write to *Penguin Books Netherlands bv, Postbus 3507, NL-1001 AH Amsterdam*

In Germany: Please write to *Penguin Books Deùtschland GmbH, Metzlerstrasse 26, 60594 Frankfurt am Main*

In Spain: Please write to *Penguin Books S. A., Bravo Murillo 19, 1° B, 28015 Madrid*

In Italy: Please write to *Penguin Italia s.r.l., Via Felice Casati 20, I–20124 Milano*

In France: Please write to *Penguin France S. A., 17 rue Lejeune, F–31000 Toulouse*

In Japan: Please write to *Penguin Books Japan, Ishikiribashi Building, 2–5–4, Suido, Bunkyo-ku, Tokyo 112*

In South Africa: Please write to *Longman Penguin Southern Africa (Pty) Ltd, Private Bag X08, Bertsham 2013*

BY THE SAME AUTHOR

The Death of the Heart

Sixteen-year-old Portia comes to live with her wealthy older half-brother and his wife, Anna, in London during the thirties. Tormented by the agonies of her first love affair, she is obsessed by the feeling that everyone is laughing at her. And when she discovers that Anna has been reading her diary, she takes a sudden explosive step which pulls everybody up short. 'One of the most sensitive novels written during this troubled century' – John O'London

The Collected Stories of Elizabeth Bowen

'If there is anything to the catchphrase "felt life", it is here . . . Many of her stories start like Saki and end like Edgar Allen Poe. It is that paradox which gives the edge to her writing and contributes to the sharpness of her vision' – Peter Ackroyd in the *Sunday Times*

The Heat of the Day

Wartime London and Stella's lover, Robert, is suspected of selling information to the enemy. Harrison, shadowing Robert, is none the less prepared to bargain, and the price is Stella. 'Rarely, to my knowledge, has the late flowering of love in war-time been more poignantly described in fiction' – John Hayward in the *Observer*

Eva Trout

'Resonant, beautiful and often very funny . . . Eva is triumphantly real, a creation of great imaginative tenderness' – Julian Jebb in the *Financial Times*. 'Rarely have I come across a novel in which sexual frustration (and sexuality) have been so richly and powerfully conveyed' – *Books and Bookmen*

also published:

A World of Love
Friends and Relations
The Hotel
The House in Paris
The Little Girls
To the North